MEGAN
MULRY

Bound
with
Passion

AN EROTIC HISTORICAL NOVEL

RIPTIDE
PUBLISHING

Riptide Publishing
PO Box 6652
Hillsborough, NJ 08844
www.riptidepublishing.com

Bound with Passion
Copyright © 2015 by Megan Mulry

Cover art: L.C. Chase, lcchase.com/design.htm
Editor: Sarah Lyons
Layout: L.C. Chase, lcchase.com/design.htm

ISBN: 978-1-62649-315-5

First edition
July, 2015

Also available in ebook:
ISBN: 978-1-62649-314-8

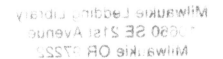

MEGAN MULRY

AN EROTIC HISTORICAL NOVEL

RIPTIDE
PUBLISHING

At one moment we deplore our birth and state and aspire to an ascetic exaltation; the next we are overcome by the smell of some old garden path and weep to hear the thrushes sing.
—Virginia Woolf, *Orlando*

TABLE OF Contents

Chapter 1

September 1810
Ajax, Southampton Harbor

Georgie swayed in the bowels of the ship. She couldn't recall the last time she'd slept in a proper bed. Not that it mattered—she was just grateful to have secured passage at all, for herself and for the two beautiful beasts with whom she shared her accommodations . . . such as they were. Her string hammock swung with the gentle currents of the harbor, just as Saladeen and Cyrus swung in their equestrian slings. The three of them were tired and filthy, and quite ready for this treacherous journey to be over.

Rolling out of her hammock, Georgie stood as best she could in the awkwardly shaped hold.

"We're almost there, my dears. We disembark today." She stroked Saladeen's neck the way the horse loved, and watched the more aggressive Cyrus out of the corner of her eye. Georgie and the larger stallion had a very cautious peace. He knew he was being taken someplace cold and inhospitable, and he was not pleased about it. But he also knew Saladeen would be there, so . . . he moped along.

"Don't look at me like that, Cyrus. I'm just as unhappy about it as you are. At least you will be coddled and prized—a lifetime of sweet oats and green pastures await you. And the beautiful Bathsheba."

She turned to dismantle her hammock and do what few ablutions she could with the bucket of cold water that sloshed near her feet. *Sweet oats and green pastures do not await me*, she thought sadly. More like an army of people who would try to convince her that spending the rest of her life in rural Derbyshire would offer some Elysian Field of perpetual pleasure.

No, thank you.

Georgie splashed her face, not worrying too much about any residual dirt. After all, it helped make her look more like the young British lad she'd been posing as for the entire trip. Her clothes were simple, masculine, and well made. She'd found a tailor in Cairo who— after the requisite horror that she was a woman—agreed to make her a full kit of men's clothing, including the stiff, unforgiving corset that flattened her troublesome breasts.

Troublesome.

She shook her head and began the familiar routine of defending herself to herself. She was quite fond of her breasts, actually, when occasion warranted acknowledging them—when strong or soft hands liberated them, caressed them, toyed with them. But for the most part, her life did not revolve around such occasions. Lady Georgiana Elizabeth Cambury lived her life at a full gallop, demanded that all doors be open to her, and none of that happened while reclining on a palanquin, having one's nipples fondled.

Putting an end to that fruitless line of thinking, Georgie continued packing her flannel and soap and other small items with military neatness, buckled up her leather bag, and took one last look at the two beautiful horses. "Now I have to leave you for a short while to deal with the captain and the customs officials. Don't bite anyone, Cyrus."

He stared at her as if he didn't understand. She leaned in and kissed Saladeen on his satiny nose. "Be good, handsome." She patted each of them one more time for good measure.

Then she turned out of the grimy stall where she'd spent the past three weeks, and with a masculine swagger she'd perfected over the past few years in Egypt and Syria, she strode up on deck and prepared to begin greasing the palms of everyone who was going to help her get the horses off the ship and on their way to Derbyshire.

By midday, they were on dry land—or rather, seeing as she was back in dreary England, moist land was more the truth. She hired a carriage and two men to accompany her north. While she rode Cyrus and led Saladeen, they drove the carriage with her trunks and all of the additional saddlery and equipment she had bought as a present for Trevor. At least the promise of spending time with James and Trevor was one glimmer of sunshine in what felt like an otherwise gloomy errand.

For as far back as Georgie could recall, she had loved Trevor Mayson. Not romantic love, of course—she'd decided at the age of seven that she would never do something as stupid and self-defeating as fall in love. And Trevor had decided . . . or rather, it hadn't been a decision at all, had it? It was simply a wonderful fact: Trevor loved James Rushford. The two of them had been attached to each other since university, and Georgie had enjoyed getting to know James better in the intervening years—or as much as she could in her perpetual absence. She knew Trevor loved him, and that was enough for her to love him as well.

As her little caravan made its way north, the air turned surprisingly restorative, despite the thick, cool, humidity of it. Georgie gradually let Cyrus have his way, and she enjoyed the prick of cool autumn wind as it swished past her cheeks. Occasionally, she'd loosen her neckcloth, welcoming the cool air against her skin, and let him ride harder. She'd taken to tying Saladeen to the carriage after lunch, warning the two coachmen that she'd cut off their bollocks if anything happened to the prized stallion.

Along the way, they bedded down in Sutton Scotney, Newbury, and Oxford, staying well out of the town centers so Georgie wouldn't run the risk of seeing any familiar faces. She had plotted an overland trip that would take them about twenty miles a day, getting them to Derbyshire by the middle of September. She'd thought of sending her mother and Nora another letter once she landed in Southampton, but it would arrive only a few days before she herself did, so she didn't see the point. She had managed to dash off a quick note to Trevor and James to say she'd landed.

As the days passed, the horses became accustomed to the lush greens and autumn ochres that were so foreign to their native Arabia, while Georgie feared she would never become accustomed to England again.

The idea of her native land tortured her. Yes, of course, she felt filial responsibilities, love even, but the closer she got to Derbyshire, the more she missed the Levant. The freedoms she'd enjoyed in the Middle East were impossible here—both in terms of her outward appearance and simply speaking her mind. Everything in England was prescribed; everyone was meddlesome and opinionated and irksome.

She gave Cyrus a spurring kick and he quickened his pace—at least she was going to enjoy riding astride for a day or two more. As soon as they reached Castle Donington, Lady Georgiana Cambury would be required to make her appearance. Until then, Georgie prevailed.

Chapter 2

On the ninth night after they'd set off from Southampton, Castle Donington rose up in the distance, a fine spread and one that held fond memories from her childhood. Georgie had released her pair of employees that afternoon, sending them back to Southampton, planning to hire two more local men in the morning. That evening, young master George checked into the Lion and Lamb—chosen primarily for its immaculate stables—and informed the innkeeper that his cousin, Lady Georgiana, would be arriving at some point, but George was not certain when. The proprietor hadn't seemed to care much one way or another. As usual, once money changed hands, that was the end of it.

She'd decided to spend the next two nights and days at the Lion and Lamb, shedding George and becoming Lady Georgiana. *Shedding* was quite the right word, she thought, like peeling off a second skin. It didn't hurt, exactly, but it made her think of a cobra she'd seen in the desert marketplace, as it slowly rubbed its nose and slid out of the glaucous wrapper that had served its purpose and must now be left behind.

But Georgie never really left it behind.

The supposedly masculine way she felt and acted when she was dressed as George—confident, outspoken, resilient—was part of her now, neither masculine nor feminine. In fact, she bristled at the idea that men should arbitrarily have those excellent qualities under their sole purview. And she was not alone in that view.

She had become friends with an older English woman in Cairo and had finally confided to her about her alter ego, George. Sibylla Tickenham had laughed and laughed, and had then reached for the shelf and opened a collection of drawings that showed a young Sibylla in traditional Bedouin attire. Traditional Bedouin *male* attire.

They'd spoken late into the night and on many occasions after, about the freedom and risk, the danger and the pleasure of appearing in public as a man. Sibylla said she believed the masculine and the feminine coexisted inside everyone, but the extent to which one cultivated their varied natures was up to them.

"I believe you are a perfect Janus like me, dear Georgie, swinging like a pendulum from extreme to extreme, and loving both."

At the time, Georgie had been reclining on a pile of ornately brocaded pillows at Sibylla's feet, her head resting casually on the older woman's lap. She'd taken a sip of Sibylla's brandy and thought about that. "I do love both."

Sibylla had nodded her encouragement, and made Georgie believe—or begin to believe—that Janus heads were in fact perfect, that being open to all things in every direction was a sign of vitality and strength, not a sign of duplicity or ambivalence.

Now that she was back in England, loving both—in herself and others—seemed a preposterous, distant dream, something misty and forbidden that she could only do in a faraway land where her family and connections were all severed. One more reason to sigh and hope for the shortest trip possible, after she'd delivered Cyrus and Saladeen to Trevor. And one more reason to get completely slewed in the meantime.

So, that first night at the Lion and Lamb in Donington, Georgie sat in her room and got summarily drunk. Without making a big stink in the bar downstairs, she simply drank alone and let the alcohol do its job. She wallowed in a bit of self-pity during the first few glasses. Then she laughed at herself—her wealthy, independent, spoiled self—during the next few glasses. Then she ordered a large tub to be delivered and sat staring at the steaming water for a few moments after the male servants had left with their empty buckets and their laughter.

That was another thing she was going to miss while she was all trussed up in lace and fripperies here in England. When she was George, other men—from haughty valets and rumbustious stable boys to enigmatic pashas—were accessible to her in an utterly nonsexual way. Well, in a sexual way too, on occasion, but it was the easy pedestrian camaraderie that was the most enjoyable. They would make rude jokes and laugh and speak *inappropriately* around each other, around *her*. Around her when she was George Camden, that is.

No one dared speak inappropriately around Lady Georgiana Cambury—no one dared do much of anything interesting around Lady Georgiana Cambury, heiress, sister of the Marquess of Camburton, daughter of Lady Vanessa Montagu Cambury.

After tossing back a fifth glass of Scotch, she set the crystal decanter down and began to untie her neckcloth. She removed her small amber pin and set it next to the liquor. She pulled off her close-fitting jacket, and then bent to remove her boots. Her buckskins came off next, then her stockings. She pulled her shirt over her head and let it float to the floor with the rest of the clothing she wouldn't be wearing again until she returned to Egypt.

Then she began unlacing the intricate corset-vest she'd designed with the tailor. It was similar to a woman's stays, but she'd designed it so it went over her shoulders like a skintight, sleeveless waistcoat. While it flattened her breasts, giving her the masculine appearance that let her be George, it also gave her back support while riding.

When her breasts were finally free, she arched her back, contemplating the unfamiliar weight of them, then slid into the hot water. The silky heat enveloped her and helped facilitate the mental and physical transition from lad to lady. While she lingered in the tub, she tried to envision herself perhaps enjoying the next few weeks as the jaunty Lady Georgiana. She sank deeper into the water and smiled, reminding herself that hot baths and silky undergarments were hardly trials to be endured.

An hour or so later she was languishing under the covers, in a light cotton night rail, slipping her feet around the clean sheets that covered the feather bed. For a brief moment, she missed the dank confines of the shipboard stable and the nearness of Cyrus and Saladeen, but quickly let go of her perverse sentimentality, burrowed deeper into the luxury of freshly laundered linen, and fell asleep.

The next morning she woke to a spectacularly sunny day, as if the weather were eager to provide a fresh start on this, her first day as Lady Georgiana. She narrowed her eyes against the brightness—that fifth Scotch might have been a mistake—then let the curtain fall back into place. She drank as much water as she could stomach, then opened her trunks filled with pantaloons and chemises and ribbons and gowns and riding habits. She opted for a dark blue velvet habit and a hat that would cover most of her short hair. By comparison, her female corset was softer, looser, and emphasized her breasts, and although it was supportive, it was far less constricting. She liked constricting, damn it.

When she was ready to go downstairs, she took a long look at herself in the mirror. Her face needed powder—she was far too dark by British standards of femininity—but otherwise she looked, well, rather pretty. She smiled at her reflection, grabbed a parasol, and tried to enjoy the swishing fabric around her legs and the luxury of so many layers cosseting her.

As she began to make her way down the stairs, she realized she was quite out of practice when it came to moving with all that skirted fabric. The silk velvet was everywhere, and there was so *much* of it. She nearly tripped on the last step and had to steady herself before continuing into the parlor where luncheon was being served. As she was turning in to that room, she heard a familiar deep voice coming from the front hall behind her.

"She should have arrived by now. Are you certain? Lady Georgiana Cambury?"

She wheeled around and was unable to repress a squeal of delight. "Trevor!"

He glanced in her direction and his face bloomed with pleasure on seeing her. "There you are!" He turned with a lordly look of disappointment to the innkeeper. "She is right there and she is quite obviously the most beautiful creature this side of the Channel. How you could have missed her arrival, I cannot understand."

Georgie smiled benevolently at the innkeeper, then back to Trevor. "I slipped in late last night—"

"Yes, the other gentleman said you would—" began the innkeeper, eager to preserve his reputation.

"What other gentleman?" Trevor interrupted with a raised brow.

Georgie slid her arm through his and turned him toward the parlor. "Let's catch up over lunch, shall we? The innkeeper must mean one of the men I'd hired to carry all my trunks and my special gifts for you and Rushford."

The innkeeper shook his head and went back to his bookkeeping.

Trevor tipped his hat to the man and then squeezed Georgie to his side. "I am so pleased to see you, darling. And looking so well."

"You're such a charmer. I know I must look like I've been dragged through the Sahara. My skin has become coarse, my arms thick."

"Your strength has always appealed to me, you know that." He smiled and showed her to a table near the window.

His compliment gave her an unfamiliar blush. "Where is Rushford?" she asked quickly. "Did he also ride ahead to meet me, or are you traveling alone?"

"No." Trevor seemed preoccupied, and he kept looking at her in an unusually *assessing* way. "I wanted to speak to you privately."

"Truly? I can't imagine what you could possibly have to say to me that you wouldn't say in front of Rushford. Is he as darling as I remember? I'm hoping we can spend lots and lots of time together on this visit, so I can get to know and love him as thoroughly as you do."

If Georgie hadn't known better, she'd suspect that her innocuous statement was making Trevor blush. He looked unaccountably shy.

Before she could press him for details, the serving girl came over and asked what they'd like to drink, and told them what was on offer for lunch. They ordered, and then Georgie gave Trevor her full attention, reaching for his hands. "What is it, my dear? You look troubled. You know I'll do anything you need. Is it money?"

He narrowed his eyes and exhaled. "In a way . . ."

"Well, that's easily solved! It turns out I'm quite clever with my finances—my mother's daughter, in that at least. How is Vanessa, by the by? Still managing everyone?" Georgie knew it was wrong of her to cast her mother in this negative light, but Vanessa *was* managing, and it *was* tedious.

"She and Nora are wonderful."

Georgie looked at the wood of the round table, where the sun caught the high polish. "Nora has always been wonderful."

"Vanessa has always been wonderful too, Georgie."

She looked up. "Yes, yes. Of course she is. So how much do you need? I'll have it sent up from London."

When their drinks arrived, Trevor looked politely at the serving girl, then refocused on Georgie. "It's a bit more complicated than that, I'm afraid."

"Complicated?"

"This is rather more awkward than I thought when James and I were speaking about it."

Georgie smiled and took a sip of her lemonade—her lady's drink, she thought with a wrinkled nose—and set her glass down. "You don't ever need to feel awkward with me, Trevor. We've seen each other through every possible stage of our silly lives, haven't we? Remember when I first got my courses? What could possibly be more awkward than that?"

He paused, then looked straight into her eyes. "I want to marry you."

She choked on the second sip of lemonade, and within seconds Trevor was standing behind her, patting her back and giving her one of his perfectly monogrammed linen handkerchiefs to help contain the spray that was threatening to explode from her nose. Several other patrons of the inn turned to make sure she wasn't actually choking to death, but with a quick smile and nod from Trevor, they were assured of her non-imminent demise.

When he sat back down across from her, he simply stared. And she simply stared back. And then she started laughing uncontrollably. Her eyes watered, her nostrils burned. He smiled at her and let her mirth run its course.

"I've missed you terribly," he said at last.

She breathed deep to prevent a new wave of merriment from overtaking her. "So much so that you now want to marry me?"

"No!" He smiled through his words. "I mean, yes, of course I've missed you desperately and wish you would just move home already, but this isn't about that."

"Are you certain?" She ventured another sip of the lemonade and prayed he didn't say anything equally absurd while she attempted to swallow it. The idea of Trevor having romantic notions about her was just . . . preposterous. And yet, a silly flush was creeping up her cheeks at the mere idea of it. What if . . .? Of course not!

"Yes." He was quite serious this time. "I'm certain. This is not some ploy to bind you to a life you despise." It was a life he adored, so she always felt small when he said it like that.

"Oh, don't say it that way, darling. I don't *despise* England. We're just . . . a poorly matched pair." She smiled at the equine reference. "Speaking of pairs, have you seen Cyrus and Saladeen?"

"I have, actually." He sat back and gazed at her. "I went into the stables a few minutes ago, and there they were looking as regal and out of place as you promised. I was surprised you weren't bedded down with them in the hay."

His good humor was contagious. "Truth be told, it was the first night in many that I didn't bed down with them."

"You can't be serious." He looked appalled at the idea. If he only knew.

"Quite serious." She waved her gloved hand to swat away that conversation. She'd tell him about her life as George—at some point, or maybe never—but not now. "Now, go back to this perplexing marriage proposal. You must be serious about it or you never would have risked sending me into convulsions. Why?"

He tapped the table with his index finger several times, then stopped and looked up at her. "It's my father. He's gone a bit berserk ever since my mother died—"

"I'm so sorry for your loss—you received my letters, yes?"

"Yes, thank you. It wasn't awful—as far as these things go. She was in fine fettle, and then last winter she fell ill, and she was gone in a matter of weeks. I understand my father's misery—he was entirely devoted to her—but her absence has, well, made him quite . . . difficult. He's threatening to withhold my inheritance if I don't marry . . . a woman."

She smiled at the unnecessary addendum. Of course, James and Trevor had been living together as bachelors for many years, but Trevor's father had never—would never—accept the truth of their partnership. "Thank you for clarifying your father's preference for the gender of the person you marry."

When he looked at her then, Georgie saw something so much deeper, so much tenderer than her light words could possibly allay. The man was in trouble. Not because of who he was or whom he loved, but because this damnable society was punishing him for being the wonderful person he was. Her heart hammered for him.

"What about my assets?" she asked pragmatically. "I'm generous, but I shan't become *feme covert*, even for you, my sweet. I shall never be a man's property."

"Are you s-saying—" He stuttered. "Are you even willing to entertain the idea, if we can iron out the logistics of you retaining your independence, financial and otherwise?"

She spread her arms wide. "As you can see. Here I am, entertaining the idea of marrying you."

"Oh, my dear, dear friend."

"There are many particulars, I presume. Your father isn't going to simply accept a marriage of convenience. First off, I shan't have children under any circumstances—"

"Oh! Of course not! No. I mean—" He stuttered again, and Georgie reached for his hand and held it in hers. "Not that I wouldn't, you know, if you ever wanted that, I mean—"

The poor man. "I love you, Trevor. You know that. Just tell me everything and we will sort it out. You won't ever need to bed me, if that's what you're getting to." The words came out sounding cavalier enough, but something went a bit haywire in Georgie's chest when she uttered the words *bed me* while looking into Trevor's eyes and holding his hand in hers.

He squeezed her hand and breathed a sigh. "James thought I was crazy to even suggest it—the marriage, I mean!—but I knew you would be your breezy self. I'm so relieved you didn't take offense."

"Offense? James must think very little of me if that's what he thought."

"No. Quite the opposite. He thinks very highly of you and didn't want you to think I was—oh, I don't know—toying with you or forcing you into anything."

"Well," she chuckled, "then he and I really do need to get to know each other better, because you of all people know that I will not be forced into anything . . . ever."

Trevor laughed and then leaned across the table and kissed her cheek. That damn flush crept up her neck again, and she shivered and pretended it was the draft that had just come into the parlor as the front door swung open.

"That's exactly what I told him," Trevor continued. "That's why you were the perfect person to ask. You would never be coerced into doing something you didn't want to do."

She smiled back at him. "Quite so."

"James then made a joke about whether or not you could be coerced into something you *did* want to do."

"Oh, I like him all over again for saying that." Georgie patted Trevor's hand and slipped her own back into her lap. There had been some sort of tingling in her palms when she held Trevor's hand in hers, and that needed to stop immediately. What in the world had got into her? Her best friend was asking her for what amounted to a legal favor; he was not pledging his troth, for goodness' sake.

She sat up straighter, took another sip of lemonade, and then looked him straight in the eye. "How soon do you want to call the banns?"

They spent the rest of the afternoon meticulously sorting out the details of a settlement. It turned out Trevor really had no need of her funds; once he married, according to the terms of his father's wishes, he would inherit both the real property and a sizable portion of the income from his mother's myriad investments. His family home, Mayfield House, was a vast country estate in need of renovation and attention. All of the agriculture had stagnated under his father's less-than-watchful eyes, and Trevor was eager to implement the latest crop rotations and irrigation schemes.

Knowing this, Viscount Mayfield was threatening to halt any financial support for the modernization of Mayfield House and the surrounding lands. If that occurred, Trevor was sure the place would descend into bankruptcy within five years, if not sooner. How his father could allow that to happen—to embark upon a self-destructive path that was so obviously motivated by spite—Georgie did not want to contemplate. The viscount had always preferred his life in London, and the glory of Mayfield was lost on him. Not so Trevor, who had inherited his mother's love of the land.

The next day they rode into Derby and met with their respective solicitors. It was all *very unusual* according to Messrs. Ward and Wooley, but they drew up the papers nonetheless, and everything was sealed with wax and rings and stamps.

As the somber clerks went about their business, Georgie turned to Trevor. "I am finding this all quite delightful! To be poking fun at the law satisfies my rebellious nature, and to be helping you attain what was rightfully yours suits my heart."

He lifted her ungloved hand and kissed it. "You suit me, Georgie." There was nothing more to it, she told herself. They were best friends. That's all he meant. Of course that's what he meant. He loved James Rushford. Why was her silly heart fluttering, then? Preposterous heart.

"I am to marry my best friend. How lucky am I?" She turned to Trevor and laughed from the sheer joy of it all, then handed him the pen for him to sign the rest of the documents that granted her complete financial independence.

The lawyers and clerks merely shook their heads while Georgie and Trevor laughed and signed page after page. When Trevor had signed the last line, he set down the pen and looked at her. "There. Now you will be my wife." His smile was tentative and adorable, filled with wonder and gratitude.

In name only, she reminded herself briskly.

They reached Mayfield two days later, and Georgie decided to stay on with James and Trevor for a little while longer—ostensibly to settle Cyrus and Saladeen into their new home, but mostly to postpone seeing her mother and having to remove to Camburton Castle for the remainder of her visit.

James was waiting for them at the front door when they rode into the forecourt of Mayfield. Trevor leapt off his horse and tossed the reins to a groom who waited nearby, then took the front steps two at a time to get to James.

Georgie dismounted more slowly, breathing in the familiar air of home, and trying not to be too obvious about her interest in how Trevor and James behaved in front of the servants. Did they embrace? Shake hands? Nod?

A second groom took hold of Cyrus for her and she turned casually to see James and Trevor by the front door. They were somehow intimate and appropriate all at once. Trevor had one strong hand gripping Rushford's firm upper arm and was laughing and talking all at once. Georgie heard bits of the conversation on the wind—"she said yes" came out clearly, and James turned to catch Georgie looking at them. He mouthed a *thank you*, then returned his attention to Trevor.

She ascended the steps with ladylike poise, taking care not to stumble on the reams of fabric. She'd got back into the habit of being a lady over the past few days, but it still felt like she was playing a part.

"Lady Georgiana!" James patted Trevor once on the cheek, then walked around him to greet her. "It's such a pleasure to see you again after all these years." He took her hand and kissed her gloved knuckles. "I've missed your sparkling company."

"It's a pleasure to see you as well, Mr. Rushford."

"What's all this Mr. Rushford and Lady Georgiana blather?" Trevor asked on a laugh. "Come inside at once and let's the three of us have tea and cease with these silly formalities. There's much to celebrate, and I want to be festive with my two favorite people in the world."

Rushford held out his forearm for Georgie to take. Very formal. Very appropriate. She rested her hand lightly on the fine fabric of his jacket and accompanied him into the grand front hall. "Thank you. A million thank-yous," he said in a low, intimate tone. "You have saved this place, but more importantly, you have saved Trevor. I am indebted to you forever."

He spoke with such earnest regard, and in a way that was a bit close to her ear. The hot breath of his words tickled Georgie's neck and she had a strange sensual response to the man's nearness. Her breasts tightened and a fizzing awareness simmered low in her belly. Perhaps she'd been too long alone on her journey, or perhaps being in England was doing something to her, because it seemed as if every man of her acquaintance was suddenly making her think of . . . fornicating.

She inhaled to clear her muddled thoughts and then smiled brightly up at James. "It was nothing at all. A favor from one friend to another."

He looked taken aback, almost hurt. "Oh, no. It was so much more than that, Lady Georgiana—"

"Please call me Georgie. I insist."

"Very well, Georgie. But you must know what an enormous gift you've given him, and how hard it was for him to ask. He simply adores you, you know, and the idea that he was perhaps risking the intimate friendship that you've shared all these years. Well, it has been quite a difficult few months while he tried to figure out how best to broach the topic."

Perhaps a cold bucket of water was required, thought Georgie, because that devilish flush returned when Rushford said the words *he adores you.* And worse, she had an image flash in her mind of what it would be like if her *intimate friend*—and his partner—happened to *simply adore* her body. The vision was quite abrupt and quite clear. And then it was gone in a snap. She opted for silence, lest her voice betray her bizarre imaginings.

"I am garrulous and you must be tired from your journey." James laughed at himself and Georgie felt it rumble through her. "I beg your pardon. I did not mean to launch into an endless stream before we'd even reached the drawing room. I'm just so grateful, on Trevor's behalf of course. So grateful."

He quieted until they reached the splendid drawing room. When they entered, the fire was crackling and a large tea had been laid out in advance of their arrival.

"Here we are," James announced, patting Georgie's hand where it rested on his forearm, then releasing her and crossing the room to join Trevor.

The two men stood close together, not actually touching, yet an undeniable heat arced between them. Heat, or love perhaps. They seemed relieved and happy to be in one another's company, and Georgie enjoyed the simple pleasure of being with like-minded friends. She hoped her strange attraction to Trevor—and now, it seemed, James—would wear off in the next few days, and if it didn't, at least she would be on her way back to Egypt soon enough. Neither of them fancied her, and it would be preposterous to pursue anything in the bedroom even if they did.

Preposterous.

At least that's what she kept telling herself as one day passed into two, and then a week. She was avoiding going to see her mother, and spending time with James and Trevor was distracting and joyful. Trevor was as mad about horses as she was, and the two of them would ride for hours each day. James was quick-witted and charming, regaling them with stories over dinner about the latest on-dits from London. On-dits that nearly always featured titillating escapades of the aristocracy, which he would finish telling and then raise an eyebrow toward Trevor. The sexual tension between the two men was palpable.

And no business of Georgie's.

At the end of that enjoyable week, Trevor finally played the adult and prodded her about visiting her mother.

"The longer you put it off, the more put out she is going to be. You know how she is."

"Unfortunately, yes, I know exactly how she is."

"What's all this?" James slowly swirled his glass of claret as the three of them sat around the fire after dinner. "I adore Vanessa. We should all be so lucky to have a mother of such open-mindedness."

"She's not quite so open with her daughter."

"I don't believe it."

"Tell him, Trevor." Georgie lifted her chin.

"She loves you, that's all. She—"

"If love is a noose, then yes, that's precisely true—"

"Now, Georgie," Trevor soothed. "She misses you terribly when you're gone, and then she's all nervous that everything has to be perfect for the short times you're here. Try to see it from her point of view."

"Oh, enough! I'll go tomorrow." She looked at Trevor, then at James. "Will you two accompany me? It will be easier somehow."

"Of course. We wouldn't have it any other way. Plus, you need to announce your engagement!" James stood up and grabbed her around the waist and lifted her off the chair where she'd been curled up with her legs tucked beneath her. He twirled her around and then set her down with a quick kiss on the lips. She laughed and tried to ignore the spike of sexual awareness that accompanied the buss. She'd had a few blessed days of *not* being overly aware of the two men around her. They were her friends, damn it.

She set herself away from him and caught Trevor looking longingly at James when she bade them goodnight. "Until tomorrow, then."

She raced up the stairs and tried *not* to imagine what the two of them were getting up to in the drawing room after she left. Once she'd undressed and changed into her night rail, she slipped into bed and gave up trying. She let her imagination run riot, picturing Trevor and James in every sordid, compromising position she could conjure, until her own climax overtook her and she needed to bite the edge of the heavy duvet to muffle her own pleasure.

The next morning, feeling as if she were on her way to the gallows, Georgie chose one of the calmer horses and trotted from Mayfield to Camburton with James and Trevor beside her. They took the longest way round and still arrived sooner than she'd hoped. It was probably petulant or incendiary of her to do so, but she'd decided to wear buckskins for her first reunion with her mother. She was also wearing a jaunty hat with an outrageous lavender ostrich feather, so she couldn't be accused of being entirely masculine. *Begin as you mean to go on*, she thought sullenly.

It turned out Camburton was filled to the gills with more than the usual assortment of poets and painters and hangers-on, including a young Spanish woman named Anna de Montizon who turned out to be Nora's long-lost daughter. Georgie was thrilled for Nora, her de facto stepmother, and thrilled to meet Anna—a new sister of sorts. Anna was an exuberant, confident woman, and Georgie was especially pleased to speak with her at length because their meeting distracted Vanessa from focusing so much negative attention on Georgie's numerous shortcomings: the fact that she'd been staying at Mayfield instead of coming straightaway to Camburton; the fact that she'd cut of all of her beautiful blonde hair; the fact that she was, well, Georgie.

"Why did you cut it so short? You used to be so pretty!" Vanessa cried at one point. Georgie wanted nothing more than to hurl her glass at the side of her mother's thick skull.

"Used to be?" she couldn't resist taunting.

"Oh, you know what I meant."

"I live in the desert, Mother. With sand."

There was no point in explaining anything to Vanessa because she knew everything already. Women, no matter how liberated, were supposed to be *pretty*, don't you know. Georgie shrugged it off, like she shrugged off every other thinly veiled insult her mother tossed at her. It was endless. And tiresome. And soon enough she'd be back in Egypt.

Why was she the only one who saw Vanessa for the calculating, manipulative matriarch she was? Everyone else was fooled by all of her *great works* and *social reforms*. Georgie sighed and looked away from her mother. No point in hoping the woman would ever change where she was concerned.

Her sweet twin brother Archie, the Marquess of Camburton, swept in to repair the emotional damage, as he always did, but Vanessa still ended up making Georgie feel like she simply didn't measure up. In light of Vanessa's obvious disappointments, Georgie decided not to tell her just yet that she'd agreed to marry Trevor—having to explain the rather callous nature of their arrangement was beyond her at the moment.

After an hour or so in Vanessa's drawing room, Georgie finally escaped with her dear Archie. James and Trevor took her horse and Archie walked her home—or rather back to Mayfield House—and he talked at length about his growing attraction for the novelist in residence, Selina Ashby.

After she bid Archie farewell late that afternoon, she looked forward to relaxing with Trevor and James for a few hours before returning to Camburton for the dreaded family dinner to which they'd all been invited.

Chapter 3

Relaxation was the last thing Georgie got when she entered the drawing room at Mayfield that afternoon.

"Why didn't you tell them about our plans?" Trevor was the picture-perfect country gentleman. Quite literally. Nora White had painted his portrait so many times, he had become a sort of pastoral ideal in the picture galleries of London and drawing rooms across the continent. He was tall without being overbearing, elegant without being too feminine. His wide shoulders and muscled thighs were the result of constant sport and manual labor around his vast estate, not the work of fashionably deceptive cotton wadding. His dark hair curled carelessly around the folds of his collar—apparently bucks in London were already trying to imitate said carelessness, with great care.

Georgie sighed and shook her head—she'd taken to staring at Trevor far too blatantly. "Unfortunately, after you two left, the absence of my hair caused a commotion, then Pia announced she was *enceinte*, and then it turns out Archie has fallen hopelessly in love with some writer named Selina Ashby, so he spent the entire walk back spilling his poor heart out to me, and well—" She threw up her hands. "There really wasn't a spare moment."

"As bad as all that?" Rushford asked. Whereas Trevor was the picture of a vigorous country squire, James was more like a greyhound: whip thin, sinewy, quick-witted, and razor sharp. He set down the fabric trim he was working on and gave Georgie an assessing look. "You could have left your hat on and avoided the discussion about your hair altogether. It's a fabulous hat."

"You and your damned hats!" she joked.

Rushford laughed. "Women in London pay spectacular sums for those *damned hats* of mine, so you'd best keep your opinions to yourself."

Georgie flopped on the large sofa next to Trevor, tossing the aforementioned hat to Rushford, who caught it with a quick one-handed grab.

"What am I to do?" she said on a moan, leaning her head back against the sofa cushion and looking at the angels across the ceiling. "I've only spent thirty minutes in her presence and already my mother's driving me berserk. She willfully misconstrues everything I say or do."

Trevor reached for one of her hands and took it between both of his, massaging her knuckles and wrist. "Stop worrying. You'll be back in Cairo in no time. Anonymous and living your Bedouin existence."

"Is that so wrong?" She shut her eyes and relaxed into his firm touch. "When you say it, I feel happy and free. When she says it . . . I feel as if I'm being irresponsible and running away. Why does she make me feel so *wrong* all the time?"

"Maybe you make *her* feel wrong, did you ever think of it that way?" Trevor was always trying to see every side. "Maybe her idea of being a good mother means her children are always near."

She opened her eyes to look at him. He was so damnably perfect: the kind green eyes, never judgmental; the slight lift of his full mouth, always sympathetic, never sardonic. "Oh, Trevor. You must be understanding like that for all of us—I couldn't possibly manage it." She turned to James. "How can you bear it? All his kindness? It almost makes it worse. Now I feel heartless around my mother *and* heartless around Trevor for not being more understanding of my own heartlessness."

"Come, Georgie. It can't be as bad as all that. Vanessa is so *loving*." James abandoned his work and joined them on the sofa. He was watching the way Trevor's hands worked on hers, probably thinking the massage was wasted on her.

"I know!" Georgie exclaimed. "That's why it's so dispiriting. She's so kind and open and generous and *perfect*, and then she looks at me and I can practically feel the disappointment roll off her in waves. Because I'm none of those things. I'm selfish and closed off and—"

"Oh, do stop it. That's simply not true." Trevor finished squeezing her pinkie, then rested her hand back on her thigh. "You are always helping others, even if you are not *effusive* about it. Look what you're willing to do for me."

Georgie waved her hand in front of her face. "Oh, that's nothing."

"Marrying me is nothing?" Trevor laughed and shook his head. "Saving this estate by fulfilling the outrageous demands of my father's entail that I marry a *woman*. Emphasis his."

"Well." Georgie smiled at the way he said it. "When you put it that way, I see what you mean. But you know, even that, Vanessa is going to be appalled—tormented that it's not a *love* match. Because it's obvious I'm not in *love* with you or any such foolishness."

She caught the glance that James and Trevor exchanged. "I mean, it would be foolish for *me*. I mean . . . See, when you two look at each other like that, that is *love*. Of course I love you as my dearest friends—I can tell you anything, say anything, do anything. But really? All that gooey emotion is just . . ." She shivered at the thought. "So *cloying*."

Both men laughed, and then James stood up to pour them all drinks. With his back still turned, he asked, "If you're really able to tell us *anything*, Georgie, have you ever . . . you know . . . been with anyone?"

Georgie smiled at his back and then looked at Trevor to see what he thought, if it was just a silly question. But his lips were quirked and he seemed genuinely interested.

"Fine," he admitted. "I've also wondered."

"Really?"

He shrugged adorably. "I mean, I haven't spent a lot of time thinking about it. But you know, you're fabulous and my closest friend, and you deserve to have a bit of fun like the rest of us."

"I'm so flattered you two have taken an interest in my *physical needs*."

"Oh, never mind." James obviously sensed her sarcasm. He crossed the room and handed them each a glass of whiskey. "I shouldn't be so crass, but I always think of you as one of the boys, so I figured I might as well ask what I'd feel comfortable asking . . . one of the boys."

Georgie loved that idea. Why shouldn't she tell them about her rather blasé attitude toward her sexual activities? It was nothing more than a physical appetite she satisfied when the need arose, akin to eating or drinking. "Well, when you put it that way, as long as I'm one of the boys and all, I'll tell you."

"Ooh, exotic stories from faraway lands!" Trevor settled more comfortably into his corner of the sofa.

"So, I was in Egypt first. Lots of British expatriates and French soldiers and a lot of mayhem actually. I'll tell you more about it, of course. But to get to the point, once you went behind the veil— pulled back the curtain, what have you—Egypt and Arabia were quite fantastic places as far as the sex was concerned."

James perked up. "Really?"

"Yes. Of course, in some ways it was all very physical and matter-of-fact. When I was first there, for example, I met a slightly older British woman—a widow I think, but maybe an adventuress traveling under the guise of widowhood—who took me to a bathhouse, for women only of course. And oh, how the women take care of one another's bodies, so tender and thorough. In an almost reverential fashion, they take hot baths, massage each other with splendid oils and fragrant extracts, and all that sort of thing, quite relaxing and luxurious. And trust me, there was nothing *platonic* about it. But I'm not really one for all that *lounging*, as you can imagine." James and Trevor both smiled knowingly at the preposterous idea of her sitting still for longer than a few moments at a time. "So, after I had set up my own establishment, well, I guess you could say I pursued my own desires." She sighed at the memories.

"Truly?" Trevor teased. "You were quite the belle of the . . . Bedouins?"

"Well, *beau* was more like it. All those men loved to treat me like their little British lad, to be played with, and used, you know, in all the ways men play with lads."

"What?" Trevor nearly spit out his drink. "I beg your pardon?"

James's eyes gleamed with anticipation. "Pray tell!"

"I mean, you certainly didn't think I was allowed to attend the horse-breeding establishments and sales or visit the inner sanctums of the sheikhs while I was the upstanding Lady Georgiana Cambury, did you?" She leapt up from the sofa and struck a mannish pose, one trousered leg cast arrogantly in front of the other. "George Camden at your service." With that, she sketched a perfectly masculine bow.

James bellowed out a laugh. "You passed yourself off as a chap? I adore you!"

She nodded and smiled and stood up a little straighter, feeling immediately comfortable in the confident, manly position. "Of course it was awkward at first. I felt so . . . oh, I don't know, like an impostor I suppose. But when I gave myself over to it, really let it wash over me, it was quite wonderful. It was perhaps the most comfortable I've ever felt in my own skin. Not only for the places I could finally go without raising the eyebrows of the matrons in the British social clubs in Cairo, but the actual feeling of it, of walking with my arms swinging and my legs strong. Keeping my chin up and looking out at the world instead of that mincing female business of always avoiding eye contact and staring at my feet."

Trevor was still smiling after her revelation, but he obviously had other questions bubbling to the surface.

"What else?" Georgie wanted to take all comers.

"You were never a very *mincing* female to begin with, Georgie, so I don't see how it was *that* much of a change."

"Really, Lord Mayson?" She raised a haughty brow and spoke in her deeper masculine tone. "You don't think it would be *that much of a change* for you to put on a dress and walk down Bond Street? You don't think you would feel powerfully aware of how people looked at you, how confining and distracting all the fabric and petticoats and delicate shoes would feel against your skin?"

He flushed. "Well, when you put it that way, I'm *powerfully* interested."

"Oh, you are terrible!" Georgie collapsed back onto the couch between them, all three taking sips of their drinks and sighing happily.

"He would, you know," James remarked.

"Would what?" Georgie asked, still flushed from her confession.

"Walk down Bond Street dressed in the latest women's fashions." James leaned in front of Georgie and looked at Mayson. "Wouldn't you, pet?"

Trevor smiled agreeably. "For you, darling, anything."

"Stop it at once, you two. You're far too affectionate. You know I can't stand it."

"You'd best get used to it if we're going to be married and all." Trevor gave her a conspiratorial wink.

"I shan't be a member of your household for long. After we say our vows and the terms of your father's will are met, I'll be off soon after."

"Oh, I know, but you're still here for now, and I don't like having to behave in front of you."

"Is that what you've been doing for the past week since I arrived? Behaving?" Georgie asked.

"To be honest, yes."

"Really? Well, far be it from me to tamp down your ardor. Feel free to do what you wish. I shan't bat an eye."

"Oh, how delicious! An audience!" James set his glass down on the Louis XIV table to the left of the sofa and stood up. "Move over, young Master Camden. I've some business to attend to with the lord of the manor."

Georgie laughed and scooted to the far end of the sofa. "You're terrible, James. As if you would do anything—" She gasped when James fisted his fingers into Trevor's hair at the nape and tugged hard.

"Have you missed me, pet?" James's voice had lowered to a menacing growl.

"Terribly," Trevor panted.

With that, James rested one knee provocatively between Trevor's spread thighs and dipped his mouth to Trevor's, teasing him with the lightest kisses. At first, Georgie tried to look away, but the moans of pleasure were rather . . . inviting, and after a few vain attempts to appear disinterested, she curled her legs up beneath her and turned to watch the two men with her full attention.

James was a wicked, taunting beast. Giving Trevor little bits of suction here, a trail of his tongue there, a whisper of his lip along the edge of Trevor's mouth, all the while tightening that mad grip at the base of the other man's neck. Trevor's entire huge body was coiled tight, broad shoulders and biceps flexing beneath the perfectly fitted wool of his riding jacket, hands fisted into the blue silk upholstery of the couch.

"Why isn't he touching you, James?" Georgie asked, as if watching two animals in the wild with a local guide there to answer her inquiries.

When James took his attention away—reluctantly—from Trevor's moist, swollen lips, he turned to answer her. "Because he's not allowed to touch me today."

"Really? How divine."

"It is. Quite," James agreed. "He has to sit there patiently and take it. And it makes him quite exercised, doesn't it, darling?" James pressed the palm of his free hand into the straining crotch of Trevor's buckskins as he spoke casually to Georgie. "He gets delightfully frustrated, as you can see. Barely able to reply."

Trevor moaned unintelligibly to prove the point.

Seeing this huge, capable man willfully—happily—reduced to this moaning, desperate pile of desire made something flip in Georgie's belly. She stood up quickly and set her empty whiskey glass on the side table. "I'll leave you to it, then."

"You're welcome to stay," James called playfully after her, but she knew he didn't really mean it.

"Three's a crowd," she responded over one shoulder, her voice echoing his levity. James laughed darkly, and she heard Trevor moan again.

Georgie pulled the door to the drawing room shut behind her, and leaned against it with a heavy sigh. She shut her eyes and let her heart race unfettered. She was such a liar.

In fact, it hadn't been a crowd at all. For the first time in Georgie's life, she had actually wanted to be an intimate part of something— and not merely physically intimate. Georgie had wanted to feel what James and Trevor were feeling, to give of herself the way they gave of themselves to one another.

And it terrified her.

She stood in the dim hallway and tried to catch her breath. She'd been in any number of unwelcome scrapes over the course of the past five years—contending with runaway camels, fending off angry sheikhs, and being held at knifepoint . . . Well, that last wasn't entirely unwelcome, come to think of it. She smiled ironically and took another deep breath, forcing herself to calm. If she could handle marauding gangs of Bedouins, she could certainly handle a bit of intimacy between the two men in the other room.

Right as she had the thought, Trevor let out a cry of sensual pleasure, and even though it was slightly muffled by the two-hundred-year-old oak door behind her, Georgie leapt away from the sound as if she'd been burnt. She strode across the black-and-white marble floor of the grand front hall, stepping only on the white squares, as she'd always done on her frequent childhood visits to this majestic country house. Hands clasped behind her at the base of her spine, bounding toward the large front doors, she jumped when the housekeeper, Mrs. Daley, called out, "Lady Georgiana, is that you?"

"Oh, do stop with the formalities, Daley." Georgie let out a sigh and plopped down on the bench near the front door that had been there for decades to accommodate unwelcome visitors.

"Well, I can't be calling you Georgie-girl if you're to be the lady of Mayfield House, now can I, miss?" Mrs. Daley stared with narrowed eyes at Georgie. "It's still hard for me to look at you with all your beautiful blonde hair disappeared into the desert wind. But it will grow back and you'll be as pretty as ever. Though you'd make quite a dashing lad, I must say."

Georgie smiled up at dear, dear Mrs. Daley. The woman had been sneaking sweetmeats and biscuits to Trevor and Georgie since the two of them were in apron strings. "Oh, Daley. I think I'm in need of a bit of cake. Have you got any?"

Mrs. Daley nodded and extended her hand in a welcoming gesture. "Come on." Georgie stood up, towering over the servant who resembled Napoleon in both stature and authority.

"Thank you."

"I've got just the thing for a frazzled day." Mrs. Daley nudged Georgie back down the hall, steering her to the kitchen with chatter and bustle. "A nice cup of tea and something sweet to tide you over until supper. And you'll be needing the carriage to take you back to Camburton, of course. And you're going to put on a pretty dress for dinner at your mother's house and not vex her. All right? All right."

Even though Georgie might be on the verge of becoming the *lady of the house*, there was only room for one at the top, and Mrs. Daley was already firmly ensconced on her domestic throne. Georgie had no desire to unseat her. Instead, she gave herself over to the comfort and familiarity of the well-run manor.

The pace and rhythm of a large country estate—here at Mayfield at least—was a soothing current, like the rolling surf along the Barbary Coast, repetitive and reassuring. She heard the kitchen maids discussing something while they cleaned pots; the scent of the promised cake wafted down the servants' hall; two footmen polished silver in a side room as Daley and Georgie passed.

Georgie wondered why she was able to feel a hint of admiration for this estate and its goings on, but the house in which she'd been raised, little more than a mile away—even though it was run in a very similar fashion—made her feel like a prisoner in the hulks.

Her mother had never been overly disciplined or draconic with them. Georgie and Archie had been afforded what many would consider an idyllic childhood. When their father had died at sea, Vanessa must have decided that one tragic childhood event was more than enough to build a seven-year-old's character. Most of their time had been spent in Derbyshire or London, but they had also traveled occasionally with their great-uncle, the diplomat, social reformer, and scholar Fitzwilliam Montagu, to Spain and Italy. They had hardly been restrained at all.

But that just added to Georgie's sense of her own inability to value life for what it was now. She had been raised in a world of exquisite privilege—and she thought she had appreciated it to the fullest—but her mother still made her feel she was, and always would be, lacking proper gratitude.

"You mustn't think so hard, Lady Georgiana. We don't want those lines of worry forming between your beautiful eyes, now do we?" Mrs. Daley set a plate of cake in front of her, along with a cup of black tea. Georgie always preferred eating in a kitchen—whether it was here in windy Derbyshire or in a grand city house in Cairo. Georgie felt closer to the earth, closer to what mattered, when she ate food near the hearth on which it had been prepared. There was honor in kitchens.

There was honor in the running of this grand house, an honor Trevor was eager to preserve. And that was a small something Georgie could do for him by agreeing to be his wife, even if it was in name only.

Once his father's wishes were fulfilled, however, Georgie would leave Trevor to James and be on her way back to North Africa. She was already desperately missing the smells and the sounds, not to mention the wild freedom she had secretly carved out.

Until then, she would stay close to the kitchens, close to the ground.

"You mustn't frighten Georgie like that again." Trevor kissed James one last time, letting his lips linger against his lover's mouth, tasting himself and feeling a renewed sense of pleasure riding straight to his cock.

"Yes, my lord."

Still breathing heavily, Trevor felt far more like the rutty gamekeeper of Mayfield than the future viscount of anything. "God, you are fantastic."

James smiled as if he'd just been complimented for a lofty academic achievement. "Why, thank you kindly, your lordship."

"Don't even start." Trevor shoved James away with a friendly push and stood up from the pale blue sofa to fasten the placket of his buckskins.

Trevor, James, and Georgie had been talking casually and James had given him a look—one of *those* looks—and when Georgie had said it was fine with her if they were affectionate in front of her, James had leapt at the chance. Trevor had taken for granted how utterly attached he and James had become over the past few years. In the usual course of a day, when they were alone in the house or on the estate, the casual touches while they worked, the occasional buss, the brief, passionate embrace before one or the other went off to work or ride—not being able to do those little bits throughout the day had thrown them both into a sort of fever.

And it had become rather, well, *heated* within a matter of seconds. Georgie had dashed from the room like a deer getting its first scent of a hunter.

When Trevor finished with his buttons, he stared down at James Rushford, sprawling in all his masculine glory. Legs spread wide and careless, cock spent and resting against one strong, lean thigh. "Aren't you a picture?"

James raised a brow. "I am quite content, if you must know."

Trevor leaned down and kissed him on the lips one last time before turning toward the dwindling fire. "So am I." He approached the large marble hearth, enjoying the familiar languid feel of satisfaction that always pulsed through his strong muscles after he and James took each other like that. He needed that feeling, more than he had realized. He needed James Rushford's hands on him every day of his life in order to feel whole and settled in his own skin.

"Do you think Georgie's really thought this through?" Trevor poked at the fire until a few flames licked, then turned to the pile of logs at his right and tossed one on. The idea of summoning a footman to put a log on the fire had always struck Trevor as preposterous.

"She's a practical person, no question about it." James started to sit up and attend to his own clothing. "It sounds as if you'd barely mentioned the circumstances of your father's demands before she leapt at the chance to help you resolve this insane wish of his."

Poking the fire again, Trevor said, "That's what I'm worried about. She's so cavalier about everything. Even if I've no intention of bedding her—not that her virtue is an issue in any case, given her revelation about her, er, busy nights in the Levant—I think she has failed to weigh the full consequences of our actions. She will *never* be able to marry for love. Do you think she's trivializing that part of the arrangement?"

James remained quiet while he considered his reply. When the silence persisted, Trevor set the fire poker in the stand and turned to face him. "Well, what do you think?"

"Maybe she *is* marrying for love. Perhaps you need to ask yourself the same question." James had always been blunt; it was one of the things that had initially attracted Trevor to him at Cambridge. James was fearless with words. Trevor had always been fearless with his body—taking up any fight, answering any taunt with his fists, making love with fervor—but he had never had the audacity to simply speak his mind the way James Rushford did.

Trevor narrowed his eyes and thought about how best to answer. Was he falling in love with her?

He and James had been entirely devoted to each other these past five years, but both of them had enjoyed being with women before they met. And it would be dishonest for Trevor to say he wasn't at least *intrigued* by the idea of having Georgie in their bed. Initially, he'd thought of it as a possible romp, but over the past week of having her in his house, he was far more intrigued by *her*, not merely her body. His heart always raced when she entered a room—all bluster and chatter about the horses or disdain for some nodcock in the morning paper. In his mind at least—especially in his fervid imagination—she was no longer *just a friend*. Looking back over his life, he was beginning to wonder if she had ever been *just* a friend.

She was also very different from the girl he'd grown up with, the girl he'd always thought of as a friend. Her experience abroad had given her a gravity, some kind of solid bedrock he wanted to mine. And yet her heart—the fierce, joyful nature that was so distinctly *her*—was still there, if shuttered. So much like James, now that Trevor thought of it. Hard to break through, but so temptingly worth the effort. He also sensed an answering desire in her, as much as she tried to bury it beneath all her layers of independence and bravado.

"I would like to bed you both," Trevor confessed. "Together." When he saw the smile of slow, delectable pleasure spread across James's face, Trevor realized it probably wasn't the first time the idea had crossed James's mind either. He began to walk back toward the sofa with a predatory stride. "Would you like that too, James?"

James nodded slowly. "I think I might like to . . ." He hesitated. "How did she phrase it? Use her like a lad . . . or better yet, watch *you* use her like a lad."

Trevor was standing directly in front of James by then. "Tell me . . ." His voice had gone rough at the prospect of hearing James reveal what he had in mind.

"It's hard to say," James said blandly—as if he were contemplating which color velvet he wanted to use for his latest hat design—while his hand reached out and palmed the front of Trevor's buckskins. James pressed against Trevor's hardening cock as he spoke. "I think she'd like it rough and fast, maybe pinned to the bed—" Trevor's cock twitched in response. "I know you'd like that, wouldn't you? Maybe you could even hold her in place for me, let her take you in her mouth, while you watch me down the length of her back as I pound into her firm, tight arse."

Trevor moaned and pushed his hips against James's hand. "That might work," he said, his voice raspy.

"But I'm a perverse bastard, ain't I?"

"Yes," Trevor gasped, never underestimating the extent of James's sexual imagination. "You have something else in mind, I know it. What would you do instead?"

"I think—no, I know—I would make it soft and slow. She might need to be restrained much more to endure *that* kind of torture. Do you see how impatient she is? She is always in a rush and likely sees lovemaking as nothing more than an athletic exercise. A sprint of some sort."

"Ah—" Trevor was devolving into a mist of sensuality again; words were becoming vague and meaningless as James's hand smoothed and rubbed against him. "And you, you would s-slow her d-down, is that it?"

"Oh yes." James stretched the two words out until they floated around the room like some sort of heady smoke. He pulled Trevor to the sofa and then slid down to kneel on the floor between his legs.

"I'd want to go very, very slow . . ." James unbuttoned Trevor's fall (again) and pulled his straining hard cock into his mouth. No urgency. No force. Just long, slow, languorous licks. Delicate, easy, sucking pulls. Light kisses. It was entirely maddening. And entirely delicious. "Slow . . . like this," he said when he released him.

James kissed the tip of Trevor's cock, trailing his tongue lightly over it. He licked at it, the flat of his tongue barely moving as he teased Trevor slowly. Trevor couldn't help picturing Georgie's mouth, imagining Georgie's moans, as James worked on him—and the effect was stunning.

With one hand, James reached between Trevor's legs, up, and behind—still at that delectably glacial pace—until he fitted the side of his hand into the crack of Trevor's arse. "She would be forced into patience, wouldn't she?" Trevor moaned as James began stroking, lightly at first, then deeper, until he was pressing the entire side of his palm gently and firmly into Trevor's crease. The look James gave him—filled with awe and trust and desire—promised everything.

They could have this, damn it; the three of them could have a beautiful life together.

"And then I would just make her . . . love it." And with that, James dipped his head fully and pulled Trevor's cock into his mouth, sucking hard and relentlessly, but still slow . . . slow . . . slow. He pulled his mouth away for a second while his hand kept working. "Because you know it now, don't you? It's not just her body you want to claim, is it, Trevor?" Trevor gasped when James squeezed his bollocks. "You are falling in love with her, aren't you? You want the three of us to be together in truth?"

Without waiting for a reply, James opened his mouth and resumed his slow, patient torture of Trevor's cock, until Trevor cried out his release. He may have said yes or he may have just screamed out something unintelligible—but that was the truth of it. He was indeed falling in love with Georgie.

James Rushford might have been born in the wrong century. As he moaned through Trevor's release—deriving as much pleasure as Trevor did from the act, his own seed spilling in the same desperate pulse as Trevor's—James had visions in his mind of being a dedicated Roman slave, with Trevor as his patrician lord and master. Then, some days, it was the other way round, with James wielding all the power, binding Trevor to their enormous bed and grabbing his dark hair from behind and thrusting into him like Trevor was nothing more than a stable boy, there to be fucked, used, and discarded.

Or perhaps the two men would have been better suited to a life in India in the fourth century, exploring a shared world of fleshly delights amid the freedom and curiosity of that society so focused on voluptuous pleasure. Men. Women. Tenderness. Seduction. Lovers.

Regardless of time or place, Trevor and James were meant to be together in any century, under any social circumstances. The bond between them went far beyond any role or socially prescribed behavior. Whether they had been born men or women, had met when they were old or young, they both believed they would have found each other. They were simply a part of one another's being.

But Georgie's presence was causing something more complex to surge between them, something that felt like it could enrich what they already had—something profound that they would need to act on with unusual haste if they were ever to get her to at least consider the *possibility* of a true marriage.

"You are relentless." Trevor breathed heavily as he fell back against the sofa. "Honestly. If anyone could get into the hidden heart of Lady Georgiana Cambury, it would be you."

James smiled softly. "I would certainly like to try, but I think we need to be a bit . . . careful about it."

Trevor was coming back to himself, his eyes turning more alert. "Careful how?"

"I think we need to seduce her without her really knowing."

Trevor laughed out loud, tilting his chin up so the strong muscles on his neck flexed and vibrated. "And how do you propose to do that?" he asked. "Seduction seems the type of thing Georgie might cotton to."

"I'm working on it." James tapped the side of his head and pulled himself up to sitting. "First off, no calf eyes or declarations on your part. And button up your trousers unless you want me to go for round three." Lightly licking his lips in memory, James looked away from Trevor's cock and stood up. "I'm as randy as a goat from not having you as much as usual this week."

Laughing quietly, Trevor did as he was told, then stood up and followed James to his worktable.

"What are you working on?" asked Trevor, resting his hand on James's shoulder while they both looked down at the sketches and fabric samples on the table.

"Oh, just something outlandish to cheer Lady Caroline Lamb. I don't think she's fully recovered from the loss of her last child, even though it's been well over a year."

"A year? That's not very long. My mother never recovered."

James turned to look at him. "She still had you to lavish all her love upon, didn't she? Caroline has another child."

"Oh, James. You really were raised by wolves, weren't you?"

James shrugged. "Mostly absentee wolves at that." His parents had been young when they'd had him, but the Rushfords wouldn't have known what to do with a child even if they'd waited until the supposed maturity of middle age. Both of his parents were actors and they'd traveled around Europe with a troupe of motley thespians. While they were away, James was farmed out to several less-than-welcoming tenuous connections in Wales. He learned early on that it was best not to rely on anyone to pave the way for him, much less love him.

"Yes, Caroline still has her son, but it's not the same," Trevor continued. "At least I don't think it was for my family. It was almost as if when my mother had me—an heir!—she was relieved, because that's what she was obliged to do, what society demanded. But when she had my little sister, Cynthia, it was so much more, meant so much more, for herself I mean, for the joy of it. So when Cynthia died before her second birthday . . . " His voice trailed off.

"Well, it's all finished now. Your mother—and your father, even now, in his backhanded way—adored you. You can hardly fault them for it."

James watched as Trevor fingered a piece of crimson velvet. "I think I would love to have children," Trevor said. It came out like a breath of sadness.

Tempted to joke about how there was a limit to what even he, with his boundless imagination, could provide, James caught himself before he made light of the tender confession. "Maybe Georgie would—"

A tap at the door interrupted him.

Trevor called, "Come."

The door opened and Georgie poked her head in. "Are you two decent?" Her smile was tentative and confident all at once.

"For now," James said suggestively.

She rolled her eyes and entered the room, shutting the door behind her. "Mrs. Daley has ordered the carriage for half six." She looked at the mantle clock and saw that granted them an hour to prepare. "Does that give you both enough time to get ready? I don't want to antagonize my mother by being late."

"How thoughtful of you." Trevor smiled. "Taking your mother's feelings into account? What's come over you?"

She walked over to the table where they were looking at the swatches. "Mrs. Daley's lemon cake came over me. That confection seems to soothe all my irritations with my mother. I've even agreed to dress like a proper lady for the occasion."

"How charming!" James held up a piece of lavender silk next to her face. "I want to make you more hats and dresses in this color."

"Don't bother." She waved her hand dismissively over the table and all the samples. "I'll be gone before I have the opportunity to wear them anyway. And you know I find British hats so deplorably structured and confining."

"I've already made you one and sent it up to your room. I did my best to keep your preferences in mind. It is neither structured nor confining."

"Oh, very well. I suppose it would be rude not to wear it at least once."

He nodded his approval, then held up another piece of fabric in a deeper purple. "This one is perfect; it makes your eyes look like burnished copper. You must allow me." He let the soft fabric touch her cheek faintly before he pulled it away.

"Are you flirting with me, Mister Rushford?"

He stared at her eyes, then at her lips, where the hint of a smile played. Then he simply leaned in and kissed her cheek.

She stiffened immediately. "James. Do stop being ridiculous."

He shrugged and lined all of the samples into a neat pile, not really looking at her as he did, but he'd felt the shiver of physical recognition pass between them, and it had not been one-sided. "You and Trevor have been best friends your entire lives," James said. "I feel like the odd man."

Georgie smoothed her bodice with a quick, jerking motion. "Well, that would be a first. Trevor told me you were notoriously popular at Cambridge and universally adored in London."

James looked at Trevor with a smile, and the other man lifted one shoulder. "What? It's true," Trevor said.

Georgie continued, "I suspect you've never been the odd man a day in your life, James."

He finished organizing his work area and looked at Trevor, then back at Georgie. "Have you?"

"Have I what?" Georgie glanced around the room as if she were looking for viable escape routes.

"Have you ever been the odd . . . person?"

She sighed impatiently. "I am *always* the odd person. I don't know what in the world I was thinking to make that offhand comment about my willingness to tell you *anything*. That was entirely shortsighted on my part."

"Is that a renege?" James parried.

"Are we playing whist?" Georgie shot back.

Trevor sighed. "Do stop squabbling."

"No, we're—or at least *I*—am not squabbling. I am merely trying to deepen our friendship." James said, keeping his focus on Georgie.

"You are as much a friend to me as anyone, James Rushford, and you know it. I have no secrets, isn't that right, Trevor?"

James watched as Trevor tried to suppress his true thoughts—that there was much more he wanted to know about Georgie, about the woman she had become.

Georgie obviously noticed Trevor's hesitation, and she appeared to be . . . hurt.

"What's this?" Georgie asked with a bit of anger tingeing her voice. "You think I'm secretive, Trevor? You know me better than I know myself!"

Trevor smiled and kissed her on the other cheek. "Go change for dinner, sweetling. Of course I do. But you are different somehow— which is as it should be after all your adventures."

She looked confused. "I—I mean, of course I'm changed. Did you think I would always be the same ninny who used to steal your horses and ride them to Camburton in the middle of the night?"

Trevor put an arm around one of her shoulders and walked her to the door of the drawing room. "Come, let's all get changed for supper and forget this who-am-I nonsense. We'll be ready in good time for the carriage ride to your mother's."

James followed close behind as the other two ascended the wide marble staircase that rose through the center of the grand hall.

"And you must learn to ignore James. He's entirely too persistent."

James smiled at Trevor's back. "Yes, I am. Relentless even."

Georgie shook her head and looked at him over her shoulder, rolling her eyes again. "Honestly, you two are like puppies. Does anyone do any work around here?"

Despite their afternoon of languorous lovemaking, Trevor and James were arguably two of the most productive men in the north of England. Trevor managed over ten thousand acres of properties in Derbyshire and London, and James had created the second largest hat business in the British Isles. "We manage to get a few things accomplished now and then," James drawled.

She laughed through her words. "I bet you do."

As they preceded him up the stairs like the old friends they were, James was overcome with a flash of unfamiliar passion. Unfamiliar, because it wasn't the slow, seductive eroticism he had described to Trevor earlier when he'd taken him a second time in front of the fire. This was something deeper, a momentary vision of what it could be like if the three of them were truly bound together, if the three of them were walking up the stairs like this in some imaginary future, toward their communal bed and into the comfort of one another's arms.

James wanted to *see* Trevor and Georgie joined, not in some carnal, voyeuristic heat, but in a reverential way. He wanted to prepare them both, as if for some ritual—their marriage, he supposed. He wanted to bathe them and anoint them and make sure they were wet and eager for one another. He wanted to shepherd them through the process: to lick Georgie while Trevor watched with trembling patience; to suck Trevor while Georgie was forced to be the languorous woman who must exist *somewhere* inside that curved, luscious body of hers.

For all her talk of mannish poses and how they helped her gain access to the top stables in Arabia, James suspected—nay, knew—that Georgie was capable of loving as deeply and honestly as Trevor and James did when it came to the most fundamental elements of their desire. They loved both: male and female; mastery and subservience; the steely power of demanding what one wanted and the liberating courage to beg for it.

He'd seen the way she looked at them when he and Trevor were kissing. He'd seen the longing in her eyes, and it wasn't mere physical lust; Georgie was filled with longing in her heart. The question was whether James and Trevor would be able to peel away the years of protective emotional armor she'd built up.

Chapter 4

Georgie parted from James and Trevor at the first-floor landing and turned to the guest quarters where she was staying—for a little while longer, at least. The moment her mother got wind of her upcoming marriage, there was no chance Vanessa would countenance Georgie staying at Mayfield.

They'd agreed to meet in the study in forty minutes—or sooner if they happened to be ready. Georgie was in no mood to primp and had planned to sponge off quickly and put on a serviceable dress for the dinner at her mother's.

Mrs. Daley had other ideas. Georgie's room was candlelit and scented with attar of roses. A large tub had been brought to the room and filled with steaming hot water and aromatic oil.

"What's all this?" Georgie asked, looking up to see Mrs. Daley herself, along with one of the younger maids she'd seen in the kitchen. "I don't require any assistance with my toilette."

Mrs. Daley pursed her lips and tilted her mobcap-covered head. "Let's not bicker, shall we, Lady Georgiana? If you are going to be the lady of Mayfield House, I cain't show my face in town if you are parading around in—" The solid stump of a woman shook her hand in Georgie's direction. "That."

Georgie looked down at herself and smiled. She'd had the trousers made in Cairo and they were a splendid deerskin, sueded to the softest nap. Her shirt was mannish, but not entirely without feminine flourishes at the cuffs and collar. Her jacket, likewise, was a luxurious velvet that had been embroidered with meticulous care, but in a matching thread that only shone in the sun or candlelight. "I think I look rather fine today." She struck a pose.

Without softening her pursed lips, Mrs. Daley shook her head. And continued shaking her head. "You do *not* look fine. You look like you are on your way to the stables or some bawdy house twenty years ago—"

"Well, I often *am* on my way to the stables, so that is as it should be."

Striding toward her, Mrs. Daley continued. "This is Franny. She is your new maid."

"But I've just told you I do not need a maid." Georgie let Mrs. Daley help her out of the tight-fitting velvet jacket.

"And I've just told you that you now have one. Are you going to put the poor gel out on the street?"

Franny gasped as if that was the first she'd heard of being sacked.

"Of course you wouldn't do such a thing." Mrs. Daley was now beginning to unbutton Georgie's shirt.

Which was simply not on. Georgie swatted her away. "I'm perfectly capable of removing my own shirt. Now off with you both."

Mrs. Daley shook her head again. "You need a proper bath, and I'm not leaving until you are in the tub and Franny has scrubbed that beautiful blonde hair of yours—what little of it you've left."

Georgie smiled despite herself, rubbing the palm of one hand back and forth along the crown of her head. "This is getting quite long actually. I was thinking of shaving it again next week."

Franny covered her mouth.

"Don't worry, Franny." Mrs. Daley was taking a pair of very ladylike shoes and silk stockings out of the wardrobe and setting them near the bed, where a lovely gray-green dress lay flat on the coverlet, next to some feather-covered contrivance that must be the hat. "Your mistress enjoys shocking people for no apparent reason. You must learn to pay her no mind much of the time."

Georgie laughed and set her shirt on the back of a nearby chair when she'd finished removing it. "That's rich. I'm to be the lady of the house, but she's to pay me no mind?"

Mrs. Daley turned her attention from where she was fussing with the fabric of the dress she'd laid out on the bed, and gasped. "What in the world?"

Poor Franny was getting one shock after another—if her wide eyes were any indication—but she was obviously too shy to say a word. Georgie was wearing one of her stiff close-fitting vests under her clothes. It was like a second skin in both color and texture, and poor Franny must have thought, at first glance, that it *was* skin—that Georgie had been born without any female parts whatsoever.

"It's a girdle of sorts . . . a corset . . . more or less . . ." Georgie explained as she undid the ties at her waist that worked as a belt and attached to the lacings up the back. She'd had several of them made in a flesh-toned fabric, so when she wore it under her riding clothes, it was invisible.

"Where's your bosom?" Franny asked, affrighted.

Georgie laughed again, stepping closer to the maid so she could see the construction. "If Mrs. Daley is sincere in her declaration that you are to be my maid, you must acquaint yourself with my oddities."

"Oh posh. You are not so odd, Lady Georgiana," Daley said. "You just make yourself out to be so."

Georgie looked at Daley, then back at Franny and smiled. "Daley's always taken me under her wing and tried to make me feel better about it, but I know what I am. And I'm an odd duck."

Georgie struggled a bit to get out of the stiff undershirt and started to shimmy it over her head as she always did. "Oh miss, please let me help you, at least." Franny reached for the ties and loosened them more and helped ease off the contraption.

"Ah, that does feel nice." Georgie breathed when it was off her. She watched as Franny held it with the tips of her fingers and well away from her body, as if it might cast a dark spell.

"Get her boots and pants off, Franny. Don't be standing about starin'," Daley said.

Franny set down the stiff girdle next to the wardrobe and stepped quickly back to help Georgie with the rest of her clothes.

Franny removed her boots and socks, but Georgie pushed her away again when she tried to help with the breeches. "Honestly, when I'm dressed like a man, you'd best treat me like one. I'll feel ridiculous having you help me take my own pants off. I'm not infirm!"

Blushing furiously and looking like she might cry, Franny curtseyed, probably not knowing what else to do.

"Oh, I'm sorry, Franny," Georgie apologized with a sigh. "I will try not to be so strange around you." Georgie finished taking off the pants and set them down atop the shirt, so they were both hanging at the back of the chair. She stood naked for a moment and stretched up to the ceiling. She'd never suffered from any false modesty, or any modesty whatsoever for that matter. Public baths from Paris to Alexandria had afforded her the pleasure of communal bathing, and she was grateful to Daley for making the effort after all. "A bath is a perfectly luxurious idea. Thank you, Daley. I appreciate it very much."

With that, she lifted one leg and stepped into the large copper tub that had been hauled up and filled just for her. As she lifted her other leg and was about to sink into the deliciously hot water, the door to her bedroom opened and Trevor walked in casually, looking down at the jacket buttons he was fastening as he spoke. "James is taking nigh on forever to fold his cravat with seventeen pleats, and I thought you'd be ready in a snap—"

"Lord Mayson!" Mrs. Daley was appalled.

"Eeek!" Franny squealed, looking right and left as if *she* were the one who had been caught naked.

Georgie simply smiled and sank slowly into the wonderfully hot water. "Apparently I'm to be a lady this evening, so it will take me a few minutes longer to finish my toilette." She smiled at his embarrassed face. "You may go now, Trevor. Unless you wish to scrub my back."

"Lady Georgiana!" Mrs. Daley was beside herself, poor thing. "You are incorrigible!"

Finally recovering his voice, Trevor muttered his apologies and left the room in a hurry.

She held her nonchalant smile until he quitted the room and then pretended to herself that her wildly heated cheeks were the result of the hot bath, nothing more. But lord, the way he had looked at her— and the way it had made her feel. There was nothing friendly about it, and she would do well to tamp down her foolish libido lest she get drawn into some greater foolishness.

Georgie slid all the way under the water, then rose up like a seal and let little Franny scrub her clean.

He hadn't even recognized her! Trevor was barely breathing. He finally remembered he needed air somewhere around the second or third step from the bottom of the stairs. He inhaled sharply. She'd been so damned beautiful, half turned toward him with one strong, long leg in the tub and her rounded hip tilted at that provocative angle, and her breasts—dear God, he didn't even think of her as having breasts, much less a pair as splendid as any he'd ever clapped eyes on.

Trevor had been so aroused this afternoon—with all of James's talk about how he planned to slowly, ever so slowly, peel away the layers of Georgie's resistance—that perhaps he was on some sort of residual high alert. He rubbed his moist palms along the superfine wool of his dinner jacket and turned toward his study.

He hoped reviewing the latest crop rotation analysis in the south pasture would help take his mind off the man and woman abovestairs who were making him feel like a damned teenager. Not that anything would take his mind off Georgie's splendid body—or James's imaginative plans for it—anytime soon, but it was worth a small effort.

For as long as he could remember, working on estate business had calmed and restored him. After he came down from Cambridge, Trevor knew Mayfield House was the only place he wanted to be, the only place he could ever imagine spending the rest of his life. Of course he'd spent a year or so in London—who wouldn't? What young man didn't want to sample the variety and crammed thrills of the capital? But after he and James had decided that no amount of variety or thrills would ever surpass the simple pleasure they took in one another's company, they decided to move to the country all the year round.

In a little under four years, James had managed to employ close to thirty local women in his hat factory, which he was now operating at a very tidy profit. For his part, Trevor had been implementing a slew of agricultural advances on the estate, and the results were starting to bear fruit. Everything had been running quite smoothly.

Right up until her death, Trevor's mother, Lady Penelope Mayson, had held the purse strings. In an unusual settlement similar to the one he and Georgie had negotiated, Trevor's mother had retained control of much of her vast inheritance. She had been exceedingly generous regarding agricultural developments, and she'd also been exceedingly lenient in terms of James and Trevor's living arrangements.

Of course she never spoke of anything outright—as the daughter of an earl and the wife of a viscount, she would never speak of anything so *private, dear*—but she had accepted the *friendship* between James and Trevor in every way that mattered.

Meanwhile, his father had always followed his wife's lead, and his attitude toward James had appeared to be no exception. That's why the past few months had proved so upsetting. Before his mother died, Trevor had never come close to imagining the depth of his father's spite—since it had been so carefully concealed while his wife was still alive. Lord Lawrence Mayson had been a destitute viscount when he'd fallen in love with the blindingly rich Lady Penelope Culverton. In 1785, there'd been a few raised eyebrows—she was delicately beautiful and possessed a great fortune; he was ruddily handsome and possessed (very tenuously) a vast expanse of land in Derbyshire at the center of which sat (also very tenuously) the dilapidated Mayfield House.

Lawrence and Penelope—Trevor very rarely thought of them as Father and Mother—had been ideally suited to one another. Lawrence adored her tenderness and care; Penelope adored his masculinity and rough humor. Unfortunately, when the tender, caring side of the equation died of a particularly aggressive pneumonia shortly after Christmas, all that was left was the rough. His father was devastated and angry after the loss of his beloved wife . . . and for some reason he chose to direct all of his rage at Trevor. Which brought them to their present circumstances.

Trevor was still staring at the portrait of his parents above the glass display case when James strode into the study. As he turned, Trevor caught sight of the snowy white cravat: it had at least seventeen folds, if not more. James was as impeccable about his sartorial decisions as he was about every other form of personal expression. Tonight he sported a fitted wool jacket of the highest quality, which emphasized his lean strength.

"What has you so quiet?" James asked, crossing the room and resting a hand at Trevor's back.

"Just thinking about my father."

"That doesn't usually end well." James pulled his hand away and went to sit on the large Chesterfield sofa that dominated the masculine room.

"I can't imagine how he could turn so quickly. Not that I ever thought he was entirely *happy* for you and me to be such particular friends, but I believed him to be, at worst, ambivalent."

James pretended to pick at something on his immaculate sleeve. "I'd say it's slightly worse than ambivalent. He despises me."

Talk of Trevor's father always put James in a peevish mood, not that Trevor could blame him. "I think *despise* is an awfully strong word."

"I think your father would agree with the strength of it."

"Well, it's no matter now, I suppose. It is his right to do as he wishes with the estate."

"Not really. It was your mother who transformed this place—saved it really—from the near ruin of his side of the family. And she passed that love of the place to you. It was always her wish that you would carry on in her footsteps, keeping it going for future generations." James stared at Trevor for a moment. The mention of future generations hung in the air until the fire popped and cracked loudly, as if to puncture the weighted silence. "It was a malicious thing for him to do and you know it," James continued in an even tone. "What difference would it be to him if he left the trust and estate as your mother intended, with a generous portion going to maintain his life in town and the lion's share going to the preservation and modernization of Mayfield? He of all people knows you can't maintain an estate of this size without the cash to support it."

Trevor sighed. They'd been around this track so many times. "Look, it's all going to work out fine, now that Georgie has agreed to be my baroness, my future viscountess. It's not overly taxing after all. He's exercising a bit of paternal will, nothing more. So I have to marry before the end of the year—and Georgie is perfectly happy to oblige." He shrugged and walked across the room to fix himself a drink. "All will be well. My father can die happy, with some absurd image of me standing at an altar with a woman, and then we can all proceed apace. Maybe even have a spot of fun along the way."

James smiled and stood up to join him at the drinks tray. "You would find the silver lining in a black plague, I swear it."

"No point in fighting the tide, my sweet grandmother always said. I shall marry Georgie. Hardly a trial. Even if we don't get to implement any of your diabolically tempting schemes in the bedroom, she's a sweet friend to do it. Otherwise, I'd be left with Mayfield House and no resources to preserve it—which would be almost worse than getting nothing." He handed James a crystal tumbler.

"And your father knows it. He knows you would never abandon this place." James gestured around the room, then took a sip. "Still . . . if you were willing to walk away, to call his bluff . . ." James's voice faded away.

"I could never play that deep. I could never pretend to abandon the tenants and laborers and, well, you know how I feel about it. I know you're beginning to feel it too. It's part of my muscle and bone. I don't think I could really survive anywhere else." Trevor finished pouring his own drink, then turned to look James in the eye.

"I know, darling." James's face softened. "That's why you are who you are. And I shan't ever wish for you to be any other way. You are a loyal, devoted creature. The marriage to Georgie will satisfy your father's controlling nature, and that could be the end of it." James's face turned serious. "But I don't think either of us want that to be the end of it, do we?" James reached up to caress Trevor's cheek. "What is it?" His thumb passed knowingly along Trevor's brow. "Something's happened." Trevor's face colored at the words. James narrowed his eyes and looked at him speculatively. "Did I miss something while I was putting these endless folds into my cravat? You look a little flushed at the mention of your intended."

"If you must know, I accidentally walked in on her as she was stepping into her bath." Trevor tried to appear disinterested in his own report.

James let his hand curl around to the base of Trevor's neck and moved in close, until their bodies were nearly touching. "Really? Accidentally, you say?"

Trevor nodded, but with James crowding him and the topic so . . . distracting . . . it was hard for him to concentrate.

"Was she very beautiful, Trevor?" James set down his glass and pressed his other hand against Trevor's rapidly hardening cock.

"Please don't," Trevor whispered hotly, obviously warming up to the memory of Georgie in the tub.

"Was she wearing a clinging chemise, like some of those modest females are wont to do?" He trailed the knuckles of his right hand up the silhouette of Trevor's erection where it pressed against the elegant silk breeches he'd changed into for supper.

"She was not." Trevor's voice lowered an octave as James gripped him harder.

"So she was very naked, then?" James gave Trevor one more meaningful squeeze, then pulled his hand away carelessly. "I see."

Trevor exhaled. "She was so lovely, James." His voice was still strained, but he appeared to have regained his senses now that James had taken his hand away. "I was . . . dumbstruck. And I know she was as well; I could feel it. She might deny it to high heaven, but I know she felt it too."

James looked into Trevor's eyes. Deep shades of green and brown and goldenrod—like the best elements of the rich late summer fields that surrounded the estate—were all drawn together in those beautiful, loving eyes.

"I want to give her to you like a present," he whispered.

"How primitive of you. Will you wrap her in white linen and carry her to me on the back of an ass in exchange for a cow and a bolt of silk?"

James smiled at the idea. "I would, you know."

Shaking his head, Trevor said, "I know you would, that's the problem. I think there's a movement afoot here in England to stop selling human beings. And the minor point of her free will."

"Free wills can be . . . bent," James taunted.

The fire crackled and the door opened at the same moment. Both men turned, and the butler announced Lady Georgiana Cambury.

She swept into the room as if she were the queen herself. Her dress was exquisite—James reminded himself to thank Mrs. Daley for her part in that—and her face and bosom were a delicate, fresh pink from the warm bath. And perhaps from her encounter with Trevor, James suspected. Her hair—what little of it there was—had been pulled back from her forehead with the hat James had made for her: a matching gray-green bandeau of pleated fabric with a spectacular peacock feather shooting off the side. The entire effect was magical.

Both men bowed and gave a leg as she approached.

"Oh, do stop with the courtly bows. It's still me, after all."

James reached for her ungloved hand, not caring if she bristled at his warm attention. Kissing the backs of two knuckles lightly, he breathed in the scent of her skin and felt the answering quiver of desire course through her as plainly as he felt it in himself. Then he let her hand go. "You are simply stunning, Lady Georgiana."

She laughed lightly. "Such enthusiastic praise is so silly under the circumstances, Rushford. Honestly." He smiled at her use of his last name, as if that could defuse the scintillating awareness that snapped and sparked among the three of them. She turned to Trevor, apparently hoping for a voice of reason in this storm of flattery and ardor, only to find him even more smitten than James had been. "Trevor?"

He also reached for her hand with the slow grace of a full-blooded nobleman. "My lady." He kissed the back of her hand and his eyes lowered slightly. James was unable to look a moment longer or he was going to do something completely barbaric—like hold Lady Georgiana Cambury pinned with her back to his chest, while Trevor lifted her skirt and made her scream with abandoned pleasure as he brought her to the heights of ecstasy with his mouth.

Instead, James coughed into his hand softly and suggested they go to the carriage and get to Camburton Castle in time for drinks before dinner with Vanessa and the rest of the family. Georgie readily agreed, leading them out of the room with a businesslike stride—and a rosy bloom on her chest.

The carriage ride was a silent business. James certainly wasn't about to reveal the rude nature of his desires; Trevor looked like he couldn't articulate his affection, even if he could find his voice; and Georgie, poor Georgie. She looked like she was on her way to a funeral—a perfectly beautiful, closed-up bud of a woman, on her way to a funeral.

James wished he could make this woman enjoy her own beauty. Not merely the physical grandeur of her Olympian body, but the beauty of who she was as a *whole* person with all of her myriad interests and conflicting desires. He wanted to prove to her that there need be no conflict; that there was variety in every lamb that was born in springtime in the west pastures; that there was artistry in every hat that was made in his factory; that there was a life, a beautiful life, to be lived in this place she considered lifeless.

Trevor and James could show her—through the daily practice of their own love for the place, through the deep rhythm and natural pace of it—that she could have a deeply fulfilling life with them, that the three of them could build something lasting and beautiful if she would let herself feel, let herself believe. Georgie would refute it of course; she would claim it was a monstrous show of their swagger, their eagerness to impose their wills upon her, their desire to *change* her—but that was not the case, and he was going to prove it to her.

And this wasn't an attraction that had formed over a matter of days. The seeds of Trevor and Georgie's intimacy had been planted decades ago, James was certain.

"How shall we tell them?" Georgie asked, breaking the silence of the fifteen-minute carriage ride as soon as the horses turned from the country road into the private lane that signaled the entrance to Camburton Castle.

Trevor was agitated. "You don't have to do it, Georgie. I mean it. It's too much to ask. I shouldn't have asked."

"Oh, it's really nothing. And it's all done and dusted with the solicitors at this point anyway. We might as well go through with it." She tossed her hand in the air as if it were all a bit of nonsense.

James saw how her careless words tore at Trevor, even if she didn't.

"But if you marry me, even though we know it is, well . . ." Trevor crossed and uncrossed his legs. ". . . whatever it is. The fact remains: you will *never* be able to marry for love if you are married to me." He stared at her, and she narrowed her eyes at him but didn't reply. "Don't you want to take more time to contemplate the ramifications of that decision, of what that means for your future?"

"I have contemplated the decision, Trevor." Raising her hand, she began to tick off her reasons. "As I've already mentioned, we've drawn up the paperwork—everything is signed and official. Next off, it's quite convenient for me, actually." James watched her take on that blasted look of assumed carelessness that was becoming so familiar. She was a terrible liar to everyone except herself. "I no longer have to be seen as the dreaded *single woman* at the party—threat to man and wife the world over. Furthermore, I no longer have to see that desperate longing in my mother's eyes for me to be the happily paired-off daughter she's always wished for." She stopped enumerating and let her hand fall to her lap. "Are *you* having second thoughts about marrying me, Trevor? Am I so troublesome, even on paper?"

"What? No! Of course not. Why would you ask such a thing? I've never been so enamored—" He stumbled over the words. Poor Trevor, thought James. He was already wanting to throw himself at her feet. "—with an idea. I've never been so *grateful* in my life."

James suspected that hadn't been the best choice of words; Georgie didn't seem the type who appreciated being seen as a debt to be repaid. She looked as if she was about to speak, then decided not to. Perhaps she believed gratitude was slightly less terrifying than Trevor declaring his undying love.

The carriage came to a halt, and the footman opened the door for Georgie to step out. She looked from Trevor to James, then back to Trevor. "So it is settled. I will tell my mother immediately." She turned to the footman, rested her gloved hand on his, and stepped from the carriage like an empress.

Chapter 5

eorgie lifted the hem of her gown and more or less stormed out of the carriage. Her emotions were careening around in a most unpleasant manner—she did not countenance emotions, damn it, much less the careening variety! One moment she had thought—had hoped!—the man was going to make love to her in a hot bath, and the next moment he told her he was grateful.

Grateful? Trevor was merely grateful? That was the best he could muster? After all those heated looks and whispered compliments in the library? After seeing her stepping into the tub? She'd hoped he would at least suggest something a little more, well, *bawdy* than gentlemanly gratitude!

Bawdy?

What was the matter with her? Of course he was grateful; that was quite the most appropriate feeling a man in his position should profess. Very appropriate indeed.

So then why did his gratitude make her feel like something flat and empty, a shirt box that had been sent up from Jermyn Street? *Lord Mayson is very grateful for his latest delivery from Ede & Ravenscroft.*

He was respecting her wishes. Perhaps she should do the same.

Georgie held her spine straight and lifted the edge of her dress slightly higher so it didn't drag along the pebbles of her ancestral home's forecourt. She'd been practicing walking in dresses ever since that first tripping bout at the Lion and Lamb. Georgie knew full well how to be a British lady. It was a role like any other. Just as she lifted her chin to congratulate herself, she stubbed her (elegant, Italian silk-covered) toe on the last step and swore under her breath when a junior butler pulled open the two front doors. Swanson, the head man, must already have been in the drawing room, serving drinks.

The servant bowed, and she nodded to him as she passed.

"Is my mother already in the drawing room?"

"Yes, m'lady," he replied.

She continued walking down the hall while Trevor and James presumably removed their gloves and hats and handed them to the butler behind her.

"Georgie?" Trevor called.

She paused and shut her eyes without turning. What was happening to her? This was Trevor! Trevor Mayson of rock skipping and horseback riding and rabbit trapping. Why was his voice starting to make her so . . . edgy?

"At least let us accompany you into the drawing room, darling."

She opened her eyes to see Trevor standing to her right, and her damnable heart began to race. And then she felt the heat of James to her left, and her pulse redoubled. None of it made any sense—this was an arrangement, nothing more! Helping her friends, nothing more! And yet, it seemed her heart had other notions.

"You wish to escort me as if this were my debut season? You're too kind. But I'm an old maid, Lord Mayson." She snaked her hand through his arm and set it on his forearm. James placed her other hand on his forearm in a similar fashion. When she shivered at the jolt that cracked between them, she exaggerated the moment, attempting to render it meaningless with silly humor. "Well if it isn't Georgie girl with two of the handsomest men in all of England. I'm all aflutter!"

"So am I," Trevor whispered, then cleared his throat. "And you shan't be an old maid for long, Lady Georgiana." He smiled, and it was the comforting, familiar smile of their youth—but it was also something so much deeper, something so much *more* everything.

She faltered for a moment—damned useless Italian shoes—but she felt James's hand tighten over hers where it rested on his arm.

"Are you well?" James asked in a low voice.

She turned to look at him, expecting to see a casual interest in his eyes, but what she saw made her stomach clench. He meant it; he was genuinely concerned about her welfare. It was off-putting—people who cared expected things; people who cared deeply eventually made demands.

"I am. Thank you for asking, James." She lightened her voice and forced herself to lighten her mood. "It's just these silly shoes."

He patted her hand and smiled. She felt instantly relieved that the look of real concern had passed. The three of them walked down the hall until they were standing by the large doors to the drawing room. Evening was beginning to descend, and the room was lit with candles and filled with late summer blooms. Nora adored fresh flowers all year, and Vanessa lived to indulge Nora in all things.

"Georgie!" Her twin brother Archie saw her first, as always. Lord Archibald Cambury, physician and philanthropist, was standing by the fireplace. The minute he caught sight of her, he was crossing the room with long, confident strides. "You change course like a Barbary wind, Gorgeous Georgie!"

When Georgie had turned thirteen, she'd demanded that everyone cease calling her Georgie girl at once. Archie had started calling her Gorgeous Georgie the very next morning.

"Oh, Archie. Do stop with that."

"I shall never." He bowed and kissed her hand formally. "You are divine."

She reached up and patted his cheek. "As are you, sweet Archie. Perfectly divine." He blushed slightly. The glow led her to believe he'd had some sort of assignation this afternoon since she'd last seen him. He appeared to be far more at ease. "Did you enjoy the rest of your day since you left me at Mayfield?"

He nodded. "I did." She thought he was going to elaborate on some aspect of his affection for the writer he'd mentioned on their walk earlier in the day, but she should have known that the light in his eyes could spring from several sources. "I've heard from Jenner that some of the vaccinations we've been working on have proved successful. He may even come for a visit this winter."

"Ah, the medical world. You are a saint."

"A very selfish saint, if at all. The diseases are crafty little adversaries, and I feel like a bounty hunter as I track them down. I love it, you know that."

She did know it. He was dedicated to his work—as only a very lucky few were—not because of family obligation or moral commitment (though both of those were part of his constitution), but because of his pure love of the subject. Her brother had spent his childhood staring at small things: blades of grass, ants, miniscule insects, and the slightly larger insects that ate those ones. It was probably thanks to his fascination with all things microscopic that Georgie had developed a contrasting love of everything large and free—horses, birds, oceans. Unfettered things.

"You will save us all one day, Archie. Have you inoculated anyone yet? I heard Jenner is having luck with the cowpox instead of the smallpox variolation."

His eyes widened at her informed interest. "Yes, he is having luck. But there is so much more to be done. He's just received a grant from an anonymous donor to pursue his research—"

Georgie laughed and patted Archie's upper arm. "I've no doubt the *anonymous* donor bears a striking resemblance to a brilliant blond researcher who continues to hide his light under a bushel in Derbyshire."

Archie narrowed his eyes—it was like looking into a mirror. She must appear just as skeptical and stubborn when she did that, as she'd done when she looked at James and Trevor mooning at her in the carriage on the way here. "Oh, don't look at me that way. Your secret is perfectly safe with me."

"Thank you, Georgie."

Vanessa turned from where she was speaking animatedly to Anna de Montizon, Nora's daughter, and caught sight of Georgie in all her feminine splendor. "Georgie!"

Oh, Mother. Why was it that a woman who heartily defied nearly all social conventions wished her own daughter would abide by them? Vanessa, Nora, and Anna walked to the middle of the room and Georgie did the same, meeting them halfway. They'd all seen one another earlier in the day, but Georgie's appearance tonight dressed as *a proper lady* was apparently cause for great pomp.

"You are fabulous!" her mother declared, reaching up to touch the delicate edge of the peacock feather that was part of her headdress.

"Thank you, Mother." She even curtseyed a little. She could do this.

"Did James make it for you?" Nora asked.

"It is perfectly wonderful," Anna added. "I must have one. It's not quite a hat and it's not quite a turban. Plus, the color makes your skin look so beautiful."

"This is far too much attention on behalf of a bit of fabric," Georgie said. "But yes, it is some confection of James's." She looked from Anna to see said milliner standing right beside her. He was taking on a rather protective air. "Something about me needing to be more feminine or some such nonsense."

James nodded his agreement and Nora smiled; Georgie felt instantly better. Whereas her *real* mother usually made Georgie combative, Miss Nora White, the famous portraitist and her mother's partner of twenty years—and Georgie's *other* mother—always made Georgie feel like she was quite fine exactly the way she was.

Trevor watched from a small distance as Georgie suffered through all those compliments. She had always despised being the center of attention, and it was only going to get worse when she announced their betrothal. Like tearing off a plaster, Trevor wanted her to make the announcement and be done with it, but he had to trust she would tell her mother any moment now when she found the opportunity.

"She is lovely, isn't she?" Sebastian de Montizon was standing to Trevor's left, watching the women dote on Georgie in her new feminine attire. Trevor turned to look at the handsome Spaniard. They'd become acquainted over the past month, while Sebastian and his wife, Anna, and their friends, the Duke and Duchess of Mandeville, were staying at Camburton Castle.

"I find Georgie more enchanting every day," Trevor confessed. "It's quite unexpected . . . *she's* quite unexpected. The future feels suddenly . . . promising."

Sebastian took a considering sip of his whisky, keeping his eye on his wife and Georgie. "She's not going back to Egypt, then? Vanessa will be thrilled."

"Well, that remains to be seen. Georgie will be here for a month or so. Perhaps longer."

"Perhaps much longer if you have your way, you mean?"

Trevor tried to get a better read on Sebastian. The man obviously adored his wife; he could barely look away from the vivacious Anna for more than a few seconds at a time. But Trevor had recently suspected Sebastian also had a deep connection to Farleigh and Pia, the Duke and Duchess of Mandeville. The four of them traveled together, lived together, and basically looked as though they planned on spending the rest of their lives together. There wasn't really a polite way to inquire about an arrangement like theirs, but Trevor was extremely curious. On his own behalf.

"Shall we go for a ride tomorrow, Lord Mayson?" Sebastian's voice was provocative. Not seductive exactly, but there was definitely a hint of something covert in his invitation.

"I—I've much to do in the morning with the harvest beginning, but yes, that would be fine."

"Very good." Sebastian dipped his chin slightly, a courtly nod of agreement. If they'd met five years ago, at a time when neither one was spoken for, Trevor couldn't help but imagine that tomorrow's ride would have involved an assignation between them.

"Are you two flirting?" Farleigh was even more outspoken than James, if such a thing were possible.

"Hello, Farleigh." Trevor sighed, as if every sentence proved his old friend was as much of a reprobate as ever.

"Trevor." Farleigh mimicked the deprecating tone, then smiled. "So, are you?"

Sebastian looked at Farleigh, and Trevor no longer doubted that the two shared far more than an interest in diplomacy. But it wasn't a mere tupping arrangement either; if Trevor's suspicions were correct, they were deeply in love with one another.

"Were you flirting with me, Sebastian?" Trevor asked bluntly.

"Indeed. Of course I was," Sebastian said. "Now that I'm *taken*—"

Farleigh practically snorted into his glass at Sebastian's choice of words.

Sebastian grinned and continued, "Flirting with you strapping British country gentlemen is my new favorite pastime." He turned to Farleigh. "Speaking of pastimes, I think Trevor may have some questions."

"Questions?" Farleigh cocked a brow.

"Are you two terrifying the neighbors again?" Pia interrupted. She had peeled away from the hat conversation with James and Georgie, and now entered their group, fitting neatly between Sebastian and Farleigh.

Farleigh leaned over and kissed her cheek. Sebastian looked like he wanted to.

"Your grace," she chided. "We are in company. It is not proper to kiss me in public."

"This is not public. This is Camburton Castle, where Lady Vanessa practically *demands* all these outrageous displays of *amor*." He attempted to say the last word in Spanish, but it sounded to Trevor as if he was unable to roll the *r* at the end.

"Your accent is deplorable." Pia winced. "You should keep to your areas of expertise."

"But how will I ever learn to *master your r's* if I don't practice?"

Sebastian burst out laughing, a joyful, uninhibited sound. Trevor had been watching the byplay between husband and wife, as had Sebastian. Yet, while Trevor felt like a cheerful bystander, Sebastian looked like he was very much a part of whatever intimate jests were passing between them.

Pia turned a pretty pink. "Farleigh."

"Yes, darling?" He raised his eyebrow again and took an innocent sip of his drink.

"Oh, never mind."

"Don't you *want* me to master your r's? I could have sworn you asked me to get to work on it only last evening—"

"Farleigh!" Her cheeks were bright red by then, and her voice was a whispered chastisement.

"Very well. I'll not gain complete mastery of your r's overnight in any case. I'll need years of practice."

"Impossible," she muttered under her breath—looking extremely vexed—but Trevor thought she appeared to be a very happy woman.

"Nothing's impossible, darling. You taught me that." He kissed her again with gentle tenderness, on her neck this time, and she glanced at the floor with a demure fluttering of her eyelashes. "But enough about my thoughts on your r's. Sebastian was just telling me that Trevor may have a few questions, and I suspect they are of a personal nature." Farleigh turned from Pia to Trevor. "Isn't that right, Mayson?"

Trevor had known Farleigh for years and always thought him a bit of a buffoon. His numerous affairs with handsome men were, if not legendary, at least well known within the circle of men for whom such knowledge was relevant. It wasn't a secret society—especially not in Farleigh's case because he was so flagrant about his proclivities— but Trevor and James and their group of like-minded friends looked out for one another. It always helped to have a network, but Farleigh also had the money and the unflinching moral support of his wealthy, titled mother to do as he pleased.

It seemed that Trevor, on the other hand, was the latest in a long string—as old as time, perhaps—of sons whose sexual inclinations had proved to be a terrible disappointment to their paters.

"Oh." Trevor was suddenly feeling quite awkward about revealing his deepest desires to these relative strangers. "No, it was just a bit of talk and perhaps a ride in the afternoon. Wasn't it, Sebastian?" Especially in front of the young duchess, Trevor did not want to broach the subject of polygamy. He wanted to excuse himself immediately, now he thought about it.

Pia looked up and caught his eye. "A personal nature? Oh, I do love things of a personal nature."

She really was entirely charming. Whereas the men at her sides were tender and taunting in turn, she was like a sweet angel spreading her wings between them.

"I'm afraid my British sensibilities are not easily c-cast aside," Trevor stammered. "The questions I had for Sebastian were quite, well, uh, *forward*."

"Better and better," she said hopefully. And she could definitely roll her r's. The way she said *better* in that throaty, suggestive tone made both of the men at her sides look like they wanted to ravish her.

Trevor smiled. "Well, better for you perhaps, being of a more open-minded nature. We British are not always at ease sharing our . . . feelings. Especially with charming young duchesses from Spain."

"I think it is drawing rooms that are to blame," she said. "Very confining and ill suited to honest talk." She looked into Trevor's eyes, and he felt both exposed and relieved. This woman knew how to live the life she wanted. "So, I will come on the ride as well."

"Absolutely not," both men said simultaneously, all hints of humor banished. "You are with child," Farleigh added.

Pia rolled her eyes and shook her head. "Exactly. I am going to have a child; I am not infirm. And any child of yours can handle a little pony ride." Trevor wasn't certain, but the way she said *yours*—while her lively eyes took in both men—made it seem as though the baby really did belong to all three of them.

That thought made something hot and tempting shoot straight to Trevor's cock. It was unexpected, but no less demanding for being so. He took a quick sip of his drink to cool the strange bolt of desire: the idea of a relationship like that with James and Georgie made him quake with longing.

"Yes, I see you have questions." Pia reached out gently to Trevor and let it rest on his forearm. "And you shall have answers. I would be delighted to accompany you and these two rascals tomorrow. Out in the open air, where it always seems much easier to ask all manner of questions, don't you find?"

Trevor felt like she was casting a spell over him, an incantation that made it perfectly acceptable for him to reveal the forbidden thing he craved most in the world. He glanced quickly at Georgie and James where they were talking to Nora, Anna, and Vanessa a few yards away. It all seemed suddenly—perfectly—clear. He yearned for both of them, for the three of them to be woven together with a passion that surpassed the consecration of any special license or bishop's dispensation.

"Yes," Trevor said, returning his attention to Pia. "I do believe I will be able to voice my, uh, opinions with far more ease when we are out of doors."

"You are doing what?" Vanessa's voice sliced through the room like a scimitar through silk. James wished he could pull Georgie against his side, but probably best to deal with one traumatic announcement at a time. First, let Vanessa get accustomed to the fact that Georgie and Trevor would be wed in the very near future. And then, many moons later, perhaps Georgie would grow accustomed to the fact that James and Trevor hoped she would be with both of them in equal partnership forever.

"I am going to marry Trevor," Georgie repeated.

James stood next to her and hoped she could sense his support, even if it he wasn't allowed to touch her outright.

"That's wonderful news, Georgie!" Nora pulled Georgie into a firm hug and whispered something James couldn't quite make out.

"How exciting!" Anna chimed in. "First Pia announces she's having a baby, and then Georgie and Trevor announce their betrothal!" Having spent most of her life in a convent, and after finally reconnecting with her mother, Anna obviously treasured the idea of Nora's family being her family.

James could see that Anna was hoping, even now, to foster a sisterly connection with Georgie. "Will you get married here in Derbyshire or in London?" Anna asked.

Trevor had crossed the room by then, dear boy. He reached possessively around Georgie's waist and answered, "Mayfield Chapel," at exactly the same moment Vanessa declared, "St. George's, Hanover Square."

James looked from one to the other, then back to Georgie. He smiled to break the tension and she smiled in return. "Let them fight it out," he whispered, and she nodded imperceptibly in agreement.

"Oh, Trevor, you can't possibly get married in Derbyshire!" Vanessa launched in. "You would never deny me the maternal joy of seeing Georgiana in all her finery, walking down the aisle with Archibald at her side to give her away. A proper wedding."

Having known Vanessa Cambury to be an easygoing, open-minded woman for the past five years, James now found her entirely unrecognizable. She was behaving like a lovesick adolescent.

"Marchioness," Trevor began carefully. James and Georgie were still smiling as they watched the other two prepare for battle.

"What would Georgie like?" Nora interjected.

A silence fell over the room. James reminded himself to make Nora a particularly outrageous hat with four-foot ostrich feathers to extend his thanks.

"Yes, Georgie," James asked. "Where would *you* like to get married?"

She stared at him and that mischievous smile played around her lips. "Is Mr. Tattersall still doing his October yearling sales at Hyde Park Corner? The timing would be quite convenient to have the wedding in London in early November."

"Now you are willfully trying to vex me." Vanessa looked as though she wanted to stamp her foot in frustration, but propriety made her refrain. "Horse sales? It's your wedding, darling!"

Georgie reached for James's forearm as she turned to face Trevor and rested her other hand on his sleeve. He felt a bolt—almost a charge of electricity—when the three of them were connected. He noticed that Trevor started as well. Georgie was not oblivious. "What do you say, Trevor? Will you make an honest woman of me in front of all the tonnish snobs in Mayfair?"

"Oh, don't say it like that," Vanessa complained. "You make it sound positively ghastly. It will be splendid. Don't you think, Nora?"

Nora was smiling at Georgie. "Yes. I think it might very well be splendid."

Then Nora turned her gaze to James, and with the slightest nod, he thought perhaps she grasped the whole complex range of possibilities the marriage might offer. And approved. Another hat for Nora, thought James. She looked like she knew very well what he and Trevor had in mind as far as Lady Georgiana Cambury was concerned. And Nora was pleased.

Vanessa couldn't contain her enthusiasm. "I've saved the dress I wore when I married your father, in anticipation of just such a day. It's been safely preserved upstairs all these years. Just waiting for you." Her voice quavered.

Uh-oh.

James felt Georgie's fingers digging into his forearm. *Do not cry, Vanessa. Do not cry.*

Sure enough, slow tears started to roll down her face. Even though Georgie had only been staying at Mayfield House for the past week or so, James already knew how she despised this sort of blubbering display of emotion. She'd practically eviscerated a chambermaid for getting weepy about killing a spider. *"Weak women infuriate me,"* she'd said at the time.

James patted her hand now and quietly whispered. "Give her a hug, Georgie. It's just a role, remember?"

She turned to look at him, probably wondering how he'd known she'd been thinking that very thing as she entered the grand castle that night. He lifted his chin. *I see you, Lady Georgiana,* he thought, *I see right to the frantic, prancing, yearling heart of you.*

She released her hold on both men and took the few steps toward her mother. "It will be quite lovely, Mother. I'm sure you will make everything perfect."

Hugging her back, Vanessa took a few more gasps, then patted at her cheeks with a linen handkerchief she'd extracted from some invisible pocket. "Well, this is a big day for news." She took a deep breath. "Shall we go in to dinner?"

"Yes, love, let's do that," Nora said, taking Vanessa's shaking hand in hers. "We'll ask Swanson to open a few bottles of M. Moët's finest, shall we?"

"Yes, yes. That's a wonderful idea. And we must remember to order many bottles for the wedding breakfast in London. There will be much to plan, and we will start tomorrow afternoon, shall we, with the planning, Georgie? And Anna will be a wonderful help as well. And there will be the guest list and the linens and the menu, of course, and the . . ." Vanessa kept talking, and Nora looked over her shoulder and winked at Georgie as she led her mother out of the room.

"So, you just decided to blurt it out then? No warning?" Trevor asked Georgie, hanging back as everyone preceded them in to dinner.

She quirked her lips and rolled her eyes. "I didn't see the point in beating about the bush. She's reacted exactly as I suspected she would. Utterly selfish."

"Oh, Georgie, do stop it." James was surprised his voice came out sounding as strident as it did. But he didn't apologize.

"I beg your pardon, Rushford?"

He took a quick breath and shook his head. "She's your mother, for goodness' sake, and every time she behaves in a remotely loving or maternal manner, you act as if she's tied you to a stake and lit you on fire. It really must stop."

She turned to Trevor to see if he would defend her, but he shook his head slowly. "James is right, Georgie. She loves you like a puppy loves the butcher. Let her have her moment, all right?"

Georgie's nostrils flared. "Do you not care that she completely ignored the fact that you two are already quite happily *together*? Does she imagine your intimacy will simply disappear so she can serve champagne in Mayfair?"

James smiled quickly so only Trevor could see, then let his face return to complete seriousness when Georgie turned to face him. "For someone who has traveled to the farthest corners of the globe, you seem to have a very limited imagination, Lady Georgiana." James extended his arm again, indicating he was formally offering to escort her into the dining room.

She shook her head and looked utterly exasperated, but she rested one hand upon his forearm and the other upon Trevor's. *That's better,* thought James. The three of them started walking toward the hall.

"And how do you find me unimaginative, James?"

"Obviously, Trevor and I have no intention of limiting our intimacy with one another, and your mother is too much of a lady to even refer to it. Perhaps she suspects you will be a wife to both of us?"

Chapter 6

Georgie stumbled at the edge of the carpet, but it hardly mattered because her feet barely touched the floor. Trevor's solid strength secured her on one side, while James's wiry intensity held her on the other. She was not a wisp of a woman, so the effect was rather intoxicating, to be as a feather between these two powerful men.

Try as she might to convince herself it might all be a bit of bawdy fun, Georgie was forced to admit the possibility that James was not joking. In fact, his voice sounded as if he had never been more serious in his life. She looked at Trevor, realizing too late that the past few times she had done so—looked to him for a bit of calm in the storm—he had sided with James.

Well, *sided* was probably too strong a word, but he certainly hadn't leapt unquestioningly to her defense as she'd always remembered him doing in their childhood. She no longer felt like he was an unhesitating ally; the thought both scared and excited her. If James was implying that they were interested in having a *real* marriage—all three of them—well, Georgie was . . . beyond her ken.

Had Trevor lied when he said that the marriage only needed to take place on paper to fulfill the terms of his father's wishes? Trevor had never told a lie in his life. It made no sense he would start now. Was she lying to herself when she said that was all she wanted?

Regardless of what the two men—or her fiery lusting—had in mind, Georgie had no plans to stay in England, much less embark on some sort of deep and meaningful emotional relationship with her childhood friend and his lover. It wasn't as if the idea of some playful bedroom antics hadn't crossed her mind—she was the first to admit that the idea of being with both of them had made her feel all manner of heated desire that very day—but the *deep* and *meaningful* parts of the equation made those desires cool immediately.

And there was no doubt James and Trevor tended to go in for deep and meaningful; it was there in the intensity that shone from Trevor's eyes, and the conviction that gave James's lips that strong, sensual turn.

"It really is only a marriage on paper, isn't it, Trevor?" she pressed. "There are no additional stipulations from your father?"

"Georgie." Trevor's voice was particularly tender; he held her forearm more tightly, attempting to stay her progress. "Please know that I would never lie to you or try to lure you into a situation that I thought would upset you." They were getting closer and closer to the dining room entrance, and she knew that now was not the best time to badger them, but she couldn't let this situation linger.

"I know you would never lie, Trevor, but I just need you to know—to accept—that there will never be anything between us—never anything like *that*, I mean." She lifted her chin toward Pia and Farleigh and Sebastian as they entered the dining room ahead of them. "Just think about it. She was an innocent convent girl, plucked from obscurity, grateful for the smallest opportunities life has afforded her." Georgie knew she was belittling Pia quite abominably—and Farleigh and Sebastian were hardly *small opportunities*—but she was warming to her theme, and the appalled reception she appeared to be getting from James and Trevor was what she wanted, after all, wasn't it? She forged ahead, feeling as if she were—quite responsibly—hammering every last nail into the coffin of their silly, unrealistic fantasy about James and Trevor and Georgie cobbling together some sort of *real* relationship . . . whatever that meant. "To put it plainly, I can *never in a million years* picture myself as a dutiful wife or doting mama here in Derbyshire." She hadn't intended for the words to sting quite as much as they appeared to; Trevor seemed genuinely heartbroken. She added a hint of levity to her voice. "Oh, don't look like that, darling. Let us go in to dinner with my mother and the rest of the company, and then we will go home and the three of us can speak plainly about what the future could hold. Something light and carefree—a dalliance, perhaps."

She kept a flirtatious smile plastered on her face, but when he looked down at her, dear lord, something hot and thick rolled through her. He was so damnably handsome, so profoundly serious, and the pressure of him on one side and the heat of James on the other—probably watching with great interest—made her flush with undeniable desire. Unfortunately, it was a desire that held none of the carefree lightness she'd blithely offered, but instead promised something dark and terrifying that made her want to throw herself into Trevor's arms and never loosen her hold on his strong shoulders. It was something that would certainly be her undoing. It was a desire she promptly tamped.

She shook it off further by removing her arms from the two men at her side and crossing the dining room with a fake smile for everyone in the room.

The meal progressed with surprising enjoyment—as long as she avoided making eye contact with Trevor or James. Nora had obviously done the seating and had put Georgie between Sebastian and Farleigh. Both men were exceedingly charming and shared her interests in horseflesh and falconry.

Over the years of her self-imposed exile, Georgie had fallen into the habit of dividing the world into several types. When it came to dinner companions, for example, there were those who saw a shared meal as something to be endured until they could return to the comfort and familiarity of their own home and their own habits. Georgie found this type could be either tediously boring or quite jovial when encouraged to speak about their own interests.

And then there were those who sought only to escape the unhappiness of their home life—an unhappy marriage, a houseful of spoiled children—and sharing a meal with them made Georgie feel like she was spending a few hours with a soldier on furlough. This could be a cause for great celebration, slipping the noose as it were, or it could devolve into a sad recitation of endless regrets.

Georgie wasn't sure she could have sustained a difficult conversation this evening, her mind still reeling after what had just transpired with Trevor and James. Blessedly, Sebastian and Farleigh exhibited nary a hint of boredom or regret. They both appeared to have an abiding ease and satisfaction when they spoke of their domestic arrangements, and they also showed a delightful curiosity about what went on in the world outside the perimeter of their homeish interests.

Sebastian was clearly the more experienced equestrian, his time in Spain having been spent almost entirely on horseback. Now that it looked as though he was going to remain in England for some time rather than going to the Americas as he had originally planned, Sebastian explained he was keenly interested in building up his own stable. Georgie invited him over to Mayfield to look at the two Arabian horses she had transported back to England.

"I would be delighted," he replied.

"I've spent most of my time at Mayfield House over the past week soothing those two precious animals, helping them adjust to the new climate and their new surroundings."

"So they're skittish, then?" Sebastian asked.

"No, I wouldn't say that precisely. I think of them as I would any displaced royalty: they appear to be quite *put out* by their new arrangements, but not really in any position to do much about it except complain."

Sebastian laughed at the comparison. "I know just what you mean. I considered bringing my stallion from Madrid, but he wouldn't have traveled well. He enjoys being the prince of the stables on my family farm, and if I put him in some cold mews behind Grosvenor Square, I suspect he would simply refuse to eat."

"Precisely." She liked this man very much. Her love of horses was not a pastime, it was a passion, and when she met others who treated it with a similar all-encompassing respect, she felt like she was meeting a friend for life. "I acquired two splendid stallions named Cyrus and Saladeen. Trevor has a prize mare named Bathsheba, and instructed me to buy him the best bloodstock I could find while I was in the desert those past two years with the Bedouins."

"Two years?" Farleigh asked with a shiver. "Were there any creature comforts?"

She turned to look at him. "Well, I suppose that depends on the creature."

"Touché." Farleigh gave a slow grin, and Sebastian laughed.

"Yes, Leigh," Sebastian taunted. "You, therefore, would be very uncomfortable."

"And you, Sebastian?" They were all on a first-name basis already. Nora was eager to have Anna and all of her group on the most intimate terms with Archie and Georgie, to foster the sense of family that had been missing for so long in Anna's life.

"I've been known to rough it," Sebastian answered.

"Really? I find that surprising." Georgie took a sip of her wine. She blessed her mother for that at least; Vanessa always kept the best vintages on hand and loved to share them.

"As Anna likes to say, I clean up well." Sebastian smiled again, and it was almost like looking into the sun. He was incredibly virile, exuding a pulsing masculinity, and he had a sense of humor about himself that made him that much more appealing.

The three of them continued to speak over the six-course meal. Sebastian was thrilled and delighted to hear the details of her voyages and the colorful adventures she had enjoyed. While regaling him with one particularly ribald tale about a sheikh whose wife claimed he was no longer up to the responsibilities of his office, Georgie caught sight of Trevor's eyes on her.

It was one thing to receive the attention of a new suitor—she knew how to flirt with men (and women) in nearly every culture she'd encountered—but it was something else entirely to discover it in someone for whom she had a deep and abiding friendship. Her heart missed a few beats, then returned to a steady, if thudding, pace. She forced herself to turn her attention back to her dinner companion.

Sebastian continued, "I believe Mayson and I will be riding out tomorrow, along with the Duke and Duchess of Mandeville." He was holding the stem of his wineglass and leaning back casually in the Sheraton chair next to Georgie. She admired the way he held his body—the way he touched things and listened carefully, the way he looked at people and processed the world around him. She shook her head slightly, trying to shake off those strange new feelings about Trevor and James, and to remember she was at a family supper in the castle where she'd grown up, and not in some sensual salon in Cairo.

"Oh, you shall all have a lovely ride, I suspect. I'm sorry I cannot join you. Alas, I will be spending the afternoon with my mother, Nora, and Anna, making early plans for the wedding."

Sebastian looked slightly insulted on his wife's behalf. "I would be happy to switch places with you, if you'd prefer. I welcome any opportunity to spend time with my wife." He lifted his glass in a small salute. When he took a sip, Georgie had the impression that Sebastian's wine—and everything else about his life—was exactly as he wished it to be.

When Trevor saw Georgie flushed and animated under the attentive gaze of two strong men, he wanted to dive at her across the table. *Never in a million years*, she'd said. *Never*.

He was barely able to keep his concentration on Pia's words as she spoke about her family's plans to return to London in a few days and her desire to study with one of the painters from the Royal Academy.

"Don't you think, Mayson?"

"I do beg your forgiveness, Duchess, but my mind is terribly distracted this evening."

"I can see that," she answered with a complicit smile. "Your fiancée is quite distracting."

He looked at Pia more closely. "You sound like someone who knows what it is to be distracted."

"I do indeed." Her eyes slipped toward Anna de Montizon. "The three people I love most in the world are sitting at this table, and I have an abiding peace whenever the four of us are together in one room. But before . . . " Her voice trailed off and she shook her head slightly. "Before we knew our way through the thicket of our emotions, it was quite . . . distracting."

Trevor smiled. "How did you manage it?"

She took a deep, satisfied breath and shrugged. "I never thought I was the managing sort; I always imagined Anna in that role. She's very . . . practical."

Anna was speaking to James about the latest news from Spain, sounding frustrated and angry that her country was still being torn apart by France and England with no end to the destruction in sight.

"I can imagine," Trevor agreed.

"I'm not sure you can," Pia said with certain respect. "She has a *very* persuasive side. In fact, I think it might run in the family." She glanced quickly at Georgie, then back at Trevor. "Did you know their fathers, the Cambury brothers?"

"I was young and inattentive when the Marquess of Camburton and his brother died in 1789. I only remember it from Georgie and Archie's perspective. They had an enviable freedom. I know that sounds quite awful, and I'm ashamed to confess it, but as they were mourning the loss of their father, I was jealous of their independence. My parents were of a rather smothering nature."

"Interesting. I never knew my parents, so I am profoundly jealous of other people's childhoods." Pia shared a few brief details of her life as a ward of the convent in Spain; even though it must have been terribly grim, she described everything with a passive acceptance Trevor found unusual. Not that she had enjoyed the cold and the deprivations, she said, but she didn't resent the circumstances either.

"You have a wonderful way of looking at the world."

"Gratitude is a potent weapon." She glanced across the table when Farleigh laughed at something Georgie said. "It can smite all sorts of ill feelings—toward others and toward ourselves." She looked meaningfully at Georgie again. "Some people are given so much from such a young age, they begin to wonder if they will ever do anything to have earned it." She turned back at Trevor, and he remembered how that very thought had plagued him his last years at Cambridge and during the year he'd spent in London. A subtle sense of worthlessness had crept into him over those years.

"If I didn't have my land and the tenants and the life that revolves around the farm and the seasons, I could easily see how I would slip into just such self-loathing."

"So why do you find it perplexing in others?"

He let a grin spread across his face. "Not so perplexing after all, I suppose."

She nodded. "We will have much to discuss on our ride tomorrow." She lowered her voice. "I don't think anyone's life is perfect, but the life we four have constructed is bursting with love. I wish that for you."

Trevor stared at the beautiful gold-rimmed plate and the cut-crystal parfait dish that now sat empty in front of him. They'd all finished dessert and the footmen had yet to clear. The silver candelabras were polished to a shimmering gleam. Suddenly, his whole world seemed far too small for Lady Georgiana Cambury. She needed space around her, adventure—things he would never be able to provide, even with all the gold his father had to give. Even in a million years.

"All will be well." Pia's voice soothed him. "You look far too sad for such a beautiful night spent among like-minded friends."

"You're absolutely right." He raised his glass. "To like-minded friends." She touched his glass with hers, her dark brown eyes sparkling in the candlelight. "It's been a pleasure getting to know you these past few weeks, Pia." He reached for her hand and gave her a quick, courtly kiss on her knuckles. She laughed delightedly and Farleigh growled from the other side of the table.

"If you please, Mayson. Hands off my wife."

Trevor released her hand and smiled good-naturedly at the duke. "Very well, Farleigh." Then he turned and spoke quietly to Pia. "Do you ever resent his possessiveness?"

Her head turned slightly, and she narrowed her eyes. "Resent? How could I resent one of the most loving and generous people in my life? Yes, he is demanding, but the rewards are great. It would be like resenting one's own child."

Trevor raised an eyebrow. "I'd venture that's been known to happen." He regretted it as soon as he said it. Pia looked like the words had punched her in the gut.

"I will pray this night for people who resent their own children."

Thinking of his father, alone and bitter in his splendid mansion in Mayfair, Trevor pictured this Spanish woman's prayers rising through the atmosphere, circling around the globe in search of souls to soothe, and landing on the east side of Grosvenor Square. They would need to be powerful prayers indeed to penetrate the hard shell of acrimony with which his father had fortified that home in recent months. "I hope your prayers are answered. For all of our sakes."

"We never know the path to our own happiness. I never thought I would be living in England, much less sitting in one of its grandest homes. The idea of being a duchess never even crossed my mind. I thought I was a twig on the river of circumstance, but one or two times I have reached for a passing chance—and held fast. I was greatly rewarded. One should at least reach for a chance, Lord Mayson, don't you think?"

"I do. But our origins couldn't be further from one another. Whereas you grabbed at a chance to be plucked from a shadowy life in a remote convent, I have had every privilege. Georgie—" His voice caught. Damn James and his imagination. Trevor could barely speak her name without wondering—wishing—for a future, or a chance at it. "When I wish for things, I feel like an ingrate, peevishly dissatisfied with all the riches and bounty that have already been heaped upon me."

"Then do it for her," Pia said softly, with the slightest tilt of her head in Georgie's direction. "If you are worried your motives are self-serving, then at least be certain they will also serve to felicitate the souls of others."

"You are wise, Duchess."

She laughed lightly. "Far from it. I am selfish like you, but I always make sure to include the happiness of others in my supplications to the Lord. Thus far it seems to have worked in my favor."

James had enjoyed speaking with Anna throughout dinner. They'd covered everything from the latest Turkish turbans to the recent political skirmishes in her home country of Spain. But they'd finished dessert, and it was difficult for James to feign patience when all he wanted to do was toss Trevor into the closed carriage and make love to him. Georgie could hang, with her *never in a million years* and her self-deceiving ways.

He was not usually one to fidget, but he must have shifted in his chair.

"You are quite finished, I see," Anna said.

She was as direct as anyone he'd ever met, and there was no point in pretending he wished to linger. "I believe Trevor is experiencing . . . something . . . and I wish to comfort him."

"He's fallen in love with Georgie, you say?"

James whipped his head around to face Anna squarely. "No. I didn't say. But of course that's what I meant, you perceptive witch. Do you always say whatever pops into your head?"

She shrugged. "Much of the time. Perhaps it's from my father's side of the family; I see something similar in Georgie. Neither one of us takes after Vanessa or Nora, obviously. People say I am the image of my father."

"I've only seen portraits of Dennis Cambury, but I'd say people are right."

"So perhaps there is a willful streak that runs through the Cambury blood." She gestured vaguely around the grand dining room, one of the finest in all of Europe. "Obviously my father's ancestors liked to aim high."

James looked up at the ornate ceiling and across the table to the lush scarlet silk wall coverings. "You may be right. Where there's a will, is that it?" He shook his head. "Unfortunately, I don't think Georgie's will and Trevor's are quite aligned at present."

"Perhaps." She looked thoughtful. "Perhaps not. I suggest, if I may be so bold, that you speak to my husband about how he finally wore down my resistance, how I came to fall in love with him, against all my best intentions to the contrary."

James slapped his thigh and hooted. Nora and Vanessa turned to see what had him so amused, but he merely dipped his chin and apologized. After their attention had turned away from him again, he looked at Anna and quietly said, "That was the very thing I said to Trevor."

"What's that?" Anna asked, popping a grape into her mouth.

"That if he— All right, if *we*—"

She smiled knowingly.

"If *we* are ever to win Georgie's heart," he continued in a low voice that only she could hear, "it has to be done forcefully yet subtly."

"Oh, I like the sound of that very much."

"So do I," James agreed, then turned serious. "So did I. She keeps saying she's not game. At all. But I see it in her eyes . . . I feel it when she rests her hand on my forearm."

Anna looked at him tenderly. "My heart and my mind were at odds for quite some time after I married Sebastian. I am forever grateful he wore down my defenses."

About an hour later, after they'd spent time in the drawing room, Georgie declared she could no longer sit still knowing the horses hadn't seen her for nigh on five hours. Trevor and James rose immediately, bidding their good-byes, and the three of them left Camburton Castle.

When the footman had shut the carriage door and they were finally alone, Georgie spoke first. She touched her fingertips to the turban-like hat that James had made for her, looking every inch the shallow aristocrat. "Sebastian and Farleigh were charming. The whole evening was charming. Even this damned hat is charming." She let her hand go back to her lap. "But now we must talk about the future."

James felt the air change inside the carriage, Georgie's words creating a not-so-subtle tension.

"We need to set up a few . . . parameters. First off, there will be no further talk of *real* marriages," she declared, as if all their group decisions were unilaterally hers to make. "Or even more preposterous, the idea of all three of us embarking on some sort of . . . romance."

James pulled Trevor's hand into both of his and spoke before Trevor could say something irretrievable. "Very well, Georgie. If that's the way of it, you should leave Mayfield at once. Everything will be far less heated once you move back into Camburton Castle and plan the wedding with your mother."

"What? Why must I move back to Camburton?" She appeared as if she'd never taken anyone's feelings into account except her own, nor had it even occurred to her that James and Trevor might have a few *parameters* of their own. "And what about the horses?"

James would have laughed if he hadn't felt so terribly sorry for Trevor—and for Georgie, for that matter. The poor man had obviously fallen in love with his dear friend, and here she was feigning concern for the cattle.

"What about them?" James asked rhetorically, taking charge of the situation, as he should have done from the start. "They belong to Trevor now. Delivered in fine fettle. Paid in full."

She looked affronted. "It's not just about paying for them. They need to be trained. Cyrus especially is already getting disobedient and spiteful. I need to—"

"Trevor is one of the finest horsemen in the country. It's not negotiable." James used the same voice he used when a vendor tried to sell him a bolt of shoddy wool.

"I beg your pardon? Everything is negotiable. And, besides, why isn't Trevor saying anything? I don't like the way you're speaking for him as if he doesn't have any say in the matter."

Trevor was holding James's hand so tight it was beginning to hurt. James welcomed the sharp pain. Without turning to look at Trevor, James continued, "Trevor and I are of one mind about this, Georgie. It's too disruptive having you at Mayfield House."

"Disruptive? This is an outrage. Tell him, Trevor. You must tell him. You are my oldest and dearest friend. Why are you throwing me out?"

"We're hardly tossing you to the curb," James said hotly. He'd had just about enough of Lady Georgiana Cambury and her willful refusal to acknowledge that Trevor's feelings had bloomed. He'd had enough of her refusal to acknowledge that *her* feelings had begun to change as well, but her dictatorial tone was making him too angry to be sympathetic. "There's no need to be dramatic. You're going to Camburton Castle, arguably one of the grandest country houses in the world, followed by a few weeks at Cambury House in London, arguably one of the grandest city houses in the world. I'm beginning to tire of your whining."

That did it. The blood drained from her face and she looked like she would have taken a swing at him if she'd been in breeches and a man's shirt that didn't restrict her ability to make a proper hit. "How dare you? You—you—you interloper! Who are you to speak for Trevor when he is—"

"—in love with you?" James interrupted, in a low voice that left her no choice but to remain silent. "Can you be so blind? Everyone at the party tonight could see that Trevor is no longer pretending anything for the sake of his inheritance. He loves you, you idiot—for reasons that elude me just at the moment. You are spoiled, selfish, and, I suspect, dishonest about your own heart."

Trevor groaned, but kept his gaze out the dark window, as if those strikes against her were just as appealing as everything else he'd come to love about her.

"Selfish? I've offered to marry my dearest friend, damn it! Spoiled? I sleep in stalls and stables without a thought for the absurd trappings of your pretentious world. As for my heart . . . well, I never promised . . . I never . . . I—I—I—" she stammered and her voice cracked with emotion.

"Yes, Lady Georgiana, it is *always* about you-you-you. Alas, I will not sit idly by and watch the man I love get stuck in a mess of unrequited feelings for *a million years*. I was quite happy for him actually . . ." James turned his head and tenderly kissed Trevor on the jaw. "In fact, I was even encouraging him to pursue this deeper affection—for all of us to pursue a deeper affection, when I suspected there was even a remote chance."

"Trevor, please say something," Georgie finally whispered.

Keeping his eyes averted, Trevor finally said, "I'm sorry, Georgie, I really am." His voice was shredded, and all James wanted to do was kiss him and soothe away the hurt, but obviously Georgie was not going to believe the truth until she heard it from him. Trevor finally turned to face her. "It was wrong of me to think I could do this. I've always loved you, darling. Before I saw you again at the inn, after so many years apart, I thought it had passed. None of that is your fault. And this is all horribly sudden, I know that. And again, I am so sorry. But yes, I think it would be best if you do as James suggests and return to your mother's house. I will understand completely if you wish to beg off the wedding altogether, but I'm afraid my feelings for you have grown immeasurably."

"Well, stop them from growing, damn it!" Georgie was on the verge of angry tears. "Get ahold of yourself and stop this obsessing!"

James nearly wept as Trevor exhaled a quick gust of air through his nostrils. "Don't you think I would if I could, Georgie? But I want you—" He pounded his chest with his fist. "Here." James wanted to smash something. Trevor took a few more calming breaths, then continued. "And even *that* I might have borne in silence, except the way you look at me—at us—the way you blush and tremble . . . I think you want it too, but you will never confess it. You will never even admit the possibility." Trevor reached for James and held his hand. "You won't allow for even a chance at happiness. You won't allow for anything. Which makes the whole situation even more intolerable. You think I don't see the way you look at James and me when we kiss or touch?" James shivered as Trevor leaned in and kissed him lightly on the neck, then looked to Georgie. "You don't think I saw the light in your eyes when I came upon you entering the tub this evening? You expect me to believe that was just childish teasing, old friends swimming naked in the pond? To anything more than that, you say *never*?"

Her lip trembled, but she said nothing in reply.

Trevor turned away from her and looked out the window again. His grip on James's hand had loosened somewhat, but his hold was still firm. Trevor began speaking again without looking at Georgie. "When you are like James and me, when you have spent a lifetime being told your desires are perverse, unnatural, you don't treat it lightly when something beautiful comes your way. You don't cast it aside because it is inconvenient—"

"But I know what it is to feel alienated from society because of my physical desires—"

"This is not a question of mere carnality, Georgie! You are not allowing for feelings to change and grow. And again, I won't fault you for it. It's all been a rushed job. Even so . . . I cannot, I *will* not, pretend that my feelings for you are overblown or mistaken. I believe in the power of possibilities." He sighed, then faced Georgie. "For the short time that I tried to deny my feelings for James—when we first met and I had never been with a man, never had the courage—I learned that I am *incapable* of denying my affection once it blooms in my heart. In fact, it only grows when I attempt to squash it, like a diamond that achieves its greatest clarity under the greatest pressure. And now I know it for a gift and not a burden. So," he said softly, but with utter conviction, "it really would be best if you returned to your mother's until our *paper wedding* in Hanover Square. After which, we will both be very much free of our disappointments. All I wanted was a chance . . . to show you . . . to love you . . ."

She was crying quietly.

So at least she wasn't entirely without sympathy, thought James meanly.

"Will you still be my friend?" Her voice was so small and hesitant; James had a very clear view of how she must have looked as a girl—all that bluster and confidence over such a tender heart.

"In time, perhaps. This is no one's *fault*, Georgie." Trevor gave the roof of the barouche a firm double knock and the driver called a whoa to the horses. "I'm going to walk the rest of the way to Mayfield. We're only a short tromp away. James will accompany me." When the carriage had come to a full stop, James opened the door and jumped down, reaching back to assist Trevor.

Trevor was about to step out into the cool autumn night, when he turned back to face her. He was slightly hunched in the enclosed space. James watched as he leaned in and kissed Georgie on the cheek. "I will see you at the altar, if you still wish to follow through on that part of the arrangement. I shan't bother you either way."

And with that, he stepped from the carriage and shut the door behind him.

Chapter 7

Georgie held back her sobs for a few seconds until she was sure Trevor and James (that bastard) were well out of hearing distance. The carriage felt cold and empty as the horses picked up speed.

Damn those two men and their emotional blackmail. She would get her things this very evening and return to Camburton Castle immediately. Knowing Vanessa's organizational skills, she could probably plan a wedding in Mayfair for four hundred people within a fortnight, and then Georgie could be on the first boat to Egypt. Yes, she would marry him—if Trevor meant what he'd said, she could still give him the gift of his inheritance, without giving in to any of her confusing passions or compromising her settlement. For the rest of her life, she would have all the protection of a marriage without any of the restrictions of a wife.

The carriage slowed and Georgie pushed open the door before the wheels had come to a complete stop. The footman jumped from his perch and gave his apologies as Georgie stormed past him. She spun on her heel and turned her fury on the innocent man.

"Do stop with that, Hartley! I can't stand how everyone is already treating me as if I am already the lady of the house, which is many years off—if ever!" She was standing very close to him, and he kept his eyes steady on some point over her shoulder. "Do you hear me?"

"Yes, m'lady."

She growled at the respectful form of address and turned back toward the house. "And do not put the horses away. I am returning to Camburton as soon as I pack my trunks."

The butler opened the front door right before her hand landed on the knob. Even the excellent staff at Mayfield made her want to scream in frustration. Why was everyone so accommodating? She needed to get out of here just as much as Trevor needed her to get out.

In love with her. She huffed and tore the stupid hat off her head, tossing it carelessly on the bench in the front hall, then kicked off the stupider Italian shoes, and lifted the skirt of her consummately stupid dress, and took the grand stairs two at a time.

Mrs. Daley was coming around the corner at the top of the stairs, probably having turned back the beds in anticipation of their return.

"Don't say a word!" Georgie cried, lifting her palm in a gesture she hoped would prevent the other woman from speaking. "I am going to my mother's to spend the next few weeks before we go to London for the wedding."

The news seemed to make Mrs. Daley well chuffed, like a little fat robin in springtime. "Well, that's quite as it should be. A London wedding! And a young miss and her mama planning her—"

"Stop!" Georgie wheeled on her. "Please." She lowered her voice somewhat, but it still came out with a hint of fury. She felt—and probably looked—like a banshee.

"Yes, m'lady." Mrs. Daley dipped her eyes and curtseyed.

"No, no, no!" Georgie cried, pulling at her short hair. "Not you as well. I forbid it. If one more person *defers* to me, I'm going to scream."

"You are already screaming," Mrs. Daley pointed out helpfully.

"That's more like it." Georgie sighed. "I treasure your serpent's tongue. Now, help me pack up my things before those two men get back from their walk. I can't take another moment of all this soppiness!"

Mrs. Daley didn't look the least put out by Georgie's tantrum. In fact, if Georgie hadn't known better, she would have said Mrs. Daley looked quite pleased about Georgie's snit. Young Franny entered the room a few minutes later and helped fold and pack all of Georgie's clothes and toiletries.

Used to traveling light and quickly, Georgie knew better than most how to decamp with admirable speed and efficiency. Thirty minutes after her arrival, she was looking around the guest room to make sure none of her effects had been left behind. She would *never* return to this place.

After she said her vows next month, it was quite likely she would never return to England at all. She watched as Franny clamped the last buckle on the third trunk and then stood back to make way for the two footmen who'd arrived to bring everything to the carriage.

They all looked like they'd been asleep and had been ordered to put on their uniforms to assist her. She realized they *had* been ordered—by her—to do exactly that, and she felt a pang of real guilt. She reached into her smaller traveling bag, where she kept her coin, and took out a few bob. "Please give my thanks to the housemen and other servants who were inconvenienced at this late hour by my hasty departure."

"Oh, I couldn't possibly," Mrs. Daley said, offended. She stuck her hands beneath her apron skirt so it would be impossible for Georgie to force the money into her palm.

"Damn you, Daley."

Mrs. Daley shook her head. "You'll be back and you can say thank you properly, rather than in this crass and unladylike fashion."

Georgie slammed the coins on the side table in the bedroom and growled again. "For the last time, I am not, nor will I ever be, *ladylike*!"

With that, she stormed from the room and felt the freedom of having abandoned that useless dress for deerskin breeches and riding boots. She practically skipped down the stairs, feeling like freedom was finally at hand.

Yes, of course she was sad about the possible loss of her friendship with Trevor, but she refused to believe it. His silly ardor would cool, and they would probably have a wonderful correspondence at some point in the future, as they always had. If he really loved her, there was no way he could expect her to shrivel up and die in a place like this.

She turned to look around the main hall one last time, catching a glimpse of Mrs. Daley at the top of the stairs, then opened the front door and saw the carriage. Her trunks were stacked neatly, two at the back and one on top, and she realized the last thing she wanted to do at the moment was step back inside Trevor Mayson's barouche.

She handed off the smaller tote she was carrying. "Take this and all the baggage to Camburton Castle at once, and I will follow on horseback."

"But m'lady, it's the middle of the night, and you'll be alone on the road—"

"Yes, Hartley. If I'm very, very lucky, I will be alone . . . *for once.* Now be off!"

She turned toward the stables and immediately started to settle—all that inquisitive, opinionated humanity behind her and her beautiful, nonchattering, nonmanaging beasts before her. Cyrus nickered when she was a few paces from the entrance of the stables. When she approached his stall, he whinnied with that aristocratic toss of his narrow Arabian head that was so particular to his line.

"Yes, your majesty. I see you. And I too wish for a fast midnight run. We've been far too complacent since we arrived." She rubbed the long, smooth line of his nose and then his buttery soft lips, slipping him one of the treats she always kept hidden in her pockets. "Shall we?"

He lifted his chin as if he knew full well what she was suggesting and agreed wholeheartedly. She turned and found a length of rope and fashioned a head-collar while she talked to him in a string of nonsensical praise. When she slipped it over his ears, he looked like he was as grateful as she was.

She'd been so concerned about making sure he was adjusting to the new routine, she had completely forgotten his need—and hers— to go at a full gallop several times a day. She reached for a crop out of habit. Not that Cyrus would need the slightest prodding to let loose, but she never felt like she was really riding unless she had it tucked in her hand.

"You want to blow off steam, my love?'

He whinnied and lifted his head twice. Saladeen looked bored as he glanced at them from his stall, while across the way, Bathsheba peered over with a disapproving look, then withdrew. Georgie laughed softly and walked Cyrus out of the stable and into the clear night. She took a deep breath and felt at peace for the first time in weeks.

She led him to the block and got on his bare back. Her thighs gripped firmly around his middle and she leaned down to wrap her arms around his neck and burrow her face into his mane, letting him know she was there and she wouldn't be going away . . . for now.

The elegant beast exhaled with a gust of satisfaction, and she did too, letting her heart slow to meet the beat of his. After a few minutes of, well, communing, she supposed, she adjusted the soft rope reins in her hands, tucked the crop neatly between arm and ribs, sat up slightly, and urged him on.

Trevor held James's hand as they walked down the long gravel lane that led to Mayfield House. Trevor looked up and saw the outline of the medieval keep under the moonlight. As they turned a bend, the rest of the large manor house became visible against the night sky. The building was a dark silhouette, but Trevor could picture it in his mind, with all the riotous reds and metallic golds of the autumnal ivy that covered the home at this time of year. "I love it here so much. Do you ever miss the action of town?"

James pulled Trevor to a halt and turned to kiss him. It was hot and passionate, not a tender, conciliatory kiss like the ones he'd given him a few minutes ago.

"I never miss anything when I'm with you, you idiot," James said breathlessly. "We could live in a bloody cave for all I care."

Trevor reached to touch James's moist lips, loving the way they glistened in the moonlight. "Did you mean everything you said to Georgie? Do you really think she is so deplorable?"

James pulled Trevor's taunting finger into his mouth for a second, then released it. "Of course not. I think she's splendid—and I think she loves you—maybe even loves both of us—but she has to come to realize all of that for herself. I was wrong when I thought we could seduce her through some version of persistent, subtle wooing."

"How do you think Sebastian convinced Anna to marry him?"

James shook his head. "Apples and oranges. Anna was a penniless convent girl on her way to becoming a courtesan. Sebastian was a step on the way to her independence, an expedient."

"You are very cold sometimes." Trevor started walking again. "Even so, after they were married, she obviously came to love him."

"Trevor, stop."

Trevor turned and looked at James. "What is it?"

James reached over and touched his cheek, where he was already starting to have a bit of rough growth after only a few hours since his last shave.

"Are *you* happy with what we have?" James asked.

"God, yes." The words came out before Trevor could even contemplate them. "I-I don't even think of myself as *me* anymore, in any real sense. I feel like you and I are part of each other."

"So do I," James whispered and leaned in to kiss him again.

Trevor gasped at the intensity of it. James was pushing him off the gravel and onto the grass, with Trevor taking precarious backward steps into the darkness. "I have you," James whispered between kisses, until he was pressing against him with Trevor's back up against the trunk of one of the large plane trees that lined the long drive. Before Trevor was really aware of what was happening, James was pulling at the fabric of Trevor's white linen shirt and reaching under to press his cool palm against Trevor's hot abdomen.

"Oh, God, you feel so right against my hand." James's breath caught.

"James, I want to take you now. Here. On the cool evening grass. We won't be able to make love out of doors for much longer this year. I want to look up at the autumn sky and feel myself inside you."

"Yes," James whispered against his ear. "God, yes."

Trevor fumbled with his silk breeches and pulled them down enough to expose his swollen, stiff cock. "I was half-hard all through dinner, thinking of the three of us in the carriage, thinking of Georgie letting me tup her while you took me—" He gasped when James grabbed hold of his cock and began stroking him with long, nearly painful pulls. James knew exactly the pressure Trevor could bear, exactly how to bring him to the knife-edge of pain and pleasure.

"My hands are aching to touch you," Trevor panted. "Get yourself free, man."

James laughed low. "My hands are busy, mate. Do it for me, would you?"

Trevor couldn't see well due to the darkness, but he thought he'd be just as clumsy if it were high noon. He'd been so aroused all afternoon, then even more excited when he let his hopes rise that Georgie shared his feelings, that his fingers felt swollen with desire. He finally got James's pants out of the way and shoved him bodily down onto the grass. Trevor was probably a good two stone heavier than James, most of it muscle, and while he didn't always take advantage of the disparity in their strength, tonight he felt like having his way with him.

And the idea obviously pleased James as well, if his guttural moans were to be believed. Swinging James's body around roughly, Trevor pressed his fingers into James's hips to hold him pinned to the ground, then took his cock into his mouth. James cried out when Trevor began to scrape his teeth along the edge of his shaft, trailing his tongue along the underside.

Being at opposite ends as they were, Trevor moaned around James's cock when he felt James's mouth take him. They clung to each other, rolling and groping, looking up at the sky when they could, bringing each other to peaks of pleasure without ever going over the edge.

Trevor was becoming frantic with wanting—wanting to fuck James, wanting James to fuck him. Their clothes were torn half to shreds. He felt a thundering desire, a pounding, quivering need to fill and be filled. And then he realized the pounding wasn't coming from his heart—or *only* from his heart. One of the horses must have got loose, he thought through the fog of lust.

"James . . ."

"I know! It's incredible—"

"James!" he yelled. "Watch out!"

He grabbed James roughly and shoved him away from the thundering hooves in the nick of time. Both of them were panting and breathless, clinging to each other as the hot energy of sexual desire was replaced by the icy vigor of battle.

"Who goes there?" Trevor called.

But he knew.

The enormous beast wheeled around and lifted its front hooves in a display of arrogance.

Trevor put James against the tree and whispered, "Set yourself to rights and don't move until I've dealt with Georgie."

Turning to confront her, Trevor tugged up the fall of his breeches, not bothering to refasten them entirely, but attaching a few buttons to hold them in place for the moment. His jacket was somewhere in the grass, probably covered in mud the shape of horse's hooves. His shirt had likewise gone missing.

His heart was pounding with a mix of terror and anger as he approached her. Riding at night without a saddle or any proper bridle or reins was sheer madness, no matter how fine a horsewoman she was. Georgie or James—not to mention Cyrus—could have been horribly injured. A morbid vision of her body thrown from the beast flashed in his mind, and caused his heart to stutter. A further image of James crushed into the earth—

Unable to contemplate that nightmare a moment longer, he let anger overtake concern for her welfare: she was a selfish brat who needed to be taught a lesson once and for all.

"Get down from there this instant," Trevor commanded evenly. He knew better than to show the least hesitation or fear around Cyrus. Over the past week, man and beast had formed a burgeoning respect. The horse was panting and flaring his nostrils, unsure of which human was his true master. Trevor murmured to the animal, reaching out to pet his neck and slowly grab hold of the primitive rope bridle. Damn her for not even saddling him properly.

The horse's eyes flashed, showing a bit of white in the moonlight. "I've got you, my man . . ." Trevor continued softly, until he had calmed the horse enough to speak to Georgie. Without changing his tone or taking his eyes off the nervous, massive animal, Trevor said, "That's right, Cyrus. You will be free in a moment. Because this wild thing on your back will dismount immediately, and I will remove this rudimentary harness that is not fit for a pauper, much less a Persian king like you."

Cyrus nodded his agreement, and even nuzzled into Trevor's neck and shoulder.

"Traitor," Georgie muttered.

For all of Georgie's posturing about how she needed to help the two Arabians adjust to their new life in the north, they belonged to Trevor now, and Cyrus knew it, sensed it.

"Get down, *George*." When she didn't move, he added more sharply, "Now."

James stayed against the tree, as Trevor had requested, but he might as well have been that bit of rope in Trevor's hand for how the man's commanding voice rolled through him. James's heart was back to a steady pounding, the frantic gallop of lust and terror having abated somewhat. The storm of powerful horse's hooves had been inches from his skull and—not that he was at all of a fearful or maudlin disposition—James's own mortality had flashed before him with harsh clarity.

And in that moment, he'd known the truth of what he wanted: if he was going to die at the hands—or feet—of this Amazonian empress, it was not going to be by accident. He watched and waited until Trevor had calmed the horse. He stared at the way Georgie sat on its bare back, her spine so perfectly straight, her chin and jaw at that aristocratic angle. She looked as if she had nothing to prove, and everything.

James couldn't hear the exact words Trevor was saying, ostensibly to the horse, but when he saw Georgie's nostrils flare and her eyes widen, he knew there was a confrontation afoot.

"Now," he heard Trevor say more clearly.

Georgie slid from the sweaty horse's strong back with one fluid, confident motion, the moonlight glinting off the horse's slick black coat where her legs had been clinging. Then Georgie watched helplessly as Cyrus nickered and whinnied contentedly while Trevor smoothed the horse's neck and face with firm, knowing passes. While he was doing that, Trevor was also removing the rope bridle that Georgie must have fashioned in her haste.

Once he had removed the rope completely and let the horse smell it, Trevor wound the length in a neat coil, talking in that murmuring, soothing way all the while. He circled the animal, rubbing him, owning him, as he checked for injuries and let Cyrus know he was loved and honored. Then, when Trevor was near his rear haunches, he slapped him with a quick, friendly spank and cried, "Off you go!"

James loved horses as much as Trevor did, but James's love was grounded in a healthy fear, whereas Trevor's was grounded in mutual adoration. The horse whinnied and sprang about, all that black, shining muscle quivering in the moonlight, silhouetted against the lake like an enormous version of a giddy spring lamb. Then Cyrus looked back toward Trevor one last time, asking for permission.

Trevor laughed and waved his arm toward the west. "Go!"

With that, the horse ran, hard and fast and blissfully free—back toward the stables and the beautiful Bathsheba, to whom he was already becoming devoted.

"Watch out!" James cried when he saw Georgie raising her crop to strike Trevor. Unflinching, Trevor turned quickly toward her, and with one easy, swift motion, grabbed the short leather whip out of her hand before she came anywhere near making contact.

Georgie was as tall as James, but Trevor was a few inches taller—and far bigger: his shoulders wide and strong, his neck thick, his hands powerful. James watched as Trevor crowded her, slicing the crop repeatedly through the air beside them with a menacing swoosh. "You would hit me, you demoness?"

She looked as if she wanted to take a step back, away from the obvious threat of Trevor's fury, but her pride wouldn't let her. She held her ground, but her head recoiled an inch.

"You would sleep in my house," Trevor continued, "eat my food, *steal my horse*, and then you would hit me? What have I *ever* done to make you despise me so, *Lady* Georgiana Cambury?"

She continued breathing hard, but refused to answer.

"Or is it Mr. George Camden?" Trevor nearly growled.

James watched how the name affected her. When she'd told them how she'd passed herself off as a man in the Middle East, she'd described the thrilling combination of power and freedom.

"What if I am?" Her voice was slightly deeper, and James realized this was *not* a role, not like it was when she wore a beautiful silk dress and Italian slippers and a peacock feather in her turban. Nor like it was when she was Georgie, wearing her mannish riding coat that was still embellished with all sorts of decorative flourishes, frilly cuffs, and other feminine concessions to some idea of herself as part male/part female.

She was no longer an idealized version of anything. This was the real person. Her shirt was a simple white cotton man's tunic that she'd tucked haphazardly into her buckskins. But she'd apparently been in too much of a rushed snit to put on her usual confining underbodice, so her full breasts were pushing erotically through the thin fabric. When Trevor spoke to her like that, accusing her of all those abuses and then taunting her with her fake—or was it her real?—masculine name, her nipples peaked beneath the fabric and her body betrayed her.

Trevor swatted the crop through the air one last time, hard, and James and Georgie gasped in unison. He was so full of power, throbbing with it. Trevor was a gentle soul, and he didn't like to bully or intimidate, but dear God, when he chose to exert his strength, it was a beautiful thing to behold.

"Mr. Camden." Trevor bowed to Georgie. "I am very pleased to make your acquaintance. Now name your weapon."

"What?" Georgie collected herself enough to force out that one word.

"If you wish to fight me, quit with the skirmishes and the sallies and make a proper attack. And don't you *ever* again raise a hand to me while my back is turned." He flipped the crop handily and presented the handle for her to take. "If you want to attack me, face me like a man."

"Trevor." Her voice—James didn't even know how to describe it. It was everything knotted together: desire, anger, frustration. But mostly, it was raw lust.

Trevor thrust the handle of the crop closer to her face. Then he grabbed the front of her shirt and fisted it into his other hand. He shook her twice, practically punching her chest while he did. "Damn you, Georgie! Fight me or fuck me! I just want to feel it. I want to feel you."

She was coiling up for action, like she was actually contemplating her chances if she decided to fight him, to force his hands from where they were gripping the fine white linen of her shirt. Pulling away slightly to test him, she was jerked closer, and the rough handling caused an immediate gasp to escape her slightly parted lips.

"Don't you dare treat me like a girl," she gritted out, her teeth clenched. It came as more of a plea than a warning. James was inexorably drawn to them, the roiling desire they created pulling him in like a whirlpool. He stepped away from the tree and moved closer to where they were standing.

Trevor whispered hotly, his face close to hers, "I will give you no quarter, George." He trailed the braided handle of the crop along her lips, down her neck. James hovered close behind Trevor and then shuddered when he felt the energy snap and sizzle around them while they stood locked in that violent clutch.

She turned to look at James, and he startled. Her eyes were mad, aflame with lust and submission and wanting. "I mean it." She was including James in her demanding confession. Then she turned back to face Trevor. James watched as a beautiful peace settled over her. The truth. "Otherwise you will be tender and gentle and *horrible.*"

"Drop your trousers, sir," Trevor ordered, shoving her away from him.

Her eyes widened. "What?"

"You heard me." He whipped the short crop through the air with powerful assurance.

"Trevor—"

"No." His voice was resolute, but he never raised it. "If you are going to act like a spoiled brat, you are going to be treated like one." He narrowed his eyes when he looked at her. "*Humiliated* like one."

She gasped, probably from a mix of shame and lust. James knew from many years of firsthand experience: it was undeniably erotic to hear Trevor speak in that way. Smiling wickedly, James said, "You heard the man." Then he tilted his head. "Or are you too much of a coward to take your punishment?" James couldn't tell in the moonlight, but he thought Georgie's skin heated even more than it had a few minutes before, when Trevor began swatting that devilish crop and telling her to show him her bare arse.

Now, here, under the moonlight, with the sound of the horse's hooves receding into the distance and the lake water lapping and the leaves murmuring overhead, they were all stripped down to bare essence. Over and above nature's whispering chorus, it was their breathing that made the most noise, three human animals preparing for battle.

For a moment, James thought Georgie was going to make a dash for it. He almost wished she would, if only to see Trevor chase after her and pull her down into the muddy grass like a lion taking down a gazelle.

But then she began to unbutton the fall of her trousers.

Trevor kept slapping the end of the crop against his palm, probably anticipating how he was going to dole out her punishment . . . and the obvious sensual implications of her bare arse right there for the taking. When she was finished undoing the buttons, her trousers were around her knees and her shirt was hanging a few inches above them, so only a strip of her pale thighs showed in the moonlight.

"Turn around, George." Trevor and that voice! James was ready to explode.

Georgie did what Trevor commanded, and James could've sworn she even let out a little anticipatory sigh. *Of course.* She wanted this as much as Trevor did. As if to prove the point, she slowly lowered herself onto her knees and then leaned forward. She used one hand to move the fabric of her shirt up to the middle of her back, so her beautiful round arse was exposed and submissively offered up to Trevor.

"Do it," she whispered, resting her cheek against her forearms on the ground, so James and Trevor could see her profile, see the desire warring with shame.

"Oh, I'll do it all right." Trevor walked around her while he spoke. "When *I* say do it."

She huffed or whimpered; James wasn't quite sure.

"In fact, I don't want to hear another word out of you. Gag her, James."

She made that whimpering sound again, but James could tell now it was a sound of eagerness, not defiance. She wanted this more than she would—or could—ever admit.

"Gladly." James found his cravat in the grass and worked it between her lips, fastening it in a tight knot at her nape. She made no pretense of resisting; in fact, she looked happier than he'd seen her anytime since she'd arrived back in England. "Oh, she's done this before, Trevor. Mark my words." James settled himself cross-legged in front of her. "I want to be right here, to see her beautiful tears."

She groaned against the fabric in her mouth, and James could see the tension in her jaw as she bit down on it. He settled her chin so she was looking up at him. Her forearms and knees were pressed solidly into the muddy earth, bracing herself. Then she stared up at James.

Trevor didn't waste another moment. He took the first swat—a fast crack—and she looked as though she might have an orgasm from that one bit of contact.

"She's already loving it," James said.

"Why don't you take out your cock," Trevor suggested.

"Better and better." James undid his trousers and his cock sprang free. Georgie's eyes widened and she moaned through another swat against her arse. Her eyes were glistening like gems. "She loves it. Don't hold back, Trevor."

And he didn't. He worked up a steady pace. With so many fond memories of being on the receiving end of Trevor's confident strokes, James could practically feel the swats against his own skin. He worked his cock in a concurrent rhythm and watched how Georgie's eyes streamed with those delicious tears that only came from the kind of release where exquisite pain and pleasure blurred. Even though the gag prevented her from using her mouth, she leaned her face down to be closer to James's cock. He laughed and called to Trevor, "She wants more. Do you think we should let her have it?"

Trevor had worked himself up into a sweat and paused to catch his breath. As if he were checking her temperature, he took a break from the crop and put his hand between her legs. "Yes. She's responding very well." Trevor reached across her back and slid his moist fingers into James's mouth. "I think she's earned a small treat, don't you?"

James sucked the taste of her off Trevor and hummed his agreement.

Trevor smiled and slowly pulled his fingers free. Then, tossing aside the crop, Trevor undid his trousers and dropped to his knees. "Because this is what you want, isn't it, George?"

She grunted against the fabric in her mouth as Trevor spread her slick moisture up and down the crack of her arse, getting her ready. "Take the gag off, James."

Undoing the knot took a few long minutes, which Trevor apparently used to test Georgie's resistance and readiness. She was obviously slick and primed when James finally got the gag free, as she cried out into the cool night with unintelligible longing.

"Answer me," Trevor ordered, slapping her arse with his bare hand. "Is this what you want?" James watched as Trevor pushed one, then two fingers into her arse.

"Yes!" she cried out as her hips canted up to receive Trevor and her head dipped down toward James's cock, without quite reaching.

"Yes, what?" Trevor removed his fingers and taunted her with the thick head of his cock. "How do you ask politely, George?"

"Yes, please," she whispered softly, right before James thrust into her mouth and Trevor thrust into her arse.

All three of them erupted into a quaking ecstasy—without a hint of tenderness. While Trevor slammed into her over and over, she moaned against James's cock with a low, desperate rumble and deep suction. The rhythm created a perpetual motion that coiled through all of them until Trevor reached around to Georgie's clit and hurled her over the edge.

As soon as she went, Trevor cried out, and then James came in her mouth with a guttural release. She kept sucking him until the last tremor had passed. All three of them fell together and lay across each other, heaving and panting like the animals they had become.

Chapter 8

Georgie was unable to differentiate her limbs from theirs. They were wound together like one of the endless knots in traditional Moroccan jewelry: impossible to tell where one strand finished and another began. Even their breathing seemed to weave them closer together. One of her hands was gripped into someone's thick hair; a hard-muscled leg was wedged between her thighs from behind; hot breaths warmed her stomach.

Two men at once—well, three if she counted herself. How glorious of Trevor to demand that of her, to treat her like George, the young man in need of discipline. She must remember to thank him for that at some point. Some later point . . . when her mind wasn't floating through the night air like a downy feather, and her body . . . Lord, her body had never felt more relaxed, more subdued and grateful.

A warm hand was circling the tender flesh of her bottom, where the crop had left its cruel marks of devotion. She bit her bottom lip and hummed her pleasure, enjoying the simultaneous comfort of that hand and the way it caused a stinging reminder of her splendid beating. "Yes, please," she whispered.

Both men pulled in closer, and she could feel them touching her and each other all around her. She had never been one for the smoky pleasure of the hookah, but she imagined this was how it must be: simultaneously attuned to every blade of grass, every human millimeter, and oblivious to everything beyond this extremely narrow perimeter.

She leaned forward a few inches into the musky darkness of an elbow or shoulder, and began to lick the salty skin—it was Trevor, she could tell immediately—then she sucked hungrily where the soft skin of his upper arm pressed against the taut muscle of his chest. Squirming to taste more of him, her mouth grazed across a few inches of skin until she found his nipple and toyed with it, her tongue playing until his skin was a hard nub. His groan of pleasure inspired her to persist.

Both men, meanwhile, had their hands all over her. A large bank of passing clouds covered the moon, and the darkness seemed to afford her far more initiative, as if she could be anonymous even in this intense intimacy as long as she was hidden. Fucking was one thing; the tender assault she was performing on Trevor's beautiful body was something else altogether—something she wanted to hide from herself and the moon.

After she became lost in licking and mapping his chest and stomach, her body was hauled roughly onto her back, and she was engulfed by four strong hands and two eager mouths. She heard and felt them kissing each other while they kissed her. Two tongues dipping and sliding around her throbbing entrance. She could feel the moisture of her previous release—and Trevor's—coating her inner thighs, and the sloppy sounds of mouths and fingers probing and seeking pleasure.

Some remote part of her brain thought she should be concerned about the men devouring her that way, but she was too consumed to care. Everything felt both dreamlike and bone-breakingly real. She normally despised having a mouth on her pussy, much less two. She far preferred the hard penetration of a cock in her arse over what she'd come to think of as the tender ministrations of some delicate flower, of mere lips against lips.

But oh God, how different it was when Trevor and James were rough and sure, so demanding with her. So when slick fingers entered her—in front and behind—and mouths nipped and sucked hard against her clit and pussy, she felt like the act was strong and right for the first time in her life. Not some weak feminine rippling, but a glorious fight to the finish. She bit her lip and cried out.

And still the two men worked on her. Fingers, tongues, the occasional hard slap, first on her ass, and then, to her shocked delight, a rain of hard taps and pinches on her clit. She began to beg—for it to continue forever, for it to stop or she would die, for it to go on and on, for it to never end—all in wordless, moaning desperation. She felt the shiver of her own approaching climax—then James with hot spurts against her back, where she'd felt Trevor handling him with sure, knowing pulls, and Trevor—glorious Trevor—released again, in warm jets onto her stomach. His hand—someone's hand—was tight in her short hair, praising her and owning her all at once.

Her own release came roaring through her then, brutal and all-consuming. She screamed into the night, squeezed her eyes tight, and dug her hands into the muddy grass so she didn't disintegrate altogether and fly off into a million particles in the night sky. Crash after crash slammed her as they kept up their hard suction and penetration, until she finally began to soften from the violent aftershocks.

A strong fingertip traced her jaw and a throaty voice whispered from far away, "That's a good lad."

Her last vague thought before she fell into unconsciousness was that she had done well.

After a time, Trevor leaned down and kissed her lips gently. Then James bent forward and kissed her as well. Then the two men kissed each other, and it was all exactly how Trevor had dreamt it would be. One part of his warm, spent body was flush against Georgie's soft hip, while his other arm and leg were slung across James's hard shoulder and thigh. Every element of his being, the hard and the soft, the brutal and the tender, had found its counterpart reflected in these two people in his arms.

For many minutes they clung to each other like that, the three of them caressing and kissing, tending to one another in the most intimate ways they could—warming each other's skin, massaging sore muscles, smoothing back disheveled hair.

"We will all catch a terrible chill if we don't get up from this cold ground," Trevor finally said, regretting that he would have to release either one of them.

"Don't make us move," Georgie pleaded on a contented sigh. "I've never known such a feeling of peace."

Trevor kissed her again. "A feeling that shall be repeated for many years to come." He felt her stiffen slightly against him.

She sat up. "Let's start with a few days, and maybe work our way up to years, shall we?" She looked from James to Trevor and smiled. "All right?"

Trevor tried to repress the look of worry that passed briefly across his face while Georgie wasn't looking, but he knew James caught it. James sat up too, then smiled and kissed Georgie lightly on the tip of her nose. "Yes, you dirty thing, we will defile you a little at a time . . . minute by minute . . . day by day . . ."

She laughed and kissed them both, then stretched her arms above her, extending her fingertips into wide-spread stars, pale white against the night sky. "I think I feel my energy returning . . . a bit." She stood up and Trevor watched the light play against her skin, giving it a luminous sheen. "What a mess!" She was peering around, naked except for her shirt, which was torn and disheveled. She looked with dismay at the scattered clothes amid the crushed grass and the overturned dirt from horse's hooves.

"I shall wear whatever I can grab." She bent down and happened to pull up Trevor's dinner jacket. She put it on and held the too-large lapels closed at her waist with one fisted hand.

James kissed Trevor's cheek, shaking him from the reverie he'd fallen into while watching her move and bend like that.

"Come on, love. Let's all get inside," James said to him.

"Thank you," Trevor whispered.

James smiled at him, and Trevor felt all that love wash over him like warm honey. Caressing Trevor's cheek, James said, "No, darling, thank you." James kissed him one last time. "Now, up we go." He helped Trevor stand and they embraced briefly. Trevor sighed into the familiar comfort of this man and made a silent prayer that their relationship would survive—and flourish—with Georgie in their life.

They walked back to the manor like a trio of drunkards, singing a few bawdy songs, Georgie teaching them some choice epithets in Arabic. They found Cyrus eating a bit of hay near the stables, as if he'd been waiting for them to put him to bed properly.

The head groom poked his sleepy head out from his upstairs rooms. "M'lord? Is everything all right?"

"Yes, thank you. Just checking on Cyrus. No need to come down."

"Yes, m'lord." Then the door closed and the three of them smiled at each other like guilty schoolchildren. Trevor and Georgie brushed the horse while James put some fresh straw down, and then they got him settled back in his stall.

When they reached the front door to Mayfield House, Trevor pulled it open and stepped back to make way for James and Georgie. James continued into the front hall, then turned back to see what was holding up the other two.

Georgie remained outside the threshold.

"What is it?" Trevor asked. James came back and stood next to him.

"I've already sent everything on to my mother's." She smiled at them, but she looked shy somehow. James reached out and said, "Come with us." She stared at his offered hand, but still didn't move. "Just for tonight, Georgie."

She nodded at that and took his hand, as if *just for tonight* was fine, but anything more was simply too much to ask. "All right then."

It was not the heartfelt enthusiasm Trevor had so dearly hoped for, but he wanted to take Georgie in any way she was able to give. *For now.*

"We won't bite," Trevor joked.

"Liar." She smiled suggestively in reply. "I most definitely recall a nip or two."

If she needed to keep everything in the realm of sexual innuendo and carnality, Trevor could try. *For now.* At least she'd be in their bed from now on, and they could conquer her body until her mind and heart were finally ready to surrender to the truth.

They went up the stairs, much as James had hoped they would when he'd been imagining them earlier: three people in love, going to end the day in each other's arms. That burgeoning hope only lasted until the first landing, when Georgie released James's hand and bid them good night with cool formality.

"Good night?" Trevor asked in disbelief.

"Well . . . uh, thank you? For a very nice evening?"

James grabbed Trevor's arm to restrain him before he could reach out for Georgie. "A *very* nice evening, indeed," James agreed pleasantly. "We will accompany you back to Camburton tomorrow, to see that you're properly settled for the next few weeks. How does that sound?"

Georgie's face cleared. "Oh, that would be wonderful. I'd forgotten about the trunks." She laughed as if the whole thing had been a silly misunderstanding. "I was a bit peeved—rousing all the servants and whatnot—but I agree it's for the best I go back to Camburton. No need to annoy Vanessa, as you say."

"Yes," James said with a smile, still restraining Trevor with that tight hold at the back of his arm where Georgie couldn't see.

"Excellent." She yawned happily and appeared to be nothing more than an innocent, sleepy girl at the end of her own very long party. "I will bid you good night, then. Thank you both. For everything." She kissed them on the cheek—first Trevor, then James—then turned and walked into the guest room, her aristocratic posture making her torn clothes look like royal ermine.

"Thank you?" Trevor asked in an incredulous whisper, sounding more gutted than James had ever heard him.

"Come on, love. It's going to take more than a right good rogering to move that mountain."

Trevor shook his head a couple of times in disbelief as James guided him back to their large master suite. After the two men entered the privacy of their room, they washed each other gently with water and soap from the basin.

"I just don't understand how she could bid us good night and say thank you after what the three of us experienced out there tonight," Trevor said.

"Really? You don't understand how she could see it—or wish to see it—as nothing more than a physical, albeit enjoyable, foray?"

"Of course I know, or at least some part of my mind tells me, the way she reacted was perfectly normal—for Georgie. But there was nothing *normal* about what happened out there." Trevor turned to look at James. "Please tell me I was not the only one who felt like something profound and wonderful was taking place under that tree, under that sky, among the three of us?"

"Of course you're not the only one who felt that, Trevor." They were lying naked under the covers by then, facing each other in the familiar comfort of their large tester bed. "I know what I felt and it was unlike anything. But Georgie—" James cut off when he realized he didn't know how to finish that thought; he did not want to hurt Trevor, but he had to prepare him for the worst.

"You really believe it is possible for someone to be that far removed from their own heart?" Trevor asked quietly.

"That's just it. Georgie is not removed, as far as she's concerned. At this point, she truly believes . . ." James paused again and tried to think of the nicest way to say what undoubtedly sounded like petty cruelty. "Perhaps it is easier for her to believe that she was simply born without certain emotional circuits. That way, she never has to feel."

"But she does feel, damn it! You can see it in her eyes, and the way she grips her fists. You can see it in the flush of her skin when she's angry or aroused."

James reached for Trevor's cheek and cupped his face. "Those are all *a show* of feelings. If she can clench her fist, or have a climax for that matter, she manages to somehow express the feeling without ever having to actually *feel* it in her heart."

Trevor rolled onto his back and gazed up at the central floret and pleated silk that radiated out to the edges of the canopy. James stared at his handsome profile for a few moments and then slipped onto his back as well. He reached for Trevor's hand beneath the coverlet and wove their fingers together. They both lay there, looking at the forest green and gold brocade fabric that had reminded James of Trevor's eyes when he'd chosen the pattern.

The two of them had become like an old married couple—or rather, a couple who loved one another so dearly that they would never subject each other to the inherent misery of being an old married couple. James felt an unfamiliar tendril of fear. After eight years together, this was the first time they had ever crawled into bed with even the slightest hint that something—someone—was missing.

James felt his throat constricting with sadness. He turned back on his side and slid one leg over Trevor's warm thigh. "Please kiss me good night."

When Trevor turned to look at him, his eyes were likewise full of sadness. "We can help her," Trevor said. "I know we can. No one deserves to go through life feeling alienated or afraid of who they really are." Trevor's eyes softened and he even managed a small smile. "Ironically, you were the one who taught me that, James Rushford. Do you remember?" Trevor leaned in and kissed James with tender gratitude.

Chapter 9

By the time Georgie woke up, it was the unconscionable hour of ten o'clock.

"Well, that was certainly a very brief journey." Mrs. Daley scowled while Franny opened the curtains and looked nervously over her shoulder toward Georgie stretching her arms and rolling her head from side to side on the pillow.

"Merely a postponement," Georgie said with a scratchy morning voice. "I will be relocating to Camburton Castle presently. I had a bit of unfinished business with Lord Mayson and Mr. Rushford last night." Smiling at poor, innocent Franny, Georgie let herself sink deeper into the luxurious linen sheets. Why had she never noticed that they were delectably soft against her skin? In fact, she might need to stay in bed until noon just to give these sheets the appreciation they deserved.

"Franny," she ordered sweetly, "do be a dear and bring me a tray of hot chocolate, two coddled eggs, four slices of thick toast, and a rasher of bacon."

Mrs. Daley had her hands fisted on her hips as she watched the young maid make a swift exit from the room. "Since when do you take breakfast in bed like a viscountess?" Daley sniped.

Georgie plumped up two of the pillows behind her and sat up straighter, keeping the bedsheet and coverlet modestly over her breasts. "You are the one who was so concerned about whether or not I was behaving like a proper lady, so you can't very well take umbrage when I do what proper ladies do."

"There is nothing proper or ladylike about you this morning!"

Georgie lifted her chin and smiled. She imagined she looked quite a lot like her mother, Vanessa, at her most imperious.

Mumbling something that sounded distinctly like *harrumph*, Mrs. Daley fussed about the room, plumping pillows on the settee and punctuating her tasks with sighs and exhales of obvious disapproval. When she was ostensibly finished, Mrs. Daley was forced to turn and face Georgie before leaving the room.

As much as the housekeeper probably wanted to depart with nary a comment, such behavior would have overturned every law that she herself had taught Georgie regarding proper manners. "If you won't be needing anything else, ma'am, I'll be—"

"Oh, but I *will* be needing something else, Mrs. Daley. As you can see, I am in desperate need of another bath. Please have one brought up and filled with the hottest water as soon as possible."

Mrs. Daley appeared to have very many choice things to say to that, but all she allowed herself was, "Yes, m'lady."

As Mrs. Daley left the room, Georgie was fairly certain she heard her say something along the lines of *now I've gone and created a monster.*

After Daley had left and shut the door behind her with a firm little *snick,* Georgie got out of bed and strolled over to the large oval looking glass situated to the right of the fireplace. She rarely gazed at her naked self, taking little interest in the curves or texture of her own body. But this morning, she fancied a good, long look.

She had not made time for even the most cursory rinse at the basin last night when she'd returned from that wild romp under the tree. No wonder Franny had looked so frightened and Daley had looked so appalled this morning: Georgie was as filthy as a pig in muck . . . and as contented.

She had mud and grass stains on her arms and neck; her fingernails were black with dirt—the image flashed in her mind of digging her nails into the earth in that moment of crying out, and it brought her body instantly to life. She tamped down the memory, and continued to take an accounting of her physical appearance.

Her breasts looked swollen, and her shoulder—dear God, was that a bite? She moved toward the glass to make a closer examination. Sure enough, the arc and indentation of teeth were neatly imprinted on her pale skin. Georgie took a moment to admire the savage mark. She let her finger trail fondly across the small reminder of their *love.*

Because that's what it was. As much as she wanted to pretend it'd been nothing more than an animalistic mating in the wild, even she—with her diagnosable paranoia when it came to intimacy—had to confess that it had indeed been an act of love.

She stared at the looking glass, her hands absentmindedly caressing her body and revisiting the sites of all that primitive passion—scratches on her inner thigh from James holding her in place, bruises on her hips from Trevor's strong fingers. She looked down at her shins and knees, scraped and scuffed, from where she had knelt. Her lips . . . She touched the swollen flesh with the back of her hand and gasped.

She tried to tell herself that all of these marks were no different from the aches and sore muscles she'd experienced after a hard race or a long trek through the Atlas Mountains. Or even one of her more sensual assignations in the back alleys of Cairo. But as she stood there trying to examine herself with methodical detachment, her body was heating and tingling from the touch of her own hand. When a brief knock sounded at the door, she turned gratefully away from the glass.

"Who is it?" she called.

"It's the footmen, come with the bath," said Franny in her tentative voice.

"Hold on a moment, Franny." Georgie reached for the robe that Mrs. Daley had kindly left over the back of the chair near the fire. Tying the cloth belt tight around her waist, Georgie walked over to the door and pulled it open to let in the four men who were carrying the large copper basin. Franny scuttled in behind them.

Trying to sound only vaguely interested, Georgie asked Franny, "Is Lord Mayson up and about?"

"Oh yes, m'lady, he's been up these four hours." Franny was showing the footmen where to place the tub. With a low chuckle, Georgie realized Mrs. Daley had installed a four-panel screen in the room, which Franny and the footmen were now adjusting so the precious future Viscountess Mayfield would no longer be taken unawares by unannounced visitors while bathing.

Several more footmen followed soon after, with bucket upon bucket of steaming, fragrant water. After the last man had finally departed, Mrs. Daley returned and shut the door behind her. Georgie looked over at Franny, hoping for a quick glance of female collusion, but Franny had her eyes downcast and was wringing her hands together nervously, until Mrs. Daley dismissed her.

"You have put me in quite the position, *Lady* Georgiana." *Uh-oh.* Formal. Mrs. Daley was in full battle mode: apron starched, mobcap perfectly placed at the top of her head, hands clasped with firm assurance at her waist. "I simply cannot stand by and watch Mayfield House turned into some wild den of iniquity!"

"Mrs. Daley—"

"If I may?"

Georgie could easily ignore the woman, pull rank and send her from the room, but the truth was she respected her and wanted to hear what Mrs. Daley had to say. Even if she didn't plan on returning to Mayfield House, she didn't wish to burn every bridge on her way out. "Do go on, Mrs. Daley."

"Thank you. Now, I know it is not for me to say, but my lord and Mr. Rushford are two of the kindest men who ever walked this earth. And I don't even quite rightly know how to put it into words—" Mrs. Daley looked beyond Georgie and out the large windows to the wide expanse of Mayfield Park. A few seconds passed as the woman tried to compose her thoughts. Then she turned to Georgie and said, "I can turn a blind eye to many things—ha! You can't even imagine all the things to which I have turned a blind eye in my thirty-two years of service here—but as long as I *am* here, I'd hoped you'd show respect for this house and for my lord and master."

Georgie was trembling. She had faced off any number of wicked adversaries in the Sahara, but she had never been as shamed as she was at this moment. Her mind went blank and all she could think was *lemon cake.* Her bawdy double-entendres and debauched appearance upon waking had come off as disrespectful. And Georgie was contrite.

"Mrs. Daley," Georgie said as she dipped a very proper and very heartfelt curtsy. "Please accept my sincere apology for my behavior these past few days." She stood up straighter and continued. "Everything has been happening rather quickly, as you know. And I believe I've been rather wild." Georgie repressed a smile when Mrs. Daley made no attempt to disagree with her. "I promise I shall not abuse your—or Lord Mayson's—hospitality in the coming weeks, before we depart for London and our marriage is official. I shall be a model of propriety."

Mrs. Daley nodded once. And that was the end of it.

"Very good," the housekeeper said in her bullying way. "Now let's get you into that tub and erase all evidence of—" The housekeeper pursed her lips, shook her head, and said, "What I mean is, let's get you ready for lunch and get you back to your mother's, where you belong."

Trevor did his level best to maintain a sense of normalcy. Both he and James had arisen with the sun—James to visit the factory and some of the cottagers who did their work at home, and Trevor to the west pastures to make sure the hay baling was coming along without incident. They often met up in the drawing room for a brief chat after the morning's tasks, and today was no different. He reached out to touch James when he passed near the writing desk where James sat composing a letter to his mother. He let his hand rest at James's nape, touching the skin just above the edge of his cravat. "Have you had a nice morning?" he asked.

James finished the sentence he was writing, then set down the pen. He looked up at Trevor with a slow, inviting smile. "I haven't felt this refreshed in ages."

Trevor leaned down and kissed his soft, smiling lips.

A slight cough near the entrance to the drawing room startled them both into a standing position, James nearly kicking over his chair as he stood.

Lady Georgiana Camburton was a glorious sight to behold. Trevor couldn't help the wide grin that spread across his face, "Well, aren't you a picture?" he declared as he strode across the room to greet her, then bowed and kissed her hand. He never ate much for breakfast and he had definitely been feeling a bit peckish, but the way his stomach felt just then had nothing to do with the missed morning meal.

Georgie was both seductive and innocent all at once. She was wearing a silk morning dress of the palest pink, made even paler by the gossamer linen overdress that pleated around her bust and then fell in an ethereal cascade from the empire waist that nipped beneath her breasts.

"Do stop gawking at your fiancée, Lord Mayson." James was also smiling, but somehow he was able to look confident, almost as if he and Georgie were accomplices. He took her hand from Trevor's, where he had still been holding it and caressing her knuckles.

Trevor tried to breathe through the onslaught of emotion, a practice with which he would have to become very familiar over the next few weeks. If Georgie was able to wake up from a night like that looking like this, Trevor might well be catching his breath for the rest of his life.

"I see you decided to risk wearing another one of my creations." James was making a slight adjustment to her turban-like hat, which he must have designed just for Georgie in the past day or two. It was made of the same material as her dress, the pale pink silk pleated and folded, then wrapped in on itself in a seemingly disorderly fashion. James had also fashioned three lovely fabric roses that dipped perfectly near Georgie's left cheekbone.

"I did, you rascal. If you keep making me things that are comfortable and not entirely ridiculous, perhaps I will change my opinion about English hats after all."

James laughed as he made one final push at the fabric, then stood back to admire his handiwork. "I knew it would be perfect for you. Reluctantly feminine. Mrs. Daley has been my accomplice, letting me peek at your wardrobe to make two or three coordinating hats this past week. The pink rose was finished yesterday."

"No wonder this was the only dress that didn't get packed last night," Georgie said with a grin. "You and Daley will prettify me yet."

Trevor wasn't quite sure how the other two were able to have what seemed like a perfectly civilized conversation, because his heart was pounding so hard and his stomach was in such a flurry of delicate wings, he couldn't find words to speak.

"Well, at least give the man a brief kiss," James said quietly. "As you can see, he is in quite a state of apoplexy upon seeing your gorgeous self."

Georgie nodded to James and then turned slowly to look Trevor in the eye. "Did you sleep well, my lord?"

Still speechless, Trevor merely nodded.

"And I trust you have had a productive morning?" Georgie asked.

Again he nodded silently.

"May I kiss you good day?" she asked.

His eyes flew up from her bosom to her lips to her sparkling amber gaze. She was not playing with him.

"I would like that very much," he said.

Keeping her eyes fixed on his, she took a step toward him; his breath was short. She leaned in slowly, but did not kiss his lips, which were moist and slightly open as a result of his ardent anticipation. Instead, she dipped her face around his jaw and kissed the sensitive skin just beneath his ear. Then she whispered, hot and close, but loud enough that James could hear in the silent room, "I adored being with you last night."

His heart only resumed beating when she punctuated that lovely remark with a feral nip at his earlobe. She pulled away and gave James a quick kiss on the cheek. "And you as well."

Then, taking a few steps away, she began pulling on her gloves and said formally, "The carriage is ready and we are expected at my mother's for lunch. And for once, I am actually looking forward to it. Gentlemen?" She held out both of her arms so that each of them could escort her, one on the right and one on the left.

After the three of them were settled in the carriage, Trevor was able to collect himself somewhat. They all sat close together on the forward-facing seat, with Georgie in her beautiful finery wedged between their strong thighs. Trevor exhaled through his nose in an attempt to steady his nerves.

"Is everything all right, Trevor?" Georgie asked as she rested one gloved hand on his thigh. His taut muscles quivered beneath her palm.

"I think I am all right, for a few minutes at a stretch, but then you speak or touch me or I get a whiff of whatever that maddening scent is coming off your silken skin, and then I don't think I am all right at all. I think I'm going quite mad."

"Oh my sweet boy." Georgie pressed her palm harder into his thigh, rubbing the length from his crotch to his knee, back and forth with slow, steady pressure. "You're quite lovely when you are so . . . distracted."

"Georgie . . ." Trevor couldn't get his brain organized enough to say more than that when her fingers came to rest around the silhouette of his hard cock beneath the straining fabric.

"Yes, my soon-to-be husband?"

"If you don't remove your hand at once, I will spend inside my trousers, and I will not be able to attend your mother's lunch, no matter how much you were looking forward to it."

Rather than pulling her hand away, she pressed harder against his straining shaft. "Oh, I don't believe that for a moment. I think you can hold it and hold it, concealing the hard strength of your desire beneath the flaps of your jacket, and then later beneath the dining room table—where I hope I will be seated next to you—I can rest my hand against the evidence of your passion while I daintily sip my mother's traditional French *madrilène*."

Trevor wasn't certain, but through the fog of his desire, he thought he heard James give a low chuckle.

"Georgie . . . You must know—" Trevor started, unable to repress a renewed declaration of his love.

"Oh! Here we are!" James cried gaily.

Georgie pulled her hand away from Trevor's lap and sat up straight in the seat. A second later, the footman had opened the door of the carriage. James stepped out first, extending an arm to help Georgie step down into the sunny forecourt of Camburton Castle.

Trevor took a deep breath and followed her and James up the grand stairs.

James kept walking at a steady pace, Georgie's hand resting lightly on his forearm, every inch of her Lady Georgiana Camburton. She appeared to be flushed and happy, comfortable in her own skin—her own *very* ladylike, *very* feminine, *very* silky skin, thought James.

"If you don't mind me saying, you appear to be much more at ease in your frilly dress today than you were last night at supper," James lobbed casually. Both of them continued to look straight ahead as the front doors opened and they entered the large hallway.

"I don't mind you saying. In fact, I *am* much more at ease today." She turned to look at him boldly, letting her glance slip over her shoulder to include Trevor in her mischief. "Your ministrations last night seem to have given me a new peace. I believe I would feel equally happy in breeches or bloomers—something inside me feels reconciled. I thank you for the much-needed rogering."

Trevor choked at her crass honesty, and then concealed his surprise with a genteel chuckle.

She kept walking toward the drawing room as if she'd been speaking of nothing more controversial than the weather. James marveled at how so much could change in such a short time. Just last night, as the three of them had stood outside these very doors, he'd thought the possibility of a future that involved all three of them equally was fading to nothingness. Although it still promised to be quite an uphill climb if Georgie insisted on reducing all of her feelings to animal lust, at least now there was a sliver of hope. Lust would keep her close while they worked on convincing her how much more there could be among the three of them.

Before opening the door to what promised to be a gaggle of family and friends—the burbling laughter and conversation already reaching them in the hall—Georgie said quietly, "Perhaps if I can be utterly free and raw at night, dressing up during the day in such refinements will be more like a delectable counterpoint."

With that, she entered the drawing room and announced herself before the butler had a chance to do so. "Mother! Nora! We're here!"

James held Trevor back with a brief touch on his upper arm, the two of them out of earshot in the hall. "How are you, my love?"

"I think I finally understand how it feels to have the fulfillment of one's deepest desires within reach—"

James smiled. "And?"

"And forever—tantalizingly—just beyond one's grasp." Trevor tore his gaze away from Georgie, where she was already laughing and talking animatedly with Anna and Pia across the room, and looked at James. "Don't you think she *belongs* with us?"

James felt the words like a solid punch in the chest, the kind of pummeling blow that could either stop his heart or start it up again after it had seized. He took a deep breath. "Yes. What you say is true . . . and terrifying. But you mustn't scare her off with your ardor. Do you understand?"

Trevor nodded his agreement, never taking his eyes from Georgie.

Both men entered the room and were quickly drawn into separate conversations. Trevor spoke to Sebastian and Farleigh about where they planned to go for their afternoon ride, and James was immediately asked for his creative opinion about the design of the grand wedding breakfast in Mayfair. They all ate lunch together, and then the afternoon progressed with delightful ease. James stayed at Camburton with Nora, Vanessa, Georgie, and Anna to lay the groundwork for the marriage that was to take place at St. George's, Hanover Square, in a fortnight.

As they worked together on the plans, James admired the unique strength of each of the four women. Anna's wedding had been a small, religious ceremony in a cold chapel in Madrid, with only a dozen or so very close relatives of Sebastian's. She was thrilled at the prospect of being part of a proper, joyful wedding celebration with her new family. She was also thrilled that the new plan meant her mother Nora would be back in London sooner than they'd thought.

Nora, who rarely spoke of her life before coming to England with Vanessa and her uncle Fitz, also shared her own wedding memories. "I was an ill-informed sixteen-year-old girl," she said thoughtfully as she looked out the sunny, sparkling windows of the morning room, where they had decided to set up camp to plan the great event. Nora reached for Anna's hand as she spoke. "I had none of the fortitude or conviction that you all seem to possess in such abundance."

Vanessa immediately tried to contradict that statement. "Oh Nora! You know you're the most courageous of any of us—"

"Vanessa, you always see the best in me, no matter what." Nora shook her head with a sad smile. "But in this you must believe me. I was like a lamb being led to slaughter. I had neither confidence nor freedom."

James watched closely to see if Georgie felt the power of those words, and perhaps for once in her life realized that it wasn't quite so dreadful to have been born Lady Georgiana Cambury, heiress and adventurer.

She slanted him a look and gave him a sly wink and a tiny nod. Yes, perhaps that little seed of gratitude would take root in Georgie's heart after all, and she would come to appreciate her true inheritance: confidence and freedom, a legacy she might eventually learn to honor and value, rather than flout.

"But that's a terrible memory to revisit now," said Nora in a more cheerful tone of voice, clearing the air with a swipe of her hand. "I only brought it up so you would see how wonderfully lucky you are, Georgie, to be marrying someone you trust and, I hope, will eventually come to love."

"Oh, I do love him already," Georgie blurted carelessly, turning her attention from James. "I've always loved him." The other four stared at her while she continued to look at some fabric swatches that Vanessa had pulled for Georgie to decide on the tablecloths at the wedding breakfast.

"Of course you have, darling," Vanessa said, patting Georgie lightly on the shoulder and then removing her hand.

"I mean," Georgie continued airily, paying no attention to the weight of her words, "who *doesn't* love Trevor?" But the room had gone quiet, and even Georgie seemed to sense her words held a whiff of insulting negligence, as if loving Trevor were some silly pastime.

James felt the hot rush of emotion rise up from his cravat and spread across his cheeks. Loving Trevor Mayson was—and always would be—the most meaningful aspect of his life . . . a sacrament.

Anna glanced quickly from James to Georgie, then pulled her lips into a firm line and looked down at the table, as if she recognized something familiar in Georgie's cavalier handling of words like *love* and *always*. From their dinner conversation last night, James suspected Anna recognized her former self.

Vanessa stared at James, and he thought she might actually cry. There was a look of such profound unhappiness in her eyes, wordlessly letting him know that she regretted having raised a child who was so utterly insensitive to the feelings of those around her.

James took a deep breath and smiled, lifting his chin and breaking the spell of sadness. "You're quite right, Georgie," he announced with perhaps a touch too much enthusiasm. "Trevor Mayson is indeed one of the most loving and lovable people one could ever hope to meet."

Georgie looked up from the various fabrics with a cheery smile, then faltered. Her brow furrowed when she looked at James, as if she didn't quite understand why it had been the wrong thing to say.

He smiled at her, feeling sincere empathy at that point, because the truth of the matter was clear: Georgie was either incapable or completely out of practice when it came to recognizing deep emotion, either in herself or in others.

"Yes," she agreed softly, still not understanding. "Trevor is the top thing." She peered around at the other three women, and James watched her look from face to face, as if she were adrift and hoping for somewhere to drop anchor. Her eyes returned to his, a ship to port, and she lifted a pale rose damask, in a very similar shade to the dress she was wearing. "Perhaps we should choose this one for the wedding celebration and table linen, James. I think Trevor thought me quite pretty this morning when I came down in this dress. What do you say?"

James smiled and nodded. "I think that's the perfect choice."

She smiled tentatively and handed the fabric to her mother. "This is the one then. If you like it?"

Vanessa took the fabric and rubbed it between her fingers. "It's perfect, darling. Simply perfect." She flashed James a look—of gratitude, perhaps—and declarations about love and forever were set aside once more.

Chapter 10

fter tea, Georgie was relieved when Trevor and his group returned from their ride. She was curious about what they'd all discussed, and, truth be told, she was jealous. As much as she'd tried to enjoy the choosing of linens and such for the wedding, she'd much rather have been riding around the estate with the others.

Pia excused herself almost immediately for a late afternoon nap, while Farleigh and Sebastian remained. Georgie watched with keen interest when first one and then the other man kissed Pia on the cheek and bade her farewell as she left the drawing room.

Trevor came and stood behind Georgie where she was seated on the yellow silk sofa. James was right: Georgie had not felt this comfortable in her own skin—especially while sitting on this yellow sofa in this damnable drawing room—since as far back as she could remember.

Leaning down and pretending to whisper something in her ear, Trevor gave her a brief, nipping kiss at the edge of her hairline instead. A shiver of delight ran down her spine, and she placed her hand over his where it rested on her shoulder. His thumb traced the bite mark lightly.

"Did you have a nice ride, my lord?" Georgie asked, feeling like the picture—already—of an adoring spouse. She tried to tell herself it was just a game, a way to pass the next few weeks, playing at being his baroness. She had always thought such conversations were pat, merely words that bored couples used to fill the day. But her heart gave a little squeeze when she realized she genuinely wanted to know if he had, in fact, enjoyed his afternoon.

He looked down at her with those penetrating green-gold eyes and long, dark lashes. "It was quite enlightening. Farleigh, Sebastian,

Pia, and I covered a lot of ground. I look forward to covering the same terrain with you and James at some point." He had said it quietly enough so no one else in the room could hear, and even if they had, it was quite likely they would think he meant the horse trails and fields they had traversed. But the slight squeeze at her shoulder let her know that her suspicions were correct: Farleigh, Sebastian, Pia, and Anna were all in one relationship.

"And how was your afternoon?" Trevor asked.

"I think we got nearly all the decisions made for the wedding. Are you certain that you have no interest in the decoration or invitations or menu?" she asked with a mischievous smile, for she knew Trevor had about as much interest in which fabrics to use for the serviettes as he did in the latest drawing room gossip in Mayfair.

"I am at your service if you need me, but I will defer entirely to your mother's wishes when it comes to these very important and meaningful decisions. The color of a tablecloth can be quite life altering, I have heard. And I would not want to go poking about when these are verdicts of such consequence."

Georgie laughed out loud, and God, it felt good to be herself in this room at last.

She stood up and extended her hand to Trevor. "Let us return to Mayfield, my lord. I am very keen to hear all the details of your afternoon ride and to share the *life-altering* decisions we made regarding the vellum that will be used for the envelopes." James had also stood up when Georgie had, and was now waiting next to the two of them.

"I thought you said you were staying here at Camburton with us," Vanessa interjected, not quite concealing a hint of worry.

"Of course I am!" Georgie laughed, having completely forgotten that business. She turned to her mother, "Do you and Nora mind very much if I go check on the horses at Mayfield? I shan't be more than a few hours."

Being asked, even on this minor point, seemed to please Vanessa greatly. She looked up from the book she'd been reading while Nora sketched her. "Of course, darling."

The three of them said quick farewells to Vanessa and Nora. They hugged and shook hands with Farleigh, Sebastian, and Anna with far more gravity. That party was returning to Cambridgeshire early the next morning, and all of them would not be reunited again until the wedding in Mayfair several weeks hence.

As they stood at the large front doors of Camburton Castle, Georgie gave Anna a firm hug. "I very much hope that this is the beginning of our life as sisters."

Anna's eyes were bright with feeling. "There is very little that can stop me once I set my mind to something. And I have set my mind to being the best younger sister you could ever wish for."

Georgie bid Anna farewell with a smile as Trevor spoke to his driver, and then the three of them stepped into the carriage and headed for Mayfield.

When the carriage door shut, a sense of heated anticipation filled the confined space. Georgie was once again tucked in between the two men: Trevor on her right and James on her left.

"So what did you say to the driver?" she asked after the servant had shut the door.

"I told him it looked like it was going to be a beautiful sunset and to take us the long way round to Mayfield. I asked that he make the journey last at least an hour." Trevor was removing his gloves as he spoke, one strong finger at a time, very methodical and incredibly provocative.

Her mouth felt dry. "And . . . how do you plan on spending this hour in the carriage, my lord?"

When he turned to look at her, she gasped at the intensity and sexual power in his eyes. "Well, I intend to ravish you, of course."

Georgie stopped breathing altogether when she felt James's hot fingertips curl around her neck. "*We* intend to ravish you," he added with suggestive promise. James leaned in and began placing small, hot kisses down the left side of her exposed neck. Georgie's body responded immediately. Her nipples tightened and her bodice felt suddenly confining; her pussy throbbed with yearning. Before she had a moment to think about what James was doing, Trevor began unfastening her dress at the back, loosening the fabric enough so he could release her bosom from the tight bodice.

She cried out when Trevor freed both breasts and reached up to hold them firmly in his masculine hands, weighing them. "We're of a mind to introduce you to the more languorous pleasures of your body . . . Georgiana. Last night was quite rushed, don't you agree?"

With that, Trevor held her left breast in an offering way toward James. "Taste her. I want to see your lips on her and your tongue, that miraculous tongue of yours . . . "

She watched as James lowered his mouth, the strong, mischievous lips curling with devilish anticipation. When he took the taut nipple into his mouth, he didn't waste a moment with any silly flicks of his tongue or dallying. He pulled with hot, powerful suction, grazing the puckered skin with his teeth, pushing his face roughly against her so the coarse stubble of his cheek and chin also inflamed the tender skin. She cried out again, both from the physical sensation and the beautiful vision of that man's avid expression while he roused her body.

Trevor raised his other hand to her face, pressing his thumb and fingers into her jawbone. She adored the way he handled her body. Those little shoves and pulls of authority made the pressure and heat between her legs even stronger.

"This is all of you, Georgie. George. Georgiana. This is all of us." He pressed his lips against hers, squeezing her right breast with more force, while James kept up that relentless suction on the other. She moaned into Trevor's kiss when his hand drifted from her face and she felt three hands snaking up the inside of her thighs. Trevor merely kissed her harder, ignoring her cries of surprised pleasure, his tongue powerful and deep, battling against hers. When a finger touched her wet folds, James pulled his mouth away from her breast.

"Oh dear God, Trevor. She's so wet and so ready." He toyed with the soaked fabric while he spoke. "She's such a pretty little thing today, isn't she? On the outside, that is." His clever fingers found her slick opening, and first one, then two fingers entered her swollen pussy. Her inner walls pulsed around his fingers greedily. James's breathing was unsteady. "But inside she's a dirty little thing. Aren't you, Georgie?"

She whimpered her agreement.

"Trevor . . . you need to feel this . . . "

Trevor tore his mouth away from hers, then looked down at her moist lips. She was also breathing heavily, panting into him, as if they were still connected even though their mouths were no longer locked. His eyes flitted from her lips to her glowing amber eyes to her flushed cheeks, then down to her beautiful breasts. He pulled his hand from her thigh so he could tease a nipple with each hand. Staring into her eyes, he spoke to James.

"Describe her to me, love."

"Gladly." James scrambled down onto his knees.

Trevor kept his eyes fixed on Georgie's the entire time. He watched her eyelashes flutter slightly while James lifted the layers of her dress. The cool air must have made contact with her sex.

"She's all flushed and swollen," James said.

"Do you have your fingers inside her now?" Trevor loved talking about her that way, as if she were some object that James and Trevor were assessing, like a fine brandy they were passing back and forth between them. And she liked it too, from the look of melting lust in her eyes.

"I do," said James.

"Is she good and wet? Ready for both of us, you think?" Her eyes widened at the suggestion, but he didn't let his gaze falter. In that considering tone of voice, Trevor continued, "Is her arse nice and slick too?" Her eyes brightened with lust. He reminded himself to keep his emotional *ardor* to himself, as James had warned. He would break Georgie just like he broke his most volatile horses, with endless patience and gentle authority.

"Yes," James said in a low, almost humorous drawl. "I'm spreading all her slick cream around her arsehole, and her body's begging for it, pulsing."

And then he could tell that James had entered her there with his finger—her body made that slight convulsion of resistance, acceptance, and then, simply, bliss.

"He's very good at that, isn't he?" Trevor whispered to Georgie. "I love the way he gets me ready."

She moaned and let her eyes slide shut, probably imagining James doing all the things he was doing to her, but doing them to Trevor instead.

"Yes, picture him doing that to me, you dirty thing."

Her eyes flew open and her little pants of hot breath against his lips had his cock even harder. They were so close that when he spoke to James, his lips nearly touched Georgie's. "I'm torn, James. I simply cannot decide if I want my hard cock in her mouth or in her arse or in her pussy."

Her eyes slid shut again while he watched, and a little mewl of ecstasy escaped her.

"I think she would like all three," James replied. "She's so damn slick. I think I want to fuck you while you're fucking her cunt," he added, as if the idea had just dawned on him.

She cried out in pleasure, then shook her head as if she needed to clear her mind. "No," Georgie whispered. "No . . . You mustn't fuck me . . . in my pussy . . . without protection . . . " Her words were coming out between choppy breaths. "I want to do everything with both of you . . . I want to crest every wave and break down every barrier"—she breathed hard through the words—"But I do not want a child. Promise me that neither of you will ever let that happen."

Trevor stared into her eyes, wishing—wishing for so much. How could he ever promise such a thing, when it was fast becoming his greatest hope that they would spend the rest of their lives together, building a family? *Don't tell* her *that, for God's sake,* he chided himself.

"You must give me your word," Georgie said to Trevor, probably suspecting what his hesitance really meant. Her eyes were beginning to lose the gleam of lust. "If you cannot promise me, this stops now."

She stiffened slightly and Trevor shook his head, barely moving but enough that she must know what it cost him. "I can—" He faltered. "I can only promise that I will never take you that way without your permission." His heart pounded. "But I will never stop trying to win your permission." He brought one hand back to her jaw and squeezed tight. "The idea of my child growing in your belly is one of the most erotic and loving I can possibly imagine."

"Trevor . . . " Her voice was a plea, desperate and frustrated.

"I give you my word. For now." He leaned in and kissed her, hot and quick, then glanced down at James. "What do you say, James? Is that a promise you can keep?"

James's smile was the picture of joyful mischief. He nodded slowly, then leaned in and kissed Georgie's sex, lapping at her moist folds. He was using both hands—one in her pussy and one in her ass—slowly, slowly working his fingers in and out of her body while Trevor watched. He had pushed her thighs wide, and the whole picture was making Trevor blind with wanting.

"I think there is very much the three of us can do—of a very *fulfilling* nature—without ever risking the creation of a child." James leaned in and sucked on her clit to illustrate his point.

Trevor smiled at James and turned his attention back to Georgie. "You see, James is the voice of reason, the middle way. While I tend toward love and sentiment, and you are all animal lust, perhaps James offers a bridge where we can both meet?"

Georgie took a quivering breath, obviously approaching her release, and nodded once. "Yes, sweet Trevor. Your love terrifies me—" she gasped again "—but with James here—" Her eyes fluttered once more and another small cry escaped her as James continued to assault her with his mouth. "Aaaah," she half breathed, half said, "it seems I'm not as hard-hearted as I thought I was."

Trevor leaned in and kissed her again, letting all the emotion and sweet desire he felt flow from his body without words. Yes, the heat of his affection might terrify her, but she was now at least willing to stand near the fire.

After a few moments, she cried out into his mouth, almost in pain rather than ecstasy. He pulled back. "What is it?"

"He—he—he stopped!" It wasn't pain; it was frustration.

Trevor smiled. "Yes, he has a habit of doing that. He loves to bring me right to the edge and then leave me there." Georgie looked past Trevor to James, where he now sat across the carriage, licking the fingertip that was slick with her essence.

"I would like to see that," Georgie whispered.

Trevor felt a fresh wave of desire rock through him. "You want to see James and me? Together?"

She nodded, keeping her eyes on James.

"Would you now?" James asked from the other side of the carriage.

Trevor couldn't resist pressing his palm against his own cock. The idea of Georgie watching while James fucked him could quickly send him over the edge.

"No touching," James ordered.

Trevor let his hand fall away. The sound of James when he spoke in that imperious way lit up every pleasure point in Trevor's body.

"Yes, sir," Trevor whispered. And then he simply let the undertow of willing capitulation drag him below the surface.

"Kneel down."

James watched with something akin to pride as Trevor obeyed him with the easy grace of a beloved pet that lives to please his master. Trevor's eyes had already taken on the smoky haze that promised the most pleasure for both of them.

"You're very sweet this afternoon, aren't you? After your ride with Sebastian and Pia and Farleigh." James reached for Trevor's lips and inserted two fingers. "I bet they gave you all sorts of notions." Trevor sucked greedily. "And now you taste Georgie on me and you're as randy as a goat, aren't you?" Trevor's nostrils flared and he sucked harder, eyes sliding shut. James ran his other hand through Trevor's thick, wavy dark hair, and Trevor moaned under his admiration. "Yes, my love, you are very good. "

Slowly, James withdrew his fingers from Trevor's mouth. He looked across the carriage and appraised Georgie. She was a sight: her dress undone, her breasts full and free, her skirts tossed up around her hips, her thighs spread wide, and her hand making languid passes along her exposed pussy.

"So what do you fancy, Lady Georgiana?"

He watched as she let her fingers wander, and then she said quietly, "I should like to see you take him."

Trevor's moan was one of unmitigated desire. James realized that Trevor's usual excitement—always keen—was going to be ten times greater now that Georgie was watching.

James said, "I think Trevor would like that as much as you would, my lady."

Whereas last night had allowed all of them to wring out every animal urge in a frantic, rutting pile, James felt like this was the beginning of the more nuanced intimacy that could be the basis of their relationship for many years to come. If Georgie didn't turn tail and run away like a coward, that is.

Even sprawled out as she was, disheveled and flushed with desire, Georgie was very much Lady Georgiana Cambury at the moment. And just like a lady who expects a gentleman to be witty and amusing to earn her regard, she wore a haughty expression that said she expected James and Trevor to make her time worthwhile.

James nodded his agreement, feeling like he understood her better than he ever had before, perhaps better than she understood herself. Trevor might love her, but James grasped her.

"Undo your trousers, man," James ordered.

Trevor had his fall unbuttoned within seconds, and his hard, red shaft sprang free. A second later, Trevor had his hands obediently clasped behind his back and made no sign of how the rumbling carriage must be pressing uncomfortably against his knees.

"He's quite something, our Trevor," James marveled.

"Shall I change seats for a better view?" asked Georgie rather breathlessly, craning her neck to get a better view of Trevor's assets.

"No, that won't be necessary," James said to Georgie. Then, to Trevor, "Come up here with me, my boy." Patting the space on the bench seat next to him, James motioned for Trevor to join him there.

"How do you want me?" All obedience, Trevor asked.

"Oh, I want you in so many ways. But for now, in these tight quarters, I think I want you facedown on the seat, with your legs tucked up to make room for me. That way the lovely Lady Georgiana will have a proper view of how *loving* we can be."

Trevor immediately obeyed, and Georgie sighed as James kneeled and positioned himself behind Trevor's upturned arse.

"That's right, Trevor, put your forearms flat against the cushion, and your face—turned, yes, right there—where you can stare at your beloved wife-to-be while I fuck you." James heard Georgie sigh again at the sound of those filthy words.

James lifted the tails of Trevor's riding jacket and exposed his beautiful bare arse. Rubbing his palms in slow, firm circles around Trevor's hips, then back toward the center crevice, James thrilled to the way Trevor's body warmed and responded to his touch. "Are you very ready for me, Trevor?"

"Yes, sir."

James adored when Trevor was this soft, welcoming man. If words frightened her, James would show Georgie this way—with their bodies—what she would be giving up if she decided to leave them. James dragged his thumb down Trevor's crack and pressed against the tight circle of muscle. Trevor moaned, and his eyes started to flutter shut.

"Eyes open."

"Yes, sir." Already Trevor's voice had taken on that dreamy acceptance.

Normally, James would trail his tongue against Trevor's tight entrance to prepare his body, but the idea occurred to him that Lady Georgiana and her slick, wet pussy were right there for the taking.

While he continued to massage Trevor's entrance, he turned toward Georgiana. "I hate to bother you, my lady. But I believe you might be of some assistance."

She had been staring with an almost scientific interest at Trevor's open-mouthed, glassy-eyed expression, so it took her a few seconds to understand James was speaking to her. "How may I be of service?"

He looked suggestively down between her legs, where she now had both hands working in unison. She stopped moving her fingers and smiled with wicked understanding. She lifted her hands, wet with her own desire. "Ah. Is this what you have in mind?" James simply nodded once, and she was up off the bench and over to their side of the carriage.

James loved how Trevor's hands gripped the cushion, all of that strength and intensity held in check. He pulled apart Trevor's arse cheeks even more to expose the tight pucker.

Georgie hummed her approval and kept her balance as the carriage swayed slightly. She hitched up her dress with her left hand, then used three fingers from her right hand to swipe at the slick juice from her own body. She dragged it slowly up and down the crease and muscle of Trevor's arse. "That's better, isn't it, Trevor?" Georgie taunted.

From years of experience, James knew that Trevor had crossed the line from speech to inarticulate moaning. Instead of replying, Trevor merely groaned and bit into the side of his own hand.

After Georgie had repeatedly coated him with slippery moisture, James turned to her and said, with his best imitation of courtly disinterest, "That will be all, thank you."

Georgie's eyes flashed to his with a mixture of confusion and anger. But then he saw she understood. She turned back to her side of the carriage, dipping her head so as not to bump the roof, and resituated herself in that languorous, legs-flung-wide pose. "Do carry on, Mr. Rushford."

He nodded and smiled, grateful once again that the two of them seemed to be developing a perfect understanding where Trevor was concerned.

Turning his full attention back to Trevor, James kept one hand smoothing along Trevor's left hip while he used his other hand to undo the buttons of his own trousers and release his cock. He smiled to himself when he heard Georgie's little sigh of pleasure. But he did not look at her, nor would he look at her again until he was quite finished.

He stroked his length several times, not that it was necessary, as he was already hard as a post, but he wanted to, for Georgie. James adjusted his position so his knees were on the cushion and the head of his cock was sliding up and down through the smooth, welcoming heat of Trevor's arse. Without looking at her, James asked, "Do you have a good view, Lady Georgiana?"

She replied, almost panting, "I do, Mr. Rushford. You may proceed. "

James watched Trevor's profile; he was staring across the carriage, eyes fixed on Georgie. James wanted him just like that. He wanted Trevor looking at that woman with whom he was falling madly in love, while he felt the physical proof of the man who always had and always would love him. James wanted those feelings to be inextricably linked inside Trevor.

James pressed his swollen, hard cock into Trevor with one powerful thrust.

All three of them cried out at once.

James stayed perfectly still, pressed to the hilt, his hands in a hard, loving grip on Trevor's hips. Then he tilted Trevor's pelvic bones with rough familiarity, and he knew immediately the new angle would be even more deliriously pleasurable for Trevor.

Then he began to move slowly—reminding Trevor, using his body to reinforce every memory, every moment that they had between them. All the while, Trevor's gaze stayed upon Georgie.

Trevor and James were soon breathing in unison: the pattern of his thrusts, the sound of their breaths, the distant huff that came from Georgie's mouth each time he thrust in, as if she too were experiencing the act as much as Trevor. Which perhaps, she was.

Chapter 11

Georgie had never felt more connected, more attuned to life and the world around her, than she did just then, even though she was quite *apart*. Something deep and real was taking root inside her. Perhaps something that had always been there, but had lain dormant until now. The way James took control of Trevor's body, the way he drove into him as both an expression of power *and* love was completely overwhelming Georgie's senses.

Perhaps it was merely the way her body was drugged with lust, her own approaching orgasm making her soft or impressionable. But she didn't feel soft when she watched those two men—so strong, so intense, and so much in love. Her eyes skated from the erotic, graphic display of James's glistening cock—in, pause, out, pause, in, pause. It was that maddening *pause*! She knew perfectly well how that felt. Last night, that was how Trevor had taken her, each one of those pauses driving her deeper into that place of profound peace and comfort, the only place where she felt all the disparate parts of her lock firmly into place, like a broken clock, with all of its faulty pinions and wheels finally clicking back into precise, humming order.

Her breath caught. Oh lord, she'd always used the same act to distance herself from anything deeper—to lose herself in that mind-numbing pounding, an animal rutting devoid of any deeper emotion. Yet, seeing James and Trevor, she realized this was no mere display of animal dominance, but an act of profound trust on one side and profound care on the other. An act of love.

She drew her eyes away from where they were joined, and let herself gaze upon the beatific face of Trevor Mayson. Eyes moist with emotion, mouth agape as he teetered on the edge of his release, holding on until James gave him permission to let go. They stared at one another like that for an eternity—all the memories of childhood friendship weaving into this adult intimacy—until Trevor's eyes began to flutter and his lips began to quiver. It was as if her own body experienced everything in exactly the same way, her lips trembling and her pussy tightening.

She looked quickly toward James to see he had picked up his pace, and his face, too, was beginning to go slack with his imminent orgasm. Then James reached around Trevor's hip and grabbed his cock, white knuckles straining with the intensity of his grip.

"Come for me now, my love. Come for me," James ordered, moving his clasped hand in time with his quickening thrusts.

The words were meant for Trevor of course, but Georgie felt the commanding power of them too.

And she went over right as Trevor did.

Her body arched away from the back of the carriage seat. Pushing her pussy hard against her palm, she ground against herself as contraction after contraction pounded through her. When her eyes slowly opened, she saw James—looking for all the world like a fully clothed gentleman—draped over the back of Trevor's coiled form. Both men were breathing heavily and looking at her through glazed, dreamy eyes.

She watched as their panting eased to a gentle rhythm of deep breaths. She looked down the length of their bodies to where James's hand was still wedged in between Trevor's hips and thighs.

"I want to taste Trevor," she blurted.

James smiled and sat up straighter, pulling his cock gently out of Trevor's body, then sliding his glistening hand slowly out from the confined space where he'd worked Trevor's cock.

"As well you should, Lady Georgiana." And with that, the diabolical man dragged his tongue along the slick remains of Trevor's orgasm where it coated his palm and fingers. "Mmm, you simply must."

Georgie was reluctant to take her hand away from her own body, loving the feel of that lingering pressure against her spent sex. "Bring it here," she ordered haughtily, as if speaking to a servant.

James continued to suck on each of his fingers, enjoying each pass like a particularly savory lick of ice cream. He shook his head slowly from right to left and said, "I'm afraid not."

"I beg your pardon?"

"You need to come and get it yourself."

She knew what he was really saying: *Trevor might be willing to throw himself at your feet, Lady Georgiana, but I am going to make you work for it.* And she realized that was what Trevor meant when he said James was the connective tissue, because if anyone could get Georgie to admit what she truly wanted, it was James Rushford.

By making her admit it, by making her cross that small distance—that tiny space in the confined carriage—James was making her acknowledge what and how deeply she wanted. *For now*, she kept telling herself.

She sighed dramatically and removed her hand from her now soaked drawers. "Oh very well. If you insist on inconveniencing me, I suppose I must."

James smiled at her, narrowed his eyes, and gave one brief but confident nod. "Please allow me to make him more accessible."

Georgie knelt on the floor of the rumbling carriage, her face close to Trevor's backside, and then watched as James stood up and slowly lifted Trevor's hips and thighs to help him turn onto his back. Trevor was like a rag doll, gloriously spent, and when she looked at his face—

Oh God. Her heart lurched into a frantic gallop. He was quite simply the most beautiful thing she had ever seen. His golden-green irises were dreamy as he stared at her down the length of his torso. So much love poured out of that gaze. Georgie was more than a little terrified.

"Oh Trevor." She moved awkwardly on top of him, all limbs and elbows, until she was clasping his face with her hands, tracing his lips with her thumbs, and kissing his eyebrows and then his lashes and then his nose. His mouth was seeking her fingers, where they were still wet from her own juices.

She let him suck on two of her fingers after she pulled her lips away. She leaned back slightly, straddling his hips, and admired his body. As Trevor continued to lick and suck her fingers, she slid down and stretched to kiss the tip of his thick cock where it lay against his firm abdomen. She left two fingers in his mouth and wrapped her other hand around his cock. James caught her eye and nodded again, telling her to take her pleasure with Trevor's body.

Georgie's mouth opened involuntarily. She felt like she couldn't get enough air into her lungs, but in some twisted way, it wasn't air that her body craved—it was the taste of this beautiful man who was sprawled out before her like a buffet of sensual delights. She leaned in and let her tongue trail slowly along the full length of his cock, from shining crown to base, where the nest of erotic black hair was still moist with his release.

She indulged all of her senses: the smell of him, musky and rich; the feel of his skin, warm and smooth in some places, coarse with hair in others; the taste of his release, salty and powerful. Georgie licked every inch of his cock, lingering around the base, and then continued up his stomach to his navel, where a delicious drop of his release had pooled. She was turning into her most basic, animal self, letting instinct and lust direct her movements. She heard and felt against her lips the moan of his pleasure. His suction on her fingertips had been rather languid, more of a caress, when he first began tasting her a few minutes ago. But now that she was focusing all of her attention on him and his beautiful, stiffening shaft, the pressure was getting progressively harder.

She wouldn't deny it: it was a heady power to have a man of this size, of this intensity, respond to her slightest attention with such complete devotion. She moaned gently in return, letting him know how much she was enjoying her task. She finished with his stomach, withdrew her hand from his mouth, and let her lips kiss a trail down to where his balls were hanging between his widespread thighs.

"Look at you," she marveled. James's slick seed was dripping out of his arse, and she couldn't resist dipping her tongue into the pungent mix—the filthy, glorious, rudimentary evidence of what had just passed between these two men. She wanted to lap it up.

Perhaps there was some small part of her that pushed her to do these seemingly disgusting things in the perverse hope that Trevor and James would see her for the twisted, base creature she really was. Some small, cruel voice in the back of her mind told her she would always be alone with her perversions. That sinister voice encouraged her to do everything that her sick mind could think of because, eventually, Trevor and James would realize she was simply beyond redemption. She would not have to wait any longer on the edge of being discovered.

And so she kept on. She pressed her lips into that forbidden place, pushing in, violating Trevor in the crudest way she could. Her nostrils flared and her eyes slid shut when she tasted James as well. She became rather frantic, thrusting with her tongue and then alternatively sucking the remains of James's orgasm from Trevor's body.

This would prove the final straw, she thought vaguely, this grotesque display of her darkest fantasies; after this, *surely* Trevor and James would want nothing more to do with her. She slowed down after a time, finishing with her task as it were, and licked Trevor one last time while his body shuddered in ecstasy.

She pulled her face away a few inches to look, to stare really. She had his balls pulled back taut. And had been using her other hand to keep his cheeks spread while she indulged. Slowly releasing her hands, she looked up at James, expecting to see revulsion. But instead, she saw . . . herself, reflected back at her.

"He is utterly delicious, is he not, Lady Georgiana?"

She stared at James for a few long moments, unable to comprehend his words. "He is . . ." She still wasn't sure if James was mocking her, if he was going to finally laugh at her, dismiss her. But he wasn't laughing; if anything, he was admiring. Tears came unbidden to her eyes.

Georgie wasn't much for crying. Of course, she loved the stinging press of tears when a cock first breached her rear entrance or pressed into that perfect place at the back of her throat, but that wasn't at all the same thing. These were hot tears of emotion—terror, relief, and something unfamiliar that was probably love. "You—you—you mean you are not repulsed?"

James's brow furrowed and he shook his head slowly. "Look at him," James whispered. "Just look at him."

Georgie turned her head to the right and saw that Trevor had slipped into an angelic doze, like one of Botticelli's putti after a wild rout. His face was the most radiant Georgie had ever beheld.

Trevor was floating somewhere between bliss and ecstasy. The movement of the carriage, the scent of Georgie's skin on his, the feel of James's warm palm where it rested with familiar ease on his inner thigh, all mingled around him in a cloud of pleasure. Everything felt light and beautiful.

He could still feel where Georgie's fingertips had played lightly against his lips as he drifted in that miraculous space. He gradually sensed that they were nearing Mayfield House, and he opened his eyes as if from a deep, deep sleep.

Georgie, face unaccountably tender, watched him from across the carriage. She and James were already properly dressed, and James was finishing gently refastening Trevor's trousers. Trevor stared into Georgiana's eyes. Everything about her was so incongruous: she was seated with her legs bent up under her, perfectly at ease, looking very much like she must when she sat on some exotic carpet in some faraway Bedouin tent, her elbow resting casually on her left knee while she stared at his mouth.

"And how are you?" she asked softly.

Somehow he couldn't find the words, perhaps because he didn't know what he felt, perhaps because he had no words to describe the immensity of what he felt.

She smiled at his silence and reached across the carriage to press her fingers against his lips. "Alas, we are in the forecourt of Mayfield House and our lovely carriage ride is at an end." She withdrew her hand from his light hold, and he missed her touch immediately. There was a moment between them then—where he let that feeling show in his eyes, the unmasked desire for her to keep her hands on him—and her answering glance showed she was unused to being wanted that openly, if at all.

He smiled again, sat up, and quickly finished putting his clothing to rights. When he spoke, his voice was rough, probably from a combination of his guttural cries of pleasure and not having spoken for much of the past hour. "You are under no obligation to love me the way I love you, Georgie." When he looked into her eyes and saw the shining beginning of tears, he wished he could take back the words. "I'm sorry—"

"No, no," she said, putting a hand on his forearm. "It is not wrong of you to express what you truly feel. I understand that now. I am the *unnatural* one who is incapable of such feelings—" Her eyes flew to the door when a double tap sounded. Trevor's driver had been well trained over many years to always knock before opening the door.

Trevor watched as Georgie stood up halfway and bent her head so as not to hit the roof. She reached for the handle and pushed open the door. The footman was already there to help her descend, and she was out of the carriage and running toward the stables before either James or Trevor had left their seats.

Trevor sat up and crossed his legs in front of him. He rested his clasped hands on his knees and stared at James.

"Well," Trevor said with a bit of sly mischief, "I'll take Lady Georgiana Cambury's version of *unnatural* any day of the week."

James reared his head back and laughed. "Come with me," James said, reaching out his hand so he and Trevor could leave the carriage together. "You had me worried there for a minute at the end," James continued, "that you were going to launch into some sort of Elizabethan soliloquy about the nature of your affection."

Trevor leaned in and kissed the side of James's neck as they crossed into the large front hall. "I may have fallen madly in love with Lady Georgiana Cambury, but I don't think I'm entirely stupid just yet. If she thinks she can scare us off with her version of the most prurient debauchery, who are we to discourage her?"

James barked out another laugh.

"Would you like to have a light tea in our room?" Trevor asked, pausing before they ascended the wide stairs.

"Yes," James replied. "That sounds ideal."

A few hours later, the three of them rode back to Camburton Castle for supper, after which Georgie would stay on for the next two weeks. She was quiet, and Trevor asked if she was well.

"I am." Her smile was wistful. "I think I'm overwhelmed. And it's a very unfamiliar sensation."

James reached across the carriage and held her hand. "Quite so. The next few weeks will be good for all of us to . . ." He squeezed her hand and paused to collect his thoughts. ". . . to settle down a bit.

And then in London, perhaps, we'll have a better understanding of everything. Yes?"

Trevor watched as she squeezed his hand back and nodded. "Yes, a better understanding, I like the sound of that. And in the meantime, I will see you both every day. You promised!"

"Of course." James patted the back of her hand kindly, then released his hold. "And you will be over to see Cyrus and Saladeen and Bathsheba. And then we'll all be together in London again. And from there we shall see, yes? Perhaps we could accompany you to Egypt for your return journey."

She inhaled sharply. "You would do that?"

"Of course," James repeated as he sat back and rested his gloved hand on Trevor's thigh. "And is it all right, Georgie, if we *hope* a little? That you might want to return with us . . . eventually? Even though it's not at all what you planned?"

Trevor firmed his lips to prevent himself from begging her to willingly agree to that slight hope.

"Yes," she whispered, as if she needed to keep her willingness a secret from herself.

The next morning, Trevor and James awoke with the dawn and went about the day with the usual purpose and structure that was both a part of who they were and what it meant to run the estate and the millinery business. Trevor spent a few hours before breakfast with his secretary, dictating a letter to his solicitor in London as well as composing a longer and more difficult letter to his father.

When he reached the stables shortly after nine, it already felt like a very long day had passed. As soon as he mounted his usual horse for making rounds about the estate, though, all the worry about his upcoming marriage began to slip away. His father would be thrilled to learn that Trevor was announcing his betrothal to Lady Georgiana Cambury. And after the wedding . . . Georgie would stay in Egypt or return, as she wished. There was nothing more Trevor could do at present.

Several days passed in that way, with Georgie spending all of her time at Camburton Castle, preparing for the wedding with her mother and Nora, and returning to Mayfield sporadically to check on the horses. Trevor wasn't sure if she was avoiding them or simply busy, but he agreed with James that they needed to let her do whatever it was she needed to do for the weeks leading up to their marriage.

About a week later, Trevor entered the drawing room, where James was putting the finishing touches on Lady Caroline Lamb's wild hat. James turned, sensing Trevor's presence, and gave him that broad, generous smile. "And how was your morning, my beautiful man?"

Trevor crossed the room and kissed him on the mouth, then caressed his cheek as he pulled away. "All the better for seeing you," he answered with a hint of melancholy.

James set aside the hat and gave Trevor his full attention. "What is it?"

"I heard back from my father this morning."

"And?"

"And I suppose I thought I would feel better once I had." Trevor shrugged and tried to smile.

James looked at him with a thoughtful, sympathetic gaze. "So," James drawled, placing his elbow into the palm of one hand and resting his chin in his other hand. "Let me see if I have this right." He tapped his lips, and Trevor knew the direction of his thoughts. "You thought that once you fulfilled the absurd demands of a selfish, lonely old man by marrying a woman who—if we are lucky—will require a lifetime of coaxing and prodding to appreciate the smallest grain of what we have to offer . . . you thought you would feel happy when that was all arranged? Is that it?"

Trevor took a deep breath. "Apparently, yes." Then chuckled at his own misguided optimism.

"Oh, my dear boy," James said, trying to maintain an air of levity. "Don't ever change. While the rest of us are forever seeing the dark despond, you always cling to the light. And I wouldn't want it any other way."

James reached for Trevor and pulled him into a hard kiss, clutching at the base of Trevor's neck. When he pulled away, he didn't move very far. "We will survive this, whatever this is," James added with a short laugh. "I'm already starting to believe that you of all people could transform even the most coldhearted, tentative, fearful creature into your devoted slave." James massaged his neck while he spoke.

"But I do not want a slave," Trevor said quietly. "I want us to be a family."

James finished rubbing the tight muscles at Trevor's shoulder and then let his hand fall away. "Perhaps that is possible, but it's clear Georgie will have to come to that conclusion on her own."

"But how? If she won't budge without excessive prodding, and then she recoils from anything remotely resembling prodding, how are we to *guide* her?"

"First off, I think it is time we both stop *trying* so hard. She has agreed to marry you. She's agreed to get married at St. George's in Hanover Square at her mother's request. She's even gone so far as to allow us to *hope*. By all accounts, Georgie is being incredibly agreeable."

James was relieved to see Trevor lift the corner of his mouth in a small acknowledgement of humor.

James continued, "Let us go to London and enjoy this wonderful celebration. Not as a farce, but in the hope that her love will blossom at some point in the future. Most marriages begin with far less." James patted Trevor's upper arm twice. "Let's go in to luncheon and cease these endless conversations about Lady Georgiana Cambury. I certainly don't want to prove her suspicions correct."

Trevor shot him a questioning look. "What suspicions?"

"That we spend all of our time speaking about her," James said.

Soon after the letters of invitation had been hand delivered, a slew of special rush orders came in for James's hats. He was relieved to be extraordinarily busy for the few remaining weeks leading up to the wedding, but Trevor was becoming more than a tad frenetic.

When Georgie unexpectedly agreed to the idea of the two men accompanying her back to Egypt, James knew that Trevor had been too elated to think past his exuberance. *Yes, yes,* Trevor would smile encouragingly as she regaled them with fabulous tales of the Sahara, but James could see his growing dismay about leaving Mayfield for *eight weeks.*

And while Trevor fretted about the estate and how it would run in his absence, James was beginning to fret about the likelihood of them ever convincing Georgie to return with them to England. It was one thing to work on Georgie here at home, to gradually show her the beauty of their life in Derbyshire while they were able to display its charms to best advantage, but it was quite another to take her back into the exotic promise of the Mediterranean and then expect her to return willingly to the harsh north.

He tried to set aside these negative thoughts, but James often found himself envisioning a desperately emotional parting on some crowded dock when it would be time to return to England and Georgie would declare she intended to remain in Egypt. Endless, unwanted scenarios played out in his mind, visions of Georgie tossing some brisk and careless farewell as she galloped off on a camel—did camels even gallop?—and leaving Trevor a passionate ruin.

The plans were set, however, and the closer the wedding day came, the less James allowed himself to think of the potential consequences.

A week before the wedding, Vanessa and Nora traveled with Georgie to London. Two days later, James and Trevor followed with the bulk of the luggage. In many ways, it was a rite of passage marking the change in their relationship: the end of their life as a couple up to that point and the beginning of their relationship with Georgie.

They allowed enough time to stop for three nights during their journey. Their lovemaking was tender and bittersweet in those inns along the Great North Road.

The roads were clear and they often went ahead of their carriages on horseback through the brightly colored autumnal countryside. While riding with Trevor, James was reminded of all the reasons he'd fallen so deeply in love with him in the first place: the gentle confidence, the unwavering conviction, the faith.

That was it, really. Trevor *believed* in humanity in a way that James feared he never would. His own upbringing had been lacking in so many ways; he didn't really understand the first thing about faith. Most of the adults who'd populated his childhood were of *very* little faith indeed, bordering on rascals. His father had been the youngest of five aristocratic sons, and the man had spent his entire life feeling robbed of his rightful share rather than earning a proper living.

Perhaps that's what Trevor meant when he said Georgie would be able to find a middle way through James. Because it was true: James understood Georgie. Lack of faith and an inherent cynicism were philosophies they shared.

On their last night together on the road, James and Trevor were entwined in one another's arms in the narrow bed of the Stag's Leap Inn. After their second round of slow, protracted lovemaking, Trevor held James close and whispered, "You will always be mine."

That one small phrase, said so lovingly, replenished all of James's faltering hope. They both slipped into a peaceful rest and awoke early the next morning, ready to close the final distance to London.

Trevor was not the only one with a troublesome parent awaiting him in the capital. James had considered avoiding his mother entirely, but Trevor wouldn't hear of it. The elder Mr. Rushford had died when James was a teenager, and his mother had miraculously come to her senses and left the stage in favor of a more reliable husband, a decent widower with a decent shop in Ludgate. She and this shopkeeper had been childhood sweethearts on adjoining farms in Hampshire before James's father, the ne'er-do-well youngest son of the local gentry, swept Dolly off her feet and got her with child—got her with James, to be precise.

Dolly's life as an itinerant actress was now behind her—and along with it the son she had never wanted. Instead of minding him as a mother might, over the years she had pawned James off on her husband's reluctant relatives in Wales. James and his mother corresponded once or twice a year, probably because that's what the decent shopkeeper husband expected more than James or Dolly actually wishing for contact.

When the roads on the outskirts of London started to become more congested, James and Trevor decided to stop for a bite to eat before riding the rest of the way into the center of the city.

"Aren't we very close to your mother's shop?" Trevor asked.

James looked around and got his bearings. "I think you may be right," he said. "But I just don't know if I have it in me to see her yet. Perhaps later in the week?"

"That's fine, of course." Trevor murmured a few soft nonsense words to calm his fidgeting horse before he continued. "But wouldn't it be easier to see her now and then not have to worry about it for the rest of our time in town?"

"Oh, very well, you are always so ready to do the right thing."

They sent the carriages on to Mayfair and directed their two horses through the crowded streets, the lanes becoming narrower as they went. When he reached a familiar-looking turn, James peered around the crowded lane and recognized the sign out front. Pickleworth's.

"Here it is." James tried to sound blithe, but he knew his voice was strained with resignation. "Why don't you hold the horses while I go in and see if there's a stable that they recommend while we visit?"

James entered the shop, and a tinkling bell above the door caused the tall, thin woman behind the counter to turn in his direction. Oddly enough, he had spent so little time with his own mother, he hardly recognized her. It was almost as if she had taken up the role of shopkeeper in one of her traveling plays, but she had been cast permanently. She stared for a few moments, the bright autumn sun that shone behind James's shoulders perhaps making it difficult for her to see. But James knew the truth: his own mother didn't recognize him either.

"Mr. James Rushford, at your service." He removed his high top hat and bowed elegantly. She had always been an easy mark for the pomp of the aristocracy. When he lifted his gaze, she had come out from behind the counter and was walking toward him with a genuine smile of approval.

"Well, aren't you the handsome one! Thank you very much for your letter informing me of your arrival. We weren't expecting you for a few more days yet, but I did see the announcement in the paper yesterday of your *friend's* upcoming marriage to Lady Georgiana." She looked over his shoulder and out to the street.

"Yes, Lord Mayson and I have traveled down together from Derbyshire these past few days in anticipation of that blessed event."

As if she needed to prepare herself to say what needed to be said, she clasped her hands in front of her and nodded solemnly. "So this will put an end to your particular *friendship* then?"

James had had many years of practice when it came to disguising how it upset him when people referred to his *friendship* with Trevor in that mincing, disappointed way. But he realized he was, quite blissfully, out of practice. The two of them lived so openly, so freely in the world they had created both at Mayfield House and at Camburton Castle, always welcomed with open arms by Vanessa and Nora or any of the artists who stayed there many months of the year. Even Mrs. Daley and the servants in both houses respected their relationship.

James had tried to prepare for this part. Outside of their protected enclave in Derbyshire, he knew it was common for people to voice their disdain for his *particular friendship* with Lord Mayson. But his own mother?

Still, he let none of that show. In fact, this was an excellent dress rehearsal for what promised to be many days of drawing room innuendos in the coming week.

"As a matter of fact, Mayson is here with me now. And I was curious if there was a stable you'd recommend nearby so we might water the horses while we take tea or—"

A curtain that led to the back of the shop was pulled aside and a round-eyed, round-bodied man poked his round head out from behind the fabric. "Is everything all right, Mrs. Pickleworth?"

"Yes, Mr. Pickleworth. Everything is quite fine." She stepped aside so Mr. Pickleworth could see that she was talking to James. "You remember Mr. Rushford."

"Very good. And a good day to you, Mr. Rushford." With that, the curtain dropped back into place and Mr. Pickleworth was to be seen no more.

"He's very busy now . . . " she started lamely.

"Oh yes, I'm sure you both must be very busy." He looked around and gestured with his arm to encompass the entirety of the shop. Orderly jars of jam and perfectly arrayed dry goods filled the neat shelves. "You have created what looks to be a very tidy establishment."

She appeared to be quite proud of herself upon hearing the compliment, or as much as a godly woman named Mrs. Pickleworth was allowed to be proud in the eyes of the Lord. "We work very hard, and we manage."

When many more seconds of silence passed, James realized she was not going to ask him to stay for tea, nor was she going to inquire as to whether Trevor would be coming inside. He looked down at his formal hat, one more thing she probably saw as frivolous, but which actually made up the fabric of who James was. He placed the hat back on his head and smiled with perhaps a hint of sadness, but at least it was honest. "It's been very nice to see you, M— Mother." For a second there, he had been quite sure he too was going to call her Mrs. Pickleworth.

"Yes. Very nice to see you, James."

"So then, please pass on my regards to Mr. Pickleworth. I will let you know when I am next in town."

"Oh, there's no need to inconvenience yourself. It appears we are all of us well and doing fine."

"Yes, that is true. We all appear to be managing." He bowed again formally, and he thought she exhaled with something akin to relief to be rid of him. "Farewell," he added.

She walked him to the door and pulled it open, that cheerful tinkling bell signaling his departure.

Trevor had dismounted and was holding the reins of both animals loosely in his right hand while he leaned casually against the hitching post. Two young urchins had set their sights on the well-dressed country gentlemen and were begging him for a bit of coin. When Trevor looked up and caught James's eye, his expression went from hope to disappointment in a flash.

James shook his head with a quick jerk as the door to Pickleworth's shut behind him. He strode across the narrow lane and joined Trevor in his negotiations with the two rascals. Trevor was trying to explain to them that if he gave them any money, he would be encouraging them to continue their life of begging. They laughed and talked over one another, promising him this would be the last time ever, smiling their best boyish smiles, tugging at their caps.

A flash of his own youth—with many moments of having to survive by his own outstretched hand—caused James to reach into his pocket and hand each of them a gold sovereign. They stared at him in grateful disbelief.

One of them had the quick wit and good humor to reply, "Well, if you go and give us *that* kind of money—of course we will spend the rest of our lives a-begging!" The other dirty-faced little boy bit on the coin for good measure, and then both of them ran and were quickly out of sight down one of the narrow alleys that wound its way through this part of London.

James kept facing in their direction long after he'd lost sight of them.

"So, am I to take it that we were not invited to tea with your family?" Trevor asked lightly.

James turned then, without a hint of irony. "You are my family, Trevor. Only you."

Chapter 12

As Franny made the final adjustments to Georgie's wedding gown, smoothing down the old-fashioned silk and checking the seams and hem one last time, Vanessa looked as if she had never been more pleased.

"You are so beautiful, Georgie."

Unsure how to respond to that, Georgie kept her attention on Franny. "That will be all, my dear," Georgie said kindly. "Thank you so much again for your help these past weeks." This was the last she would see of the sweet maid, and Georgie was surprised by the tug of emotion the realization brought. Over the past few weeks, young Franny had proved to be a wonderful helper, and Georgie was sad to leave her now that she was returning to the Middle East.

When the maid had left the room, Georgie turned back to her mother and Nora and gave a small curtsy. "Does everything really look all right?" She took a piece of the delicate dress in each of her hands and pulled it gently to spread the fabric for them to see.

Nora came over and smoothed her palm down the length of Georgie's bare arm and then held her hand away from the fabric. "More importantly, how do you feel?"

How did she feel? That was always the unanswerable question of late. She rarely knew the answer. Or rather, there were too many answers.

"I think I'm fine?" She smiled hesitantly, knowing that Nora would understand.

Nora squeezed her hand and nodded. "I think that's quite all right to own your uncertainty on such an important day. There's nothing worse than people who seethe with overconfidence, especially when one is feeling insecure." Nora smiled at Georgie and then turned to look at Vanessa. "You know you do it, darling, and we know you can't help it. But do allow Georgie to make this day her own, even if that means she shows a little hesitance or even a hint of honest fear."

Over the past few weeks, Georgie, Nora, and Vanessa had spent many long hours in one another's company. What Georgie had thought would be a torturous battle of the wills had turned out to be one of the most salutary times she had ever spent with her mother. Nora was to thank, of course—she could foster reconciliation between a lion and a lamb if she set her mind to it. But it was also Vanessa. She seemed easier somehow, less inclined to take every remark as a barb where Georgie was concerned.

The seamstresses in London had done a beautiful job transforming her mother's original wedding gown. Even by Georgie's reckoning and her limited knowledge of sewing, it was all quite splendidly done. The modiste had taken the fabric from Vanessa's nearly thirty-year-old gown and created something that felt familiar and comfortable. At an early fitting, Vanessa had spied Georgie in one of her riding corsets while she was changing.

"That looks awfully tight and constricting," Vanessa had begun.

But instead of a renewed argument, it had turned out to be yet another seed of their burgeoning mutual understanding. Georgie had simply taken a deep breath and told her mother the truth. "I like it this way, Mother. I am happier when my breasts and back are supported in this type of confining structure. I know it is odd—"

Vanessa had cut her off with a bright smile of understanding and said, "I love odd! I wish you had told me sooner!"

Instances of that sort had been happening more and more over the past few weeks, and Georgie now stood in front of her mother, on her wedding day, wondering why she had yet again been in such a rush to get away from Vanessa.

Alas, they were leaving for Cairo on the morrow, and Georgie decided to be grateful to be parting on such pleasant terms for once, rather than to question why she had such contradictory feelings about it.

She stared at herself in the mirror one last time, letting her mother adjust a flounce at her shoulder.

"Of course one's wedding day, despite every happiness, is also terrifying. I remember when I married your father . . ." Vanessa's eyes became a little dreamy, and she looked out the large window toward the gray November day. "I already knew then that I loved him, but . . . how can one possibly know the extent?" She turned back and caught Georgie's eyes in the reflection. "And then those philosophical thoughts were overtaken, of course, by my apprehension—well, to be honest, my anticipatory delight—for the night to come." Her eyes came back into focus when she smiled at Georgie. "If there is anything you wish to know in *that* regard—"

"Oh! You are very kind to offer, Mother. But I am quite sure I have the basic facts." Georgie rarely blushed when it came to talk of sexual relations, but she supposed this was a moment in every woman's life that demanded blushing. She was grateful for her mother's willingness to offer advice on such a private matter, and she was equally grateful when Vanessa nodded quietly and did not insist on providing it.

Perhaps Georgie really had sold Vanessa short all these years, reducing her to some sort of artistic, frivolous, shallow woman. Perhaps Georgie had been such a skeptic herself that Vanessa's love of all things romantic had always seemed insincere. Now that Georgie had had her first taste of what could only be described as true romance, Vanessa didn't seem quite so ridiculous after all.

"Well, I must say that *is* a relief," Vanessa said on a chuckle. "It's such a personal business, but I couldn't very well send you into the wilderness without at least letting you know that I am always here to help if you need me."

"I love you, Mother," Georgie said simply. Nora was still holding her left hand, so she reached out her right to beckon her mother. The three of them embraced, and all Georgie could think to say was "Thank you," in a very soft whisper.

Archie was waiting for the three of them at the bottom of the stairs. It had been a very hectic few weeks for him as well. Preoccupied with her own plans, Georgie regretted that she had missed hearing many of the details, but it was obvious he was deeply happy—whether from his work or from his doings with the mysterious novelist or both, Georgie was not sure. For this morning, however, he was neither scientist nor suitor, but her beloved twin brother.

Georgie had already put on her long kid gloves upstairs, but when Archie took her hand in his, she felt the strong connection immediately. They stared at each other for a few long moments, sharing so much in one of those wordless exchanges that had always passed between them, checking one another's souls.

"You are the most beautiful bride I have ever seen," Archie said gravely. "And not only due to your spectacular gown and your stunning hat. You, my sister, are simply radiant."

"You shan't make me weep, brother. A bride must not be splotchy and mottled with red patches when she first sees her intended on their wedding day." Her heart skipped when she pictured Trevor and James.

"Very well then, you look quite average, and I shan't say another word about it."

She laughed and patted his forearm. "That's much better, thank you. Now I think we'd best be off for the church so my dear fiancé is not made to worry any more than he must already when faced with the prospect of marrying me."

The four of them rode the short distance in Archie's town carriage from 74 Berkeley Square to St. George's, Hanover Square. When the carriage stopped out front, the scuttling clouds broke and a dramatic stream of sunlight shone down on the church.

Vanessa, apparently unable to help herself, exclaimed, "You see, even the sun gods are smiling on you, my darling girl." Vanessa looked back, her eyes bright with emotion, and kissed Georgie on her cheek. "Just think, the next time I speak to you, I will be speaking to Lady Mayson. And all I can think now is Trevor is the luckiest man in London."

"Oh Mother—"

"Shhh, my dear." Vanessa held both of Georgie's hands in hers. "Nora and I will go in now. You and your brother must wait a few moments and then make your entrance."

Georgie thought she really was going to cry after all. Why did it take this unexpected engagement for her to finally develop an appreciation for her mother's love?

As if sensing her thoughts, Vanessa leaned in close to Georgie one last time and whispered, "I don't care how or why it happened, but we have found each other at last, Georgiana, and I will always be grateful for it."

Nora reached for Vanessa's hand. "Come, my love. The church bells are about to toll eleven, and we need to be inside."

Vanessa nodded at Nora and then took one fleeting glance back at Georgie, both of them smiling quickly, something small and new and precious between them.

The door to the carriage shut and Georgie took a deep breath, trying to calm her nerves and collect herself. She'd spent the past week in London avoiding Trevor and James—avoiding her own feelings if she were being honest. Finally, she could no longer escape the truth of it all: entering that church represented far more than some paper arrangement.

"Are you ready?" Archie asked in a low voice, all seriousness. "We can ride on if you'd prefer."

She turned her head and opened her eyes slowly to look at her brother, her soul's mirror. Her heart had been beating like a small fluttering thrush all morning—sometimes cheerful, sometimes fearful. Staring into her brother's eyes put a stop to all that. He knew her. He knew how and why she did things; he understood her and accepted her, contradictions and all. And it came to her in a flash that if her intelligent, kind brother could manage that, perhaps she wasn't unknowable or incomprehensible or unacceptable after all. Perhaps she was even lovable.

"You are the best brother. You look at me with all that patience and love, and it gives me hope—albeit very slim—that I might find a similar place in someone else's heart."

"I'm fairly certain you already have. Trevor, and I daresay James, will be very good to you, Georgie. I think the burden will be on you to feel you deserve it."

She nodded slowly. "I think you're right."

"Then let us go in," he said with renewed enthusiasm, "and make an honest woman of you."

Trevor and James stood at the front of the church, side by side.

Viscount Mayfield had been in a seething rage when Trevor had casually informed him that *of course* James was going to stand up with him during the wedding ceremony. Ever since his mother's death, Trevor had learned that it was always best to give his father what he would consider the most upsetting bits of news while they were in the subdued reading room at White's. Surrounded by the dukes and earls whose favor he had spent a lifetime currying, the viscount would never permit himself even the slightest show of temper in that location. Yet the signs had been there and quite familiar to Trevor: the vein at the side of his father's neck had bulged, his left eye had twitched ever so slightly, and his lips had tightened almost imperceptibly.

When a shaft of bright sunlight came through the tall panes of glass at the front of the church, Trevor caught a glimpse of his father seated in one of the raised pews. The viscount was either concealing it rather well today, or some of that rage had faded. Regardless, Trevor felt he was both protector and protected having James by his side, and he would not have forfeited that feeling for anything.

Trevor turned from his father to look briefly at James, and of course James had also turned at the same moment to glance at Trevor. They smiled at one another—keeping their hands loose at their sides—and Trevor wished for an imaginary future when he could embrace this man on an altar like this, as a show of his love and respect for their union.

James must've sensed it, his eyes softening and his lips tightening with emotion. They looked at each other for a few seconds more, and then everyone's attention was drawn to the back of the church.

A single trumpet played as Archibald walked Georgie down the center of the church, where many friends and acquaintances were also standing as they passed. Suddenly, Trevor felt like a too-tall mast on a too-small boat, on the verge of capsizing. He had seen Georgie last night at yet another celebratory dinner at yet another splendid townhouse in Mayfair, but they hadn't had a chance to really talk or be together, the three of them, since that raucous carriage ride a few weeks ago. Trevor's heart began to pound, a slow, hard, rhythm against his rib cage, drumming in his ears and pulsing in his fingertips.

Once again, Georgie had transformed herself. This time, she was the elegant, innocent picture of the perfect aristocratic bride. With each step of her approach—her hand resting lightly on Archie's forearm, her gaze fixed on Trevor's—Trevor saw some new detail that made his heart thump harder. The ivory silk bonnet was close around her face, framing her cheeks and making her rosy lips look even more luscious; the shirred fabric that was meant to impart modesty across her bosom only served to draw his attention to her magnificent figure; the wide satin ribbon high and tight above her waist immediately had him picturing how his large hands would look and feel when they spanned her and how long and powerful her legs were beneath the endless fall of sheer fabric.

By the time she was standing next to him in front of the pastor, he was nearly overcome with desire. Archie passed her hand into his, and Trevor felt it like a lightning strike—at first a shock, and then a magnetic, continuous jolt that he might never be able to let go of.

And then everyone and everything simply faded into the background: the reverend's pattering voice, the shuffle and murmur of the crowded church. All Trevor could see or feel, hear or touch, was Georgie on one side and James on the other.

Perhaps his prayer of a few minutes before had been granted, because—regardless of what the congregation saw or what the reverend said—Trevor Mayson married both Lady Georgiana Cambury and Mr. James Rushford on that bright November morning.

The rest of the day passed in a flurry of champagne and toasts and hard slaps of congratulation on the back. Vanessa and Nora had done a splendid job of organizing the celebration after the wedding. Even though Trevor had made fun of the endless meetings about fabrics and flowers and foibles, he realized that every piece of candied fruit, every Spanish almond represented the love of a mother for her daughter.

Sooner than he could've imagined, the day had passed into night, and the guests were sprawling in drunkenness throughout the splendid Camburton residence on Berkeley Square.

"After these many weeks apart, are you trying to postpone having to bed me?" Georgie whispered. She had never been far from his side, but this was the first time she had actually spoken soft and close so only he could hear. Up until then, she had laughed with old friends or parried with diplomats about the true state of affairs in Cairo, often holding Trevor's hand or resting hers on his shoulder or forearm. He loved how it felt to be out with her in public, to be allowed to touch her, to declare their union in those small, tangible ways.

Throughout the day he had frequently cast his gaze around the rooms to make sure James was likewise enjoying himself. Trevor needn't have worried. They'd often spoken about how Trevor didn't think he himself would've been able to remain so sanguine if he'd been in James's position—publicly unacknowledged.

They were blessedly different in that way. Perhaps due to the cold, heartless nature of James's upbringing, he rarely felt slighted as an adult. James assured Trevor that what the outside world thought of the three of them—or, more likely, didn't think—could never alter the truth.

In fact, the moment Georgie whispered that suggestive question into Trevor's ear, he spied James laughing merrily with Sebastian and Pia across the ballroom. Georgie also looked in that direction, and James must have felt the pressure of their gazes upon him. He turned slowly and lifted his chin in acknowledgment. Trevor smiled and leaned slightly toward Georgie, but kept his eyes on James.

"I think we are all quite ready for our wedding night, Lady Mayson, don't you?"

"Absolutely, my lord." He looked at her as she spoke: her eyes sparkled, the burnished amber making her look even more like a predatory tigress. "All of my things have been delivered to your hotel, and I am ready to join you . . . both," she added, and Trevor felt his heart pick up speed yet again. "Let us say our thanks and good-byes to my mother and Nora, and your father, and then be on our way."

They crossed the ballroom to where Viscount Mayfield, Nora, and Vanessa were engaged in what appeared to be a pleasant conversation. Once again, it seemed that Nora White was able to bring out something good in even the most coldhearted of men.

"There you are, my dear!" Vanessa said to Georgie.

"Mother, I believe it's time we must go."

Trevor thought Vanessa looked simultaneously crestfallen and delighted, if such a thing was possible. He snaked his hand around Georgie's firm waist and pulled her tight into his side.

"She will always be your daughter, Lady Camburton, but now she is my wife." He thought for a moment that he had gone too far—Georgie stiffened slightly, and he suspected she was angry he had spoken of her in that possessive, objective way. Instead, she surprised him—delighted him!—when she leaned closer and rested her head gently on his shoulder and said, "He is quite right, Mother. My place is with my husband now."

Trevor turned, tilting his head to get a better look at her gentle expression. She appeared to be some combination of drowsy, tipsy, and happy. She looked like an angel.

"Perhaps you won't resent your mean old papa, then," his father said, a bit too loud from drink. "Since it's thanks to *me* you've ended up with the bonniest lass in Derbyshire." Even though Viscount Mayfield said it with more than a hint of spite, Trevor could only hear the goodness.

A brief, uncomfortable silence was cast for a moment, before Trevor turned to his father with an easy smile and said, "You are absolutely right, Papa. It is entirely thanks to you that I shall fall asleep tonight the happiest man in England."

Having clearly expected a verbal sparring match, his father was taken aback and merely replied with a blustery, "Yes, yes, yes." After saying their good-byes, the bride and groom left the grand ballroom.

A few moments later, Trevor and Georgie were in the front hall, with the sounds of the ballroom receding behind them. James emerged from another set of doors and joined them, and they made their way out of the brightly lit townhouse and into the dark comfort of the barouche for the ride over to their hotel in St. James's.

James had enjoyed the day, but dear Lord was he looking forward to this night. The three of them hadn't been alone together in weeks, and the tension in the carriage was electric.

"I have missed you both terribly!" Georgie exclaimed on a dramatic sigh after the carriage door had shut and the horses began trotting. She reached for Trevor's knee across the narrow space that separated them, but he swatted her hand away.

"Neither one of you may come near me," Trevor chided. "I have *not* requested an extended carriage ride this evening. In fact I am hoping that this is the shortest carriage ride between Mayfair and St. James's in the history of London transport."

James began to remove his gloves, slowly tugging on each finger as he spoke. "Feeling a bit eager, are you, Trevor?"

"*Eager* is one word for it," Trevor growled, staring from James's hands to his lips to his eyes and then across the carriage, perusing his bride with the same hungry look. "*Ravenous* is more accurate."

James was quite tempted to make a nuisance of himself—maybe lean his head toward Trevor's lap or let one of his bare hands slide casually across the squabs to rest on Trevor's inner thigh—but the poor man *did* look like he was about to burst, and James agreed that it would be a shame to waste all that *bursting* in the back of a cramped carriage when a very large, very comfortable bed awaited them. So they rode in silence for the few minutes, staring at each other longingly and letting the desire simmer between them.

The Primrose Hotel was aglow with streetlamps and brightly attired footmen. Barely waiting for the carriage to come to a halt, Trevor swung open the door and the three of them leapt from the carriage as if escaping from a swarm of deadly insects. Barreling through the lobby without sparing a glance or word to anyone in their path, they raced up the stairs to the large suite of rooms.

James felt giddy with joy and anticipation, the sound of Georgie's laughter winding around them and buoying them up as they nearly fell over each other in their haste. She had pulled up the hem of her dress slightly, fisting the white satin so as not to trip as she ran.

Trevor almost threw the door to their suite off its hinges when he opened it with exuberant force. A valet and another servant awaited them in the main room. One of them opened his mouth, probably to offer food or drink, but was immediately interrupted by Trevor.

"No—we won't be needing anything—thank you very much—away you go—thank you!" Trevor hustled them out of the room and shut the door behind them, flipping the lock and turning to face Georgie and James with a look of sheer delight, accompanied by those hot, panting breaths.

As if he were introducing himself for the first time, Trevor came away from the door and slowly walked toward them. "Mr. Rushford. Lady Mayson. The pleasure is all mine."

James watched as Trevor closed the distance. Past thinking, he reached for Georgie, wrapped his arm around her waist, and pulled her roughly against him, his front pressed into her back. He felt the rippling waves of excitement transfer between them. He slid his other hand along her left arm and then up to rest around her neck, fondling her with a loose chokehold. She hummed happily at the rough treatment.

His cock had been thick and dully aroused for hours, but now that he had her pressed to him, watching Trevor approach with all of that predatory greed, it was hard steel against the soft cleft of Georgie's arse.

Stroking the satiny skin of her throat and collarbone, James watched how Trevor's eyes followed the movement of his fingers, like a bird of prey follows the movement of an unwitting field mouse.

"Do you want to make love to your wife, Lord Mayson?" James gripped her neck harder and let his other hand slide lower, trailing from her waist to between her legs, settling in with a rude, possessive grab. Georgie exhaled, and the release of air only put more pressure against James's hard staff, as if she were deflating slightly to fit even more securely into his hold.

Trevor was now standing mere inches in front of them. Georgie whimpered gently—so out of character, James thought, to see her and feel her against him like this, pliant. She was like a cat waking up from a long and satisfying nap. She raised her arms, arched her back, and stretched her hands so they reached behind James's neck and clasped there.

"Yes, Lord Mayson," she purred. "Will you make an honest woman of me at last?"

James watched—and felt—as her body responded when Trevor placed his hands reverently on her breasts. James kept his grip firm at her neck and at the hot juncture of her thighs, the better to complement the soft tenderness of Trevor's hands.

"Look at you . . . " Trevor's voice was vibrating with need. "Your breasts are warm and full in my hands. Are you ready at last to be my lawfully wedded wife, Lady Georgiana?"

James held her to him, feeling every vibration of her pleasure, every hesitant breath, every small shudder as Trevor peeled away the last of her resistance with those gentle touches and those clear words. Leaning his head down, James caught Georgie's earlobe between his teeth and began to nip and suck at the tender flesh.

"Answer your husband," James demanded.

Georgie's body reminded him of the crucible steel he'd seen in Sheffield: all of that rigid strength finally burning so hot that it nearly *begged* to be bent and molded into something new and useful, unlike what it had always been.

She emphasized the arch of her back, pushing her arse against James's cock and her breasts more firmly into Trevor's hands. "Yes . . . " Her voice was low and strong. "Yes." She let her head fall against James's shoulder. Trevor leaned in and began kissing the exposed swell of her bosom.

Whatever happened in the future, James was going to make sure that this night was exactly as each of them wished it to be—unsullied by what had happened in the past or what might or might not happen in the future—because he wanted this and he was going to have it. He wanted it for Trevor; he wanted it for Georgie; he wanted it for himself.

James lifted his hand from her throat and moved his fingers to her jaw, firmly tilting her head so her lips met his. He needn't have worried about being forceful; she was as supple as a spring twig. Her kiss was dreamy at first, distracted as she was by the hand between her legs, the hands on her breasts, the lips that were now kissing the edge of her bodice and hinting where they would go next.

Then her kiss began to awaken, her tongue seeking his, her lips tasting his. She pulled her lips away and cried out. James looked down over her shoulder to see that Trevor had freed one of her breasts and had taken it into his mouth with greedy pleasure.

James stared in wonder, filled with love. It was hard to explain, even to himself. Perhaps a normal person would be jealous or harbor some secret fear that Trevor would love him less. But when Trevor looked up and caught his eye—Georgie's breast firmly pulled between his lips—James had never felt more treasured. Whether it was because Trevor had an infinite supply of kindness and a generous heart, or it was just how the two men were wired together, James felt that loving this man and this woman brought him closer to both of them, deeper in love with both of them.

Obviously sensing the depths of James's feelings, Trevor pulled his lips away from Georgie's breast and brought his mouth up to kiss James. Everything was in that kiss. Trevor dug his strong fingers into the back of James's hair, kissing him with a near-violent clash of teeth and tongue and lips, with Georgie wedged between them.

James reveled in it, but after a few seconds he wanted Georgie and Trevor to be part of the same circuit. He took his lips away and turned Georgie's jaw another inch so she was now poised to receive Trevor's kiss.

"Kiss your wife, my love."

James nearly spent into his breeches when Trevor's mouth met Georgie's, their breath and lips so close to his own. Georgie's hips canted back against James; Georgie's mouth pressed against Trevor's; Trevor's fingers dug and gripped the back of James's head. The three of them were suddenly one, attached to each another in this intimate, binding embrace.

A few seconds later, all three of them glassy eyed, open mouthed, and panting, they stared at one another with all the heat and love that had built up among them. James spoke first.

"May I prepare her for you, Trevor, as I've long wished?"

Georgie made another whimpering sound in anticipation. Trevor smiled, then leaned in and kissed James, slow and deep, and then moved his mouth to Georgie's and kissed her in the same way, both languorous and possessive. *Mine . . . and mine*, he seemed to say. These were the kisses of a man who had everything he wanted and was looking forward to finally indulging himself at his leisure.

"Yes, Mr. Rushford," Trevor said as he stroked Georgie's bottom lip with this thumb. "I believe it's time for my wife to have her next lesson in the art of slow lovemaking."

Chapter 13

Georgie awoke feeling like a well-loved book, slipped snugly between two larger volumes of the finest leather. Her smooth skin felt sensitive from overuse as she moved slightly to test the soreness in her hips and shoulders. James was still at her back; the rough dusting of hair along his chest that narrowed down to his stomach felt familiar and foreign all at once. Trevor was at her front, his chest near her bare breasts. She breathed in the entwined scents of all three of them, quickly evoking and reigniting the previous night's passion. James and Trevor had indeed taught her many new variations of lovemaking, very slow and very satisfying.

Trevor began to stir, probably sensing she was awake; he was already so attuned to the subtle messages of her body, it was almost frightening. During the night, even after they had snuffed all the candles and collapsed onto the bed for much-needed rest in complete darkness, Trevor had somehow known how to best adjust her shoulder, her knee, her wrist. He moved her body in ways that were more comfortable than she herself knew how to move.

Even now, she was surprised at how blissfully content she was, that she wasn't stiff from sleeping with two men plastered against her. In the past, she had always preferred to slip away after she had taken her pleasure. She had seen that supplicating look in Trevor's eye—after that wild night beneath the moon and trees at Mayfield House, then again in the carriage when she'd bidden him good night—and she'd avoided him ever since.

She'd thought that would be the end of it and would set the tone for their future relationship—physical contact yes, emotional contact no. But even though this large suite of rooms included three separate sleeping chambers, it had never occurred to Georgie to leave the intimacy of their large, shared bed afterward. Whether out of respect or caution, Trevor had avoided any emotional declarations during their lovemaking.

Trevor began kissing her neck, whispering a tender, "Good morning, my wife."

She shivered as he made his way past her shoulder, until she eventually heard and felt and could nearly taste when he kissed James right near her ear.

"Good morning, my husband," Trevor whispered.

Georgie had never considered herself prone to poetic fancies, but when Trevor and James spoke to one another in that intimate, loving way—so open, so honest—a hot and needy desire bloomed deep in Georgie's belly. She suspected it was something a poet might describe as *yearning*.

But the yearning, as if it sensed that it might never be fulfilled, quickly transformed into the much more easily satiable white-hot lust. When Trevor said "Good morning, my husband," and the sound of his sweet kiss against James's lips was so close to Georgie's ear, she wanted them both deep inside her again, as they had been last night.

She must have moaned at the prospect, because Trevor finished kissing James and lifted his head onto his upturned palm and stared down at her. "Are you hungry again already, my lioness?" he asked as he trailed the tip of his finger down her exposed shoulder and let it slowly pull the edge of the white linen sheet away from her body.

James began kissing the exposed flesh as soon as Trevor moved the sheet out of his way, and she reveled in the heated trail he left behind.

She stretched and rolled to her back, still snug between them, like one of the big African cats that Trevor liked to compare her to. Throughout the night, he had called her *lioness*, or approved of her satisfied purring, or noted her catlike grace. At this moment, as she felt her muscles stretch and awaken against the warm flesh of these two beautiful men, she didn't think she would balk even if he called her *kitten*.

"I think you've both cast some sort of languorous spell on me." She yawned. "I have never felt this lazy in my life. I feel as though

I could lie here in this hotel bed with your bodies pressed against mine for the rest of my life and never miss much of anything."

She had joked last night that Trevor should buy a stake in the company that manufactured the French letters they were using to prevent a pregnancy. The salesman had assured Trevor he'd acquired more than enough to last for several months. Trevor had smiled in the dim candlelight last night and said, "I didn't bother telling the poor man that we would be depleting our supply at four times the normal rate—with two ravenous men, and the insatiable woman who wanted both of them twice over."

Trevor smoothed the palm of his hand across the curve of her bare belly, and she arched her back to meet it. James kissed her shoulder again and then her breasts. Within a few moments, both men were poised to enter her yet again—this time with Trevor at her back and James face-to-face.

Their bodies—James's and Trevor's—were so different and satisfied Georgie in such distinctive ways. James was all muscle and sinew, more precise somehow, lean and forceful when he thrust into her, deep and strong and direct like a powerful oar slicing through still water. Trevor was broader, both physically and emotionally; he encompassed her, filled her, surrounded her. She felt like Trevor could wrap all three of them in some magical protective layer.

The contrast and the combination were indescribably fulfilling. Selfishly, of course, Georgie experienced peak after peak of sexual satisfaction from the physical completion of having them both inside her at the same time. But she also adored how they rubbed up against each other inside her, how they mated with each other just as much as they mated with her when they were all joined like that. She could actually feel them enjoying each other's thrusts and pulls within the adjacent chambers of her body. It was spectacular.

Over the years, Georgie had come to see her sexual appetite as simply one more thing that made her different from other people. Perhaps there was a bit of immature bravado in it—*look at me, I'm bizarre and I don't need your approval*! She hadn't been particularly interested in men—or women for that matter—until she left home. Life at Camburton Castle had seemed full and satisfying with her love of horseback riding and athletic pursuits. Then, when she arrived in

Cairo, she'd discovered there were all manner of ways to find sexual satisfaction on her own terms, and she'd set about doing so.

In the midst of those tawdry, delicious assignations, she let herself be wild. She let loose what she thought of as her primitive self. There was no shame in it. She loved the raw hunger, the scratching and crying out, yet . . . it was confined, delimited somehow. Those experiences were restricted to the physical. In fact she'd thought they were entirely physical, like eating or breathing. Of course you could have a particularly delicious meal or a spectacular ride that left your lungs burning with the pleasure of being alive, but then . . . it was over. She'd always thought there was something unseemly about constantly chasing after *more*.

So, when she had let her primitive self out with Trevor and James—exposing herself under the moon, and then again in the carriage—she had assumed that they would either be appalled or, at the very least, would wish to keep that type of lovemaking as a private, sordid secret. Or perhaps separate, somehow.

How could she have been so wrong?

They were jubilant! *"The grittier the better,"* James had growled last night. Trevor had begged her to share her imaginings; James had baited her to think up the most perverse things she could.

Then, when she had suggested something deliciously vulgar, instead of revulsion or disdain, James had raised a slightly disappointed eyebrow and replied, "Oh, is that all? You wish to have Trevor put *that* into that *orifice* while I do *that* with my tongue and he does *this* with his hands? Is that it, then?" And then she had dissolved into a fit of laughter that left her breathless and joyful.

And then, *dear God*, the two men had somehow magically transformed all of that giddy, innocent joy into hot licks of passion all over again. Nothing was ever *too much*, nothing was ever *wrong*. Who knew that marriage could be so liberating?

Trevor no longer had a single doubt. The way Georgie bent and bowed against him or leaned forward to get closer to James or demanded what she wanted from their eager hands—this was all the evidence he'd needed to prove Georgie was deeply committed to both of them and this marriage, that she loved them in a spiritual, consummating fashion. He didn't *need* the words when her body communicated so plainly the nature and depth of her satisfaction.

But for her own sake, he desperately wanted her to declare the truth of her feelings.

They spent the rest of the morning in bed, fulfilling her every whim, but by noon it was necessary to head to the docks and board their ship to Cairo.

More than twelve hours of rapture the previous night and that morning had turned Georgiana, Lady Mayson into a mellow, sensual companion. Trevor had thought she would ignore their married state, or give it only a passing acknowledgement, once the formalities of the wedding were finished. Quite the opposite. Georgie reveled in being Lady Mayson, which afforded her the right to touch or grab or lightly caress Lord Mayson—and their *dear friend* James—with frequency and openness.

As she introduced herself to the captain of the ship, for example, she reached for Trevor's hand and smiled joyfully, introducing him as her *darling* husband. Then, with equal enthusiasm, she released Trevor and put her hand firmly on James's upper arm. "And this is our dear, dear companion, Mr. James Rushford."

It had becoming quite the thing for friends to travel together for a few weeks or even a few months—if they could afford it—after their wedding. Of course, Bonaparte had gummed up the works for any of the more traditional continental visits of his parents' day, such as Rome or Paris, but the fact remained that the three of them traveling together did not raise any eyebrows. Usually it was a maiden aunt or sister of the bride who joined the party, in case the newlyweds encountered any rough patches, but as far as anyone knew, James Rushford was a perfectly appropriate friend of the family.

Trevor had booked two cabins, one with a large bed—or rather, large by shipboard standards—and the other a smaller, adjacent one for a valet or child, ostensibly for James, according to the ship's manifest.

Those two weeks aboard the *Magnolia* would stay in Trevor's mind and memory for the rest of his life as some of the most enlightening he had ever known. The ship's passengers were a mix of British, Dutch, French, Spanish, Turkish, and Egyptian nationals, with a smattering of Russians, Danes, and a few others. They weren't all wealthy or aristocratic, by any means, but there was a camaraderie that sprang up among them nonetheless. After a day or two, it was not only the ship that was free of King and country, but it seemed as if everyone on board was likewise emancipated. National rivalries forgotten, the thirty or so men and a few women would laugh and exchange stories about their childhood homes or favorite music or the running of their farms or schools or businesses. There were also a few quieter types—most likely with the Foreign Office, even if they never said so outright.

It struck Trevor as an egalitarian, utopian ideal, one he wished to recreate when he returned to Derbyshire. Georgie's mother had long held a similarly all-encompassing view of the world, and over the summer months she transformed Camburton Castle into an artistic colony to foster it. Trevor wished to do the same at Mayfield House, only focusing his efforts on agriculture, science, and social reform. If it were possible for thirty people from so many different countries to find common ground aboard a small ship, perhaps it was possible on a much larger scale.

"What are you writing so furiously?" Georgie asked quietly, a few days before they were due to arrive in Egypt. He looked up from his notebook, Georgie's voice immediately distracting him from the complex equations he'd been working on. He'd awoken early, inspired to jot down copious notes after pondering a discussion on the latest drainage techniques he'd had with his new Dutch friend Pete Voorhees the previous night.

Ever since their wedding night, Georgie had become gentler somehow. She remained opinionated and demanding in all of her usual ways—forceful in bed and out—but early in the morning, before she armed herself to face the day perhaps, she was docile. Like now, when she was just waking up, she stretched her legs, and the thin muslin of her night rail pulled taut against her round bottom. She and James were still dozing in bed, James's hand resting lightly against her neck as it had on their wedding night.

"Nothing that can't wait until later," Trevor whispered in reply. He set aside his pen and gave Georgie his full attention, as it would've been impossible to stay focused on anything as mundane as drainage when that woman and that man were sleepy, soft, and warm with the burgeoning desire of the new day floating off them in waves.

The lulling movement of the ship had added to the dreamy quality of the entire journey, and this morning was no different. Trevor stood up and joined the other two in bed. Georgie was facedown and hummed her approval when Trevor leaned in and kissed her bare shoulder. Trevor's hand followed the curve of her waist and then along her thigh until he reached the hem of her nightgown. He pulled it up slowly until her arse was exposed and he was rubbing one of her cheeks in smooth, firm circles. "You are quite delicious, Georgie. You know that, of course"—she smiled with closed eyes while James slept on—"but I must confess I've been missing someone."

Her eyes flew open. "What? To whom are you referring?" she whispered hotly.

He loved her moments of jealousy and slapped her bottom once in tender punishment. Her eyes brightened immediately, and then he resumed that lovely rubbing that got her so wet and ready for him. "I've been wanting to reacquaint myself with one Mister George Camden prior to our arrival in Cairo. Have you seen him anywhere aboard ship?"

She pressed her face into the pillow and groaned, the sound some combination of happiness and embarrassment and pleasure. He watched as her shoulders relaxed slightly and her arms moved so she could rest her cheek against her forearm. She turned to face him and her mouth had that slack, careless quality he associated with her more masculine side. "Trust me," she said, pitching her voice slightly lower, "you're going to be seeing quite a lot of Mr. Camden upon our arrival."

Trevor raised an eyebrow. "Oh really?" He saw James's eyes open sleepily beyond Georgie's shoulder.

"Yes. I was planning on traveling—" She gasped when Trevor let his fingers press deeper into her cleft. "Well," she continued rather breathlessly, "with the three of us . . . as male friends . . . looking to buy a few prime stallions... I thought—" Her eyes slid shut and she ceased talking when his fingers found the wet entrance to her pussy and began toying with her clit and then her arse, sliding back and forth, in and out, with her own slippery heat coating her and getting her ready. When she moaned into the pillow, he couldn't resist any longer.

He levered himself up and hoisted her hips so he was between her thighs and had perfect access to her upturned arse. James was smiling up at him dreamily. Trevor pressed the head of his cock against her arsehole but didn't push in.

"I am in the market for a few prime stallions," Trevor said, his voice getting rough with sexual anticipation, "and who better to guide me than the respected Mr. Camden?"

She groaned and nodded once into the pillow and tilted her hips ever so slightly to invite him in.

"Very well then, it's settled," said Trevor, thrusting into her and leaving all thoughts of tenderness behind. He wanted to pound her to dust. And by the sounds of her moans of pleasure and the erotic tears streaming down her face, that was exactly what she wanted as well.

"You two are quite busy so early in the morning," James said, rubbing his face with both hands as he widened one eye to get a better look at the way Trevor's cock was pounding in and dragging out. "What's this I hear about a visit from Mr. Camden?" he asked casually, taking hold of his own cock and moving in time to Trevor's hips, while his other hand pushed roughly into Georgie's eager mouth.

"It seems Mr. Camden will be our guide in Cairo," said Trevor, panting and smiling as he slammed into her again and again.

"Ah, an insider's look," James said, working his cock more feverishly until his orgasm plowed through him and he spent in warm spurts against Georgie's back. The feel of it must have been the final turn of Georgie's pleasure, as Trevor felt the tight spasms of pleasure around his cock. James pulled Georgie's mouth to his right as she would have screamed out her release and awoken the entire ship. The final *slap-slap*-slap of Trevor's hips against Georgie's arse was the last sound any of them heard before they collapsed atop one another and fell back to sleep for a few more contented hours.

Two days later the ship arrived in Alexandria. They had agreed it was best if Georgie continued to dress as an elegant British bride until they had disembarked and bid farewell to all their traveling companions. James watched as she said good-bye to everyone on the ship with her wonderful combination of British haughtiness and bold familiarity. Promises to stay in touch were exchanged, with Trevor giving his details to most of the men with whom he had shared his idea of starting a philosophical society of some sort, while James looked around the docks at a dazzling world he'd never thought he would see.

Once all of their trunks had been carried off the ship, James was dumbstruck. Alexandria was a braying, bustling, packed assortment of brilliant humanity. He remained overwhelmed for the entire one-hundred-mile overland journey from there to Cairo. During one of the breaks for food and water along the way, Lady Georgiana entered a modest tent, and ten minutes later a jaunty Mr. George Camden emerged. They spent the rest of the journey taking in the vast expanses of desert sands and small villages between the port city and the capital.

Where James was dumbstruck anew.

Cairo was simply dazzling. Mamelukes in glittering saddles of gold leaf and scarlet velvet pranced elegantly by, while scantily clad paupers sat cross-legged a few feet away, weaving together bits of hemp to be used as rope aboard the ships. Carts and carriages of every size and description, vendors and street urchins, but most of all it was the look in Georgie's eyes that bowled him over.

She was so alive, already arguing in Arabic with a carriage driver who was obviously trying to swindle her. She was in her element, laughing and dismissive one second, conciliatory and accommodating the next. Haggling was in her blood. He couldn't wait to see her purchase something she truly craved.

James looked over at Trevor, expecting to see similar jubilance, and was met instead with a glimpse of his sadness. The poor man still didn't understand this woman, his own wife. While she continued to berate the carriage driver, James moved closer to Trevor. "She is splendid, is she not?"

"She is," Trevor answered carefully.

"So then why do you appear as though you've just happened upon a dear friend's funeral?"

Trevor turned to face James. "I've made a horrible mistake suggesting we travel with her to Egypt, haven't I?" He shook his head and didn't wait for James to answer. "How can I possibly convince her that you and I are necessary to her happiness, to her life, when it is so obvious we are *not*? We, neither of us, speak this burbling language nor know any of the customs of this place. Within days Georgie will most likely send us packing for our uselessness."

James shook his head. "You are a very stupid man sometimes, dear heart."

Trevor opened his mouth to defend himself, but Georgie interrupted with a wolf whistle. "I've finally talked him down to a reasonable fare! Isn't it glorious?" She swung her cane around and nearly decapitated the poor carriage driver. "Welcome to Cairo!"

"She wants you to rely on *her*," James said pointedly, so only Trevor could hear. "Not the other way round, you idiot." Then James smiled broadly and joined Georgie near the coach, giving Trevor a few moments to contemplate the quandary of how his desire had very nearly been foiled by his misguided belief in his own male primacy.

By the time they had traveled twenty minutes through the crowded streets, James had fallen madly in love with Cairo. Georgie directed the driver to a neighborhood in a quieter part of the city, where she knew of several reputable guesthouses. When they pulled in front of the one she preferred, a man in his middle thirties, arrayed in gleaming white robes, was standing in the ornate narrow doorway that led to an elegant, dim lobby.

Trevor waited in the coach with the luggage, while Georgie and James entered the building to see if there were any available lodgings that would suit. Another man stood up from behind his desk and came around to get a better look at Georgie. She bowed and tipped her hat, spinning her cane and making the most of her male appearance.

The bright black eyes sparkled with enjoyment when he realized who she was.

"And is it really you?"

"Yes, Cyril. It is I, returned at last. And I have come with great guests."

"Oh, you must stay here! You are in luck, as the pasha's sister and her family have just left the upper two floors."

"That is marvelous news," exclaimed Georgie. "We've been traveling for many days and are looking forward to a short rest before I take them out for supper."

"Yes, that is what you must do. I will have some tea and sweets sent up. Please allow me to get my two sons to carry everything upstairs for you." With that, Cyril rang a small bell on the side of his desk. Within seconds two Egyptian boys appeared from a door to the left of the stairs. They bowed slightly to James and Georgie, and then, at their father's direction, headed quickly out to the street and began carrying the large, heavy trunks on their narrow backs.

The two boys made several trips while Georgie filled out some paperwork and wrote her name in a guest book. James smiled when he glanced over her shoulder and saw that she had written with a grand flourish, *Geo. Camden, Derbyshire*. She finished signing and handed the exotic quill to James.

He reached for it, but before she released it, she leaned in close and whispered, "You love it here already, I can tell. It reaches into you and grabs you, doesn't it?"

He smiled gently and nodded. "I know what you mean. I feel as though my blood is coursing through me with a new and promising rhythm, as if the city itself has entered my veins."

She smiled in return and released the quill, then waited for James to sign the register. He hesitated before putting pen to paper, looking at her for a few extra moments.

"But however much I come to love this or any other place, Georgie, I know it would feel dry as dust and empty as a robbed grave without Trevor at my side." He saw her enthusiasm dim slightly before he leaned down and wrote his name beneath hers: *Mr. James Rushford, Mayfield House, Derbyshire*.

He set the quill next to the register and stood up straight to face her. "You would be wise to remember that before you hurt him—or yourself. I will not allow the former, and I hope you have enough sense to prevent the latter."

Chapter 14

Georgie was in her element. Five years spent in and around Cairo had given her an intimate knowledge of the city, one she longed to share with Trevor and James . . . eventually. For now, she was blissfully alone. The men were still a bit groggy after the journey and were spending the first few days strolling around the quieter neighborhood near their guesthouse. Cyril had hired a cook and housekeeper for them and also made sure they always had fresh water, hot mint tea, and beautiful sweets that his cousin made at the bakery a few streets away.

Those cautionary words James had said after he signed the guest book were constantly repeating in Georgie's mind. Of course she had no intention of hurting Trevor—or James for that matter—and she especially had no intention of hurting herself. That was the *very* reason she had no intention of returning to Derbyshire. Nor had she ever made any false promises to do so. *This* was who she was—she glanced around the bustling open-air market—and she wasn't going to be made to feel apologetic about it. She'd finally resolved all those feelings with her mother on her visit to England, and she certainly wasn't about to let Trevor take on the role of her puppy-dog-eyed conscience.

Still.

Falling in love with Trevor and James was no longer some remote possibility. It was happening, damn it.

Georgie was walking through one of her favorite parts of the city, Khan el-Khalili, the most crowded, noisy, colorful souk. She snapped her bamboo walking stick into the hard-packed earthen sidewalk with a bit more force than necessary.

Her transformation back into Mr. George Camden was now complete. She'd styled her hair so she looked like any slightly effeminate British lad, just down from Oxford or Cambridge, with a taste for adventure on the Barbary Coast. She loved this freedom: walking alone through a dangerous city with long, arrogant strides, chin held high, making eye contact with anyone—merchant or mendicant—as she pleased. Quite simply, she felt alive.

The niggling problem was that she had also felt very much *alive* on a moonlit night near a man-made lake at Mayfield House. She had also felt extraordinarily *alive* in that London hotel room. And on board that ship. And this morning in their bed . . .

She tapped the cane in time with her pace, letting it strike when her left foot hit the ground. Right foot. Left foot. *Tap*. Right foot—left foot—*tap*.

Preoccupied with the disturbing direction of her thoughts—was she actually considering giving up this adventurous existence to molder away in some godforsaken pile on some godforsaken island?—BAM!—she accidentally careened into a splendidly handsome Mameluke *bey*. The Mamelukes were an ancient tribe of Egyptian warriors who had helped control vast areas of the country through both military force and diplomacy. This man in particular, Khalid Bey Abu al-Dhahab, exuded a strength and power that sprang from many generations of warfare and victory. And Georgie—or rather George—knew him well.

"Ah. If it isn't the young and biddable Mr. George Camden," Khalid said in his seductively accented English. "I'd heard you were back in town."

George's heart sped up at the memory of how this man had pushed her to her knees, rough and sure, after they'd met at one of the men's clubs a few weeks before she had returned to England. At the time, she'd been looking forward to future dalliances with the elegant warrior upon her return.

"Yes, I am returned from my tedious family errands in England." Georgie spun her walking stick around in two wide arcs with careless ease. "What've I missed? I hear Muhamed Ali Pasha's not pleased with you."

The political climate in Cairo was always heated, but lately the Ottomans, the mercenaries, and the locals were coming to a boiling point. Muhamed Ali Pasha appeared to be playing all sides against the middle.

Khalid lifted one shoulder and tossed his chin in the air, as if some mere pasha was nothing more than a gnat he could squash if he chose to. "I've no interest in talking politics with someone as young and inexperienced as you. You don't even have a beard." He reached over and slapped Georgie's cheek, firmly, but with a familiar intimacy, just as any man might behave toward a younger friend or relative for whom he had developed an innocent regard—a nephew who was a promising athlete, that sort of thing.

But Georgie knew that slap for what it was: an invitation. Khalid's dark eyes narrowed and his intense focus caused Georgie's vision to tunnel and her arse to squeeze together in eager anticipation. She was instantly excited by all the risks: of being alone in these surroundings with the city throbbing around them, of Khalid himself looking at her like he wanted to rip her to pieces, of what it would mean to betray Trevor and James. Yes, even that excited her.

She exhaled slowly and let herself savor the feelings, both sweet and bitter. Trevor had been far too protective lately, especially when they'd been out in public—whether Georgie was dressed in the diaphanous silks of Lady Mayson or the fitted buckskin trousers of Mr. Camden. For the past day or two, it had all felt . . . confining.

She knew what she was contemplating. She knew what she was about. If she could convince herself that James and Trevor were controlling, tepid conformists, she could convince herself to leave them as she'd originally planned, with far less regret and sadness than she was beginning to anticipate.

Georgie had quietly left their lodgings this morning after the other two had fallen back to sleep—fine, she'd sneaked out, having written a brief note saying she would return for supper after spending the day with an elderly acquaintance of her father's. Such a man did exist—a retired diplomat with whom Georgie had always enjoyed passing the time and hearing stories about her father—but Georgie had no intention of actually paying him a call today.

Instead, she was now standing on a crowded street, staring at Khalid—this beautiful, dark, vicious man—practically throbbing with blatant willingness. Her mind began to turn in all sorts of amoral directions. That note this morning had already made her a liar . . . so . . . it didn't really matter if she lied once or one million times, about something small or something despicable. Not paying a social call was hardly any different from letting this man fuck her, as far as being a liar went.

So why the hell not? She was never going to thrive as a baroness in Derbyshire in any case. Who was she trying to fool? Technically, Trevor had promised he would never prevent her from pursuing her own life on her own terms. Perhaps she wanted to test the limits of that promise.

She licked her lips slowly and returned Khalid's hungry stare. "You're quite right, sir. I'm very inexperienced, especially in the ways of strong, knowledgeable men such as yourself."

The corner of Khalid's mouth turned up slightly and he raised one eyebrow. "If memory serves, you're not *entirely* without experience."

Georgie was turning the handle of the bamboo cane against her palm, one hand resting atop the other as she twisted it in front of her. Khalid stared down at the thin, strong walking stick, and his smile widened.

"In fact, it appears you have everything you need for your next lesson."

She followed his gaze to the bamboo cane and began to turn it more slowly, watching her own hands and fingers as they circled around the top and moved up and down with suggestive slowness around the wide, rounded handle. She wanted this man, and that low growl he couldn't repress let her know he felt the same.

She remembered vividly how his strong, calloused hand had gripped the back of her head—demanding and unavoidable—while he pounded his huge cock into her mouth. After he'd finished, coming spectacularly all over her face, he had flipped her over his knee almost immediately. She had never removed a stitch of her masculine clothing, so he'd moved aside the tails of her riding coat and punished her backside through her buckskins with the very walking stick she now held in her hands.

Her breath was shallow with the memory, and she could tell he knew it. Here was a man who had spent his entire life contending with power: either submitting to it as a young boy, plucked from his home and chosen to be trained for his elite warrior caste; or, later, exerting it over vast numbers of people. And she had him in her thrall. She might have been the one on her knees, but he had lost control entirely. And apparently wanted to again.

When they'd last been together, Khalid had been so hard and eager that nothing short of battle would have prevented him from slaking that need, but he also had to punish her for making him want it. Of course he could not actually *thank her* for his pleasure, thus admitting that he had desired this blond infidel man. The only way he could reconcile the forbidden desire was to discipline her immediately for being the embodiment of such vile temptation. A discipline they both enjoyed.

In the bright, crowded Cairo street, Khalid slowly pulled a brilliant gold pocket watch out from one of the many folds of embroidered silk and satin sashes that constituted his uniform. He clicked it open and looked very much like a political man of affairs. "It appears I have one hour to spare before my next appointment. Would you care to join me for a cup of tea?"

The seemingly innocuous invitation immediately conjured their previous erotic assignation. Khalid, ever the elegant, educated diplomat, had first met Mr. Camden at the men's club, where he'd invited her to join him for a cup of tea. She had nodded her agreement and, instead of staying at the club as she'd expected, he'd led her out into the streets of Cairo at night, back to his splendid home, where he'd guided her far within, past courtyards and arched halls, into a devilish room with deep red silk-lined walls and several oil lanterns casting provocative shadows.

And sure enough, after he'd finished with her—no sign of sweat or seed upon him, nor the slightest hint of what had passed between them lingering on his skin—he'd served an elegant tea from a chased silver service. He'd been the picture of sophisticated control, whereas Georgie had spent that teatime—and the following week—fidgeting . . . and reveling in the tender, prickling reminders of those marks across her bottom.

Georgie opened her mouth to accept his invitation, but at that precise moment she caught sight of two men across the street. They had their backs turned, but she recognized them, of course. Trevor was testing the bend and strength of a beautiful riding crop in a small store that sold Arabian equestrian items, and James was admiring an ornate bolt of fabric.

"What is it?" Khalid asked, turning to look in the direction of what had caught her attention. "Friends of yours?"

She had the faintest memory of Trevor swishing that crop after she had ridden Cyrus through the dangerous night at Mayfield. She remembered the look in Trevor's eyes, wild and predatory. Why hadn't Georgie remembered that look until now? Her eyes swept from the saddlery back to Khalid. She stared at his beautiful, harsh face for a few long moments and then shook her head no. "I'm afraid I do not have an hour to spare, my friend. In fact, I'm traveling with two Englishmen. I think you would enjoy making their acquaintance."

Khalid's smile spread. "Alas. Not one man, but two? I should've known." Georgie smiled in return, appreciating that he would let her refusal pass, something a man with an ego his size was not always wont to do. He snapped his gold watch closed and slipped it back into the invisible pocket from whence it came.

"Always a pleasure to see you, Camden . . . and your stick." With that, Khalid made to turn.

"No, wait—" She reached for him but stopped before actually touching. His curved saber glinted at his waist. "I wish to introduce you—if you are willing."

He nodded. "Very well." They crossed the busy alley, and Trevor, probably sensing Georgie's presence, turned and exited the shop with James. Trevor's smile was so obvious, and Georgie had a moment of panic—*Khalid will know these men love me!* Then the panic turned to warm, sweet honey in her veins—*Khalid will know these men love me.*

"There you are!" Trevor called with sheer delight when he saw Georgie crossing the busy street, accompanied by some spectacularly attired sultan. Red and gold silk *whushed* around the man as he walked; a short, bejeweled sword glinted at his waist; his black hair was slick and gleaming. The man himself was shining like the bright sun.

"How did you find your way to this quarter?" Georgie asked when she reached them, her eyes sparkling with curiosity. It took all the effort Trevor could muster not to reach out and touch some part of her, but he sensed her resistance and knew he had to be less protective in any case. She was dressed in her masculine attire and accompanied by a powerful man—Trevor knew better than to appear besotted! But he shoved his tingling hands into his pockets just the same, lest he give in to the forceful desire to be physically demonstrative with her in public.

"We were bored in that quiet neighborhood where you were trying to keep us safe." Trevor remained casual, or at least he hoped he appeared so. "And James wanted to look for fabrics and such—" He turned to see James more or less salivating over the splendidly attired man to Georgie's right.

"Allow me to introduce you," Georgie said, repressing a laugh. "Khalid Bey Abu al-Dhahab, this is Lord Mayson of Mayfield House, Derbyshire, and Mr. James Rushford. My ... friends ... from England."

Trevor noted Georgie's hesitation—as did Abu al-Dhahab. Trevor watched as the man bowed to James and then to him. There was more to it than a mere greeting: the man had *been* with Georgie—Trevor could feel it in that moment when their eyes met. "Lord Mayson. Mr. Rushford." His low voice was rich with his Arabic accent.

Trevor's feelings were in a tumult. Had Khalid tupped her that very day? Why did the thought make Trevor thrilled rather than jealous? And then a few seconds later, hideously jealous? *Holy hell.* This woman was going to be the bitter end of him.

Trevor collected himself and bowed in similar fashion. "Please call me Trevor. Any friend of George's is a friend of ours." He hadn't meant it to come out like that—as some sort of declaration that she belonged to them—but he didn't regret it either.

Abu al-Dhahab smiled ever so slightly. "I agree. Mr. Camden has much to recommend him, yes? A wonderful mutual acquaintance upon whom we may ... build a future friendship?" Trevor sensed this man knew far more than he let on. In fact, Trevor sensed that Khalid knew the whole truth about the former Lady Georgiana Cambury, now Lady Mayson.

"Indeed," Trevor agreed.

"I hate to be impertinent," James interjected, "but I simply must know where you procured the fabric of your robe."

Khalid looked down with one raised eyebrow. "Fabric?" he asked haughtily.

"Rushford has a large manufacturing business in England," Georgie explained. "Hats."

"Hats?" Khalid asked. He was so deliciously pompous, thought Trevor.

James probably adored that about him too. "Yes!" James exclaimed. "Hats of every imaginable color and shape. And I am quite certain I must make many hats out of this fabric; it will be fabulously popular in England."

Trevor watched in disbelief as James disobeyed every rule of polite society and reached out to rub a fold of the man's satin caftan between two fingers. A flash of the sword in the sunlight had Trevor imagining the *bey* whipping his blade across James's wrist, right there in the middle of the day, and leaving his amputated hand on the sidewalk for his impertinence. Instead, Khalid narrowed his eyes and smiled with a basilisk grin; Trevor had no doubt lesser men had been turned to stone under that gaze.

"My two wives make all my clothes. They are skilled in many arts." He looked down to where James was fingering the rich silk. "Perhaps we will dine together at some point during your visit and you will have the opportunity to compliment them personally."

James released the fabric, and Trevor watched as the two men assessed one another. It looked as though Khalid had initially mistaken James for some flamboyant British fool and was now beginning to see him for all he was. "I would like that *very* much," James replied. His voice was always deep, but when he pitched it just like that, Trevor—and usually anyone else within earshot—was instantly in his thrall. Khalid smiled at the innuendo.

"Would you now?"

"Very much," James repeated.

"Then you must all come for supper," Khalid declared spontaneously.

Georgie gasped and Khalid turned quickly to take her measure. "Unless that is inconvenient, Mr. Camden?"

"No, no. That sounds quite . . . promising."

"In fact, I am going to my palace in the desert in three days' time, if you'd like to escape the city for a few weeks or so?"

Georgie hesitated.

"Unless you have a prior engagement?" Khalid pressed.

"No, I believe we are available," Georgie answered, sounding a bit skittish. Trevor wasn't sure if it was the mention of wives or the fact that Khalid had invited them into what Georgie perhaps considered a private part of her life. She looked quickly at Trevor and James and asked if they agreed. Both nodded. "Fine, thank you," she said to Khalid.

"Excellent." He stared at her, and the word hovered around the four of them. "Let's depart Friday from my house. You recall the address, Camden?" Khalid's voice was low, with an intimacy that was lost on none of them.

"Yes. I remember." She spoke with curt assurance, as if she was nearly insulted at the idea she would forget, but Trevor could tell she was repressing a lovely blush. "What time?"

"Midday." Then Khalid turned to the two men and bowed. "Until we meet again, gentlemen. I'm looking forward to it."

Trevor and James bowed in return.

Khalid gazed languidly at Georgie. "And why don't you bring one of your lovely French gowns? My wives will even out the numbers." He winked at her, sly and knowing, then swept away through the crowd.

All three of them watched in awed silence as the tall, beautiful man strode confidently through the crowded bazaar, his red robes swirling in a wave behind him.

"Well," James said on a sigh. "He is quite dramatic, isn't he?"

Trevor laughed. "That's putting it mildly." He turned to Georgie. "So, is that the friend of your father's you mentioned in the note you left?"

She looked pale and distracted when she faced Trevor. "No." She hesitated and licked her dry bottom lip. "I lied about that." Her voice was thin and far away, as if she wasn't even aware of what she was saying.

The bustle and hum of hundreds of pedestrians receded to a dull throbbing in Trevor's ears. "Why?" he whispered. That was all he could think to ask. "Why did you feel you had to lie to me? To us?"

Her nostrils flared and her eyes glistened. She swiped at her eye as if a bit of dust had flown in. "I don't know—"

Trevor was about to reach for her, but before he could offer a consoling touch, James shoved her shoulder—man to man—none too kindly. "You, George Camden"—he nearly spat the words—"are entirely full of yourself, and I for one have had enough. You tried to keep us shuttered up in that boring neighborhood as if we were a pair of maiden aunts. Look at us, you fool!"

Trevor looked from one to the other. James—*God*, so gorgeous and fearless in his bright, fitted coat with the satin cuffs and his perfectly tailored buckskins and his hair getting too long and a piece across his high forehead. And Georgie—looking as though she hadn't really looked at either of them, maybe ever.

"I'm sorry—" she started.

"You should be!" James interrupted. "You have been allowed—for some reason I cannot fathom—to pigeonhole everyone who crosses your path. From your fabulous mother right on down to poor little Franny the maid, who ran around like your most devoted slave for the past month. *You*! *You* are the one who is limited! *You* are the one who can only see life in black and white." He grabbed at the masculine lapel of her jacket. "Just because you don't know who you are, *George Camden*, doesn't mean the rest of us are suffering under the same misapprehensions—about ourselves, or about you for that matter!"

She turned to look at Trevor, begging with her eyes for understanding or assistance or rescue, he didn't know which. Georgie was on the verge of tears, and Trevor had to dig his nails into his palms to prevent himself from reaching out and comforting her.

"Trevor? Is that what you think, too? Is that still what you think? That I am nothing but a selfish, confused child?"

"Georgie—" Trevor stopped speaking almost as soon as he started, unsure of what he could say that would be true and right for all three of them.

She gasped slightly into the silence, probably realizing that he wasn't going to soothe away the hurt with some placating falsehoods.

"I love you, Georgie," Trevor whispered. "Deeply. Truly. In whole and in part. I don't know what more I can possibly say."

James sighed with an exaggerated exhale and released his hold on her jacket. "Nor should he *have* to say more than that, damn you, Georgie. When the finest man in the land declares his love for you, that should be *enough*. And you *know* you love him, but you're too stubborn to admit it. Because you think it's some sort of sacrifice." James huffed out a bitter laugh. "Well, I can't stand another minute of it. I'll see you both back at the lodgings." With that, James turned away from them and began walking in the direction Khalid had taken.

After a few moments of tense silence, Georgie said in a low voice, "I was confused." But the words were no longer wobbling. When she looked up into Trevor's eyes, he felt his heart drop with a mix of fear and hope. "But I don't want to be confused anymore. Come with me." Georgie pointed her cane in the direction of the equestrian shop, and the two of them went inside.

James walked home at a brisk, angry pace. Damn Georgie and her petty lies! How dare she belittle the authentic gift that Trevor offered—his heart. While Trevor might appear confident in his declarations, James knew what it cost him to be emotionally honest while Georgie waffled. When they had first met at Cambridge, Trevor had been a timid, sheltered boy. He was physically confident— handsome, to be sure, and aware of his masculine beauty—but it had taken months, maybe even years, for him to gain the conviction to express how he really felt.

Trevor's parents had loved him as one loves a precious gem: treasured but rarely touched. Yes, he had grown up next door to Camburton, so it wasn't as though he had not been exposed to free-thinking, free-spirited friends. But it was not in his nature to express himself so openly. The love that Trevor offered was something rare and profound, and Georgie needed to be made to see that, even if it meant tying her to a post until she could accept the truth of her good fortune—the truth of her own feelings.

Slowing his pace somewhat as an enchanting plan began to form in his mind, James turned a corner and realized he was close on the heels of Khalid Abu al-Dhahab. When the Mameluke warrior stopped to look at something in a shop window, James was quickly upon him.

Khalid turned and a slow smile spread across his face. "Well, if it isn't the milliner."

James smiled conspiratorially. "Yes, it is I. And I confess I'm very happy that our paths have crossed so quickly once again."

Khalid looked at James with renewed interest, gazing from his face to his chest and the suddenly throbbing front of his trousers. Smiling ever so slightly at the obvious response, Khalid's eyes swept up to meet James's.

"Is that so? Were you hoping for some sort of secret assignation?"

James narrowed his eyes and assessed the man, an activity that could go on for hours and not yield a single definitive conclusion. "Despite what George—and my physical response—may indicate, I'm inclined to believe you prefer the company of women."

Khalid lifted his chin with what might have been respect. "Very perceptive of you, Mr. Rushford. Indeed, despite Lady Georgiana's impression to the contrary, I do prefer women . . . at this time in my life. But there was a time . . ."

It was James's turn to smile. "Better and better. Shall we walk? I have something rather delicate I'd like to suggest, and perhaps it would be easier to discuss on a quieter lane or in a nearby park."

"Very well," Khalid agreed. "Come with me, this way." He led them toward what looked like a dead end, but eventually opened into a very narrow alleyway, which then opened onto a beautiful private garden. "What do you have in mind?" Khalid asked, gesturing for James to sit down on one of the stone benches that overlooked the small, burbling fountain in the middle of the shady courtyard.

"Here is what I propose . . ."

A few hours later, James was waiting for Trevor and Georgie in the shadowy living room on the top floor of their lodgings. Khalid had not only agreed to James's plan, he had seemed downright pleased with the whole undertaking. Their time at his palace near the oasis of Faiyum promised to be one that was both erotic and, if James was correct, emotionally transformative for Georgie.

Until Lady Georgiana Mayson came to realize that her life no longer needed to be an either/or predicament, she would never be able to move forward. Khalid had assured James that his wives would be more than amenable to their parts in the plan. Now the only thing that remained was to lure Georgie into their trap.

"What are you doing over there in the shadows?" Georgie asked when she flew into the room and then halted when she caught sight of James. Obviously she and Trevor had come to some renewed balance of power after James had left them on the busy street outside the leather goods shop. Trevor would forgive her anything, so it wasn't really a balance of power, thought James cynically.

Trevor came in behind Georgie, holding a neatly wrapped package, which he set down on a side table. "Yes, James, what in the world are you doing, sitting in here in the gloaming?"

James took a sip of the tea that he was coming to love—mentally adding it the list of items he would transport back to Derbyshire and enjoy for the rest of his life—then set the etched-gold glass on the ornate round table in front of him.

"I was just enjoying the passage of time as the sun set over the rooftops. It's much easier to see the subtle colors with the lanterns unlit inside."

The other two turned to look out at the splendid view. Then Georgie turned back to face James.

"I believe I owe you an apology, James." Georgie tugged off her fitted jacket and tossed it across a carved wooden chair near the door she had entered. She rolled up her sleeves as she crossed the dim room. "You were quite right the other day, to warn me off hurting Trevor, or myself for that matter." She knelt in front of where James sat, resting her hands on his thighs and then spreading his legs to make room for herself between them.

His body betrayed him immediately. His cock began to throb, and he had to stop himself before lifting his hips involuntarily closer to her wandering fingers. Her eyelids lowered slightly, and the corner of her mouth quirked up.

"Maybe you're not so angry with me after all?" Her hands slid up his thighs, nearly touching his swelling cock, only to withdraw back down toward his knees.

"Yes," he said, doing his best to keep his voice, if not stern, at least even, "I am still angry with you . . . but my body appears to want to forgive you."

She tightened her grip and massaged his thigh muscles through the taut fabric of his trousers. "Well then," she said, "perhaps if I can convince your body to forgive me, your heart will catch up eventually?"

He kept his hands resting on either side of his hips, flat against the fabric of the sofa, not wanting to encourage her, not wanting to give in. But so very much wanting to give in. "Damn you, Georgie Cambury."

"I am Lady Georgiana Mayson now," she said haughtily, lifting her chin and somehow staring down her nose at him even though she was kneeling beneath him. "And forever," she added with unfamiliar gravity. She turned quickly to look at Trevor, and it was impossible for James to remain angry after seeing the understanding and love that passed between them. Georgie turned back to face James and said, "You see? If Trevor can forgive me, so should you."

He could see it, that Georgie must have apologized to Trevor while they'd been in the equestrian shop, and something had been resolved between them. James couldn't resist that dreamy look in Trevor's eyes from across the room, the look that silently begged James to forgive her everything.

By this point, his cock was tenting the front of his trousers, and she was rubbing closer and closer but never touching the fabric there.

"I am on my knees," she said with complete sincerity. "Not that I don't enjoy being on my knees," she added with mischief, but then let her face return to seriousness. "But I mean it, James. It was wrong of me to lie in that silly note this morning, but more importantly it was wrong of me to think that I needed to lie to you and Trevor. I shan't lie to cover up who I really am. We will simply enjoy the time that's left to us here in Egypt . . . " She faltered.

Good, he thought. Perhaps the limited time left to them was no longer striking her as merely charming and insouciant. Quite right she should start to think of her future beyond the upcoming five minutes. Even so, he might as well let Georgie cling to that live-for-now delusion a while longer.

"Well, I suppose if you are feeling very apologetic," James said, spreading his palms in a gesture of surrender. "This might suffice . . . as a fair start to making amends." He lifted his hips slightly, and she leaned forward and exhaled hot breath through the fabric as her mouth surrounded his cock.

Trevor had taken a seat near the window, where the setting sun cast him in an elegant aura of gleaming golds and burnished coppers. Colors fit for a prince, thought James. For that was what Trevor was, and it was up to James to make sure Georgie knew it and treasured their love for the rest of her life. Not as some *aspect* of her life—like her penchant for horses or men's clothing—but the central, driving force of her existence.

"Very well," James said with a hint of disdain as she unbuttoned his trousers and his cock sprang free. "My body accepts your apology."

Georgie hummed her pleasure, taking him deep and firm. James could see how the sounds she made created a nearly instantaneous response across the room. Trevor had unbuttoned his fall and grabbed hold of his cock while he watched Georgie *apologize* to James. *Yes,* thought James, *this is quite as it should be.* "Come over here," James said, motioning for Trevor to join him.

Chapter 15

Georgie's nerves were ragged, despite all her efforts to remain carefree and buoyant. Now that a few days had passed and they were on their way out of the city to stay at Khalid's horse farm in Faiyum, Georgie was becoming suspicious. James had let her off far too easily. She had been so grateful at the time, because what better way to apologize for her treachery than by doing something she enjoyed in any case? But something about his uncharacteristically hasty forgiveness was not sitting well with her.

The three of them were tucked inside one of Khalid's spectacular carriages, and Georgie was nearly convinced that, far from having forgiven her, James was luring her into some new trap. He had been too agreeable over the past few days, never making any of those pointed remarks about their future or about her inadequate commitment to or appreciation of their communal relationship.

Even so, she couldn't bear to bring it up, mostly because she was beginning to believe he was right. The truth remained that, despite all of her physical courage, Georgie had never really learned to ask for what she wanted. Or thought she deserved it. Or even really understood what it meant to declare her love, to commit emotionally.

She and Trevor and James had played all sorts of sexual games—and she had always clung to the idea that it was only playing, like they were playing at lovemaking rather than actually making love. Yet the calm determination that had settled over James during the carriage ride out of the city seemed to say, *Playtime is over.*

As the bustle and chaos of the city began to fade and the desert spread out around them, Georgie felt the pressure ease somewhat. She had always enjoyed cities in doses—whether it was Madrid or London or Cairo—but she never felt completely comfortable in her own skin until she had wide-open spaces around her. She had a brief recollection of how glorious she'd felt riding Cyrus around Mayfield in the fall. No matter how she tried to sully the memory with some imposed idea that her time there had been stuffy or confining, she couldn't do it.

Georgie pulled back the window flap and realized all of a sudden how much she missed her brother. Archie had always been the yin to her yang, the day to her night. What he'd said in the carriage before walking her into St. George's kept circling around her, in much the same way the words James had said when they signed the guest register in Cairo continued to buzz around her brain.

Was it really that simple? Was it really possible that the burden was on *her* to accept the love of these two men? She let the flap drop back into place, and her gaze tripped over James and Trevor. They were reading quietly—something she'd never been able to accomplish while in motion—and both men looked up with sweet smiles, then returned to their books. Her heart sped up, as it always did lately when either of them even glanced her way.

She looked down at her beautiful dress and how her hands rested in her lap. There was no way she could sustain this carpe diem levity for much longer. A few months ago, when she had first agreed to this farcical marriage, she never could have foreseen what an emotional maelstrom it would turn out to be. Yet here she was, unable to look at either man without feeling a pounding in her heart and a throbbing at the apex of her thighs. The physical attraction among the three of them made her feel keenly alive; the emotional attraction felt like it was going to be the death of her.

Georgie must've dozed off. The carriage came to a gentle stop in the bright courtyard of Khalid's estate. Georgie stretched her arms and opened her eyes to see James and Trevor in a passionate kiss. James pulled away slowly, then turned to face her. "Looks like we've arrived, Georgie. Did you have a nice rest?"

Georgia let her hands drop into her lap as she heard the bustle of unpacking and the sounds of luggage being removed from the carriage. "Why yes, thank you, I feel delightfully refreshed." She tried not to let her eyes widen when she noticed Trevor was smiling his I-just-came smile as he buttoned up his trousers. She glanced quickly away, but James met her eyes and licked the corner of his mouth with a provocative swipe.

"You should know better than to fall asleep during a carriage ride, my dear," James added wickedly.

She watched as the two men exited the carriage to step on the immaculate raked gravel that had been baked in the desert sun to golden pale perfection. Georgie took a deep breath and, as usual lately, tried to stuff down the whirl of emotions and desires that clouded her brain. After one more quiet moment, she too stepped from the carriage into the enchanted world of the brilliant oasis.

After traveling out of the city and through the desert for several hours, it was a magical treat to be surrounded by lush date palms and rioting exotic flowers. Georgie turned her attention from the verdant plants toward the ornately carved front door, which swung open as Khalid emerged in a swirling white caftan.

Having done as Khalid requested, Georgie sported one of her more alluring gowns. When he caught sight of her, his eyes flashed greedily, and she felt a girlish blush rise up her exposed chest and neck. Had he really known she was a woman all along? He approached her quickly and then slowed when he was a few feet away. He took one of her hands and kissed it lightly on her knuckle. She felt a shiver of desire run straight up her arm.

"*Lady* Mayson, is it?"

She curtsied formally and dipped her gaze, the perfect British lady. "Yes, sir. Lady Georgiana Mayson, at your service."

Khalid reared back, lifting his chin and laughing up at the flawless blue sky. "A lady is *never* at a man's service, m'lady, and you mustn't forget it. It is the great boon of your sex. We are your devoted slaves." He squeezed her hand with an encouraging grip, then let go and turned to Trevor and James. The three men shook hands and laughed amiably, as if they were old friends. Georgie was beginning to feel faint, not from the heat or the dress or her strange surroundings, but from the heady sensation, terrifying really, that she had never been fooling anyone but herself.

"Come! Come! It is far too hot in the noonday sun. Let us eat and then ride out for a few hours. I have many wonderful things planned for your visit." Georgie wasn't certain, but she thought she saw Khalid slip James a conspiring look when he said those last few words.

They spent the afternoon as Khalid promised, eating a splendid lunch of Mediterranean specialties: grape leaves, spicy grains, warm thin breads, and tangy yogurts. His two wives floated around the four of them as they ate, replenishing their food, refilling glasses of cool water scented with cucumber, or just dipping their chins slightly with mysterious smiles in their charcoal eyes. Khalid's wives, Ansi and Oni, were each beautiful in their ways: Ansi, slightly older, had a wisdom and depth in her expression that suited her fuller, rounded shape; Oni, slightly younger and a bit taller, had more mischief to her. Both women smiled at Georgie, and toward the end of the meal, they even rested casual hands on Georgie's shoulder or arm as they offered seconds or cleared a plate. Again, Georgie felt as though everyone was privy to a secret and she was not.

Khalid's stables were splendid. He told of how an ambitious French diplomat had built the riding rings and stables to house his extensive bloodline.

"Unfortunately for him—and fortunately for me—we were successful in evicting yet another foreign invader from our beautiful Egyptian homeland." All of them had spoken at length over lunch about the current state of affairs among Britain and Egypt, Turkey and France. There seemed to be far too many players at the table and not nearly enough chips for everyone to place their bets.

Ultimately, Khalid had finished the discussion with an offhand remark that there was no need to speak of dirty politics while they were enjoying such lovely company. He had raised his glass to Georgie and then caressed Oni's cheek before taking a sip of his strong coffee. His wives had joined them in the salon after lunch, and they were resting languidly on either side of him. James and Trevor followed suit, raising their glasses in Georgie's direction, "To beauty." And the silly toast made her blush furiously.

How was it she could speak about politics or history or horses as their equals—which she had in fact done for the past few hours—but the merest compliment about her appearance made her feel like a little schoolgirl? While society at large might attempt to depict femininity as a form of weakness, no one in this room had ever done so—except perhaps Georgie herself.

That stark realization was far from comforting.

The afternoon ride proved to be a wonderful antidote to all of that blushing and confusion. She welcomed the breakneck pace and the hot wind against her face, relished the unique experience of riding in the desert. Compliments about her femininity had made Georgie feel loose and dreamy. Riding hard made her feel the familiar comfort of rigid control. Was this really something she was willing to give up? Was anyone even asking her to choose one over the other?

When they returned in the late afternoon, all four of them covered in dust and grit, Georgie had imagined she would wash up, perhaps take a brief nap, and meet them again for supper. Apparently that was not the plan.

After handing off their horses to the grooms, the four of them entered the cool stone house and were met by Khalid's pretty wives. After silent instruction from Khalid, the two women gestured for Georgie to join them in another part of the large house.

Georgie looked over her shoulder as she was being led away, and Khalid called out with a taunting wink, "They will help you . . . prepare."

She considered resisting. It wouldn't have been too hard to tear her hands away from the light hold the women had upon her. Instead, she gave herself over to the present and followed them into the private sanctum of this desert palace.

Georgie turned to Ansi, the older woman to her right, and spoke in Arabic. "Is Khalid making you do this?"

Ansi looked up. Her eyes were intelligent and bright, a golden brown that connected with Georgie's and caused something quick, unexpected, and hot to snap between them.

"I do not understand what you mean by *making*? He said it would please him. He knew it would please us. He thought it would please you. So everyone is pleased. Are you not pleased?"

George furrowed her brow, and the woman paused at a turning in the narrow hall. Ansi reached up with her satiny soft fingertip and touched the tense skin on Georgie's forehead.

"Why do you worry so? Do your men not please you?"

Georgie didn't know what to say to this woman, this woman who was such a domesticated *woman*. A woman who lived to serve and please her husband, her master. A woman, Georgie had to admit, who seemed to find deep comfort and self-respect in the act of pleasing her beloved.

"They do please me, very much," Georgie said. It was true, but it was also something Georgie felt she had to say to get Ansi to stop looking at her with that penetrating, too-knowing stare. Georgie smiled and thought of reaching up to move the woman's hand away from her face, but for some reason she hesitated.

In that moment of hesitation, the woman's eyes locked with Georgie's. Ansi let her finger trail down the center of George's face, down the ridge of her nose to the tender skin just above her lip, and then touch the sensitive edge of Georgie's mouth.

Georgie gasped at the unfamiliar burst of sexual response that accompanied the touch. "You say the words, but I do not know if you are able to feel them." Ansi leaned in and kissed Georgie lightly on the lips. "We will help you feel the truth of them."

They turned and continued down another hall, Georgie's lips and sex tingling in anticipation, until they came to an ornately carved, dark wood door. Two guards stood sentry, one on either side. Oni, on Georgie's left, smiled and motioned to one of the guards, who then pulled open the door to allow them entrance. What Georgie saw beguiled her completely.

Trevor watched from behind the carved wooden screen as Georgie entered the spectacular bathing garden. Lush plants and small waterfalls fed into a sumptuously tiled pool in the center of the space, above which the roof was open to the early evening sky. Around the perimeter of the chamber, there were smaller baths and discreet daybeds and sitting areas. Khalid quietly explained that it was based on an ancient Roman bath with pools of varying temperatures.

The door shut behind the three women, and Trevor felt a slam of erotic awareness when both of Khalid's wives removed their colorful embroidered robes with one fluid motion to reveal their supple bodies. Ansi and Oni helped each other undo their ornate hairstyles until they were both naked, with their long black hair flowing to the middle of their backs.

"They're quite lovely, aren't they?" Khalid whispered with a tender pride. "I do not understand your confining infidel ways. If you love, and provide for the people you love, what is the sin in loving two or more people at once?"

Trevor shook his head. "I do not believe it is a sin." He glanced at James and smiled. James nodded once and turned his attention back to the women, as did Trevor.

Georgie looked awkward and out of place in her dusty riding habit. She wasn't far from where Trevor and the men sat on the large daybeds behind the screen, but the combination of burbling water and rustling leaves concealed any noise they might make.

Trevor could tell Georgie was exquisitely vulnerable; he felt his body respond in kind, with every touch and breath of hers. When Khalid's younger wife, Oni, unbuttoned Georgie's fitted jacket, slid it off her body, and then removed her shirt to reveal her rigid corset, Trevor gasped when Georgie did.

How James had ever conjured up this vision of a gentle, sensual seduction, how he knew it was exactly what Georgie needed to finally embrace her *entire* self, to strike down the walls she had constructed over a lifetime of willful secrecy and self-doubt, Trevor didn't know, but he would be forever grateful. By allowing these women to glorify her body in its most natural state, Trevor was beginning to believe that Georgie would finally come to see herself in much the same way as he already did: whole. And not just physically whole, but emotionally whole. Complete.

Ever since they were children together, Georgie had never lacked confidence, but all the confidence in the world meant nothing if Georgie was unable to love all the parts of who she was. Trevor's heart clenched when he realized what it must be costing her to finally submit to the most fundamental tenderness—and it was an incredible defeat to witness.

Georgie was beginning to lose all of her bearings, while at the same time experiencing a heightened sense of where she was and what she was feeling—a heightened sense of who she was. Oni's hands were like silky ropes that coiled around her, soothing her and tempering her as she removed her clothes. Simultaneously, a piercing sexual awareness throbbed at the apex of her thighs, in her heavy breasts, low in her belly, in the tips of her fingers, on her lips, along her spine.

It wasn't a sexual attraction to Oni or Ansi, necessarily, but an awakening within herself, a slow, physical arousal that proved in the most elemental way that tenderness and passion, love and lust could all coexist within her. Oni and Ansi's ministrations communicated without speaking: one did not need to be hard to be strong; one did not need to be alone to be free.

The sweet gentleness of it all was akin to madness—the soft tracery of Ansi's fingers trailing up her arms and the warmth of Oni's breath at her ear as she spoke soft poetry in Arabic, lulling Georgie into the magic of her own physical and spiritual existence. She saw evening stars above her and smelled beautiful oils, and her skin began to spark and tingle all over.

Georgie started to tremble and her body overtook her mind. She somehow sensed that Trevor and James were close by, watching her protectively from behind those shadowy leaves or one of the mysterious perforated walls. She felt terrified and safe. For the first time in her life, she was absolutely willing to accept whatever came.

Perhaps she was even willing to accept herself.

Trevor felt it in his spine when Georgie began to tremble. Ansi was comforting her, stroking her arms and neck with soft passes, saying gentle words in Arabic, which Trevor could not understand. Oni was now kneeling on the tile floor, removing George's riding boots, one and then the other. After she set them aside, Oni rose on her knees and undid the buttons of Georgie's riding breeches.

While Oni worked on the trousers, Ansi began to remove Georgie's corset. Every layer of clothing was another layer of protection that left Georgie looking desperately exposed.

Georgie cried out when Ansi had finished with the corset and released her full breasts. Letting her lips trail after her fingertips, Ansi finally took one of Georgie's nipples into her mouth. Trevor had never seen anything so excruciatingly gentle. And oh God, how he felt for Georgie. How she must crave the whip or cane to save her from that slow, honeyed torture.

He remembered his own introduction to that kind of tender anguish. When he'd first fallen in love with James, he remembered how desperately he had wanted to slam into James, or to be crashed into by him. Over time, James had taught him what these women were teaching Georgie: that tenderness and intimacy were sometimes far more powerful than even the most violent intercourse.

Ansi finished with the left breast, kissing it gently, swirling her tongue sweetly, never biting or tugging, then did the same to Georgie's other breast. All the while her fingertips stroked Georgie with delicate, feathery passes. Oni left the room for a few minutes and returned with a tray that held an earthenware basin, several sea sponges, and a selection of colorful glass vials.

Leading Georgie over to a large stone table that was right in front of where the men were sitting, Ansi guided Georgie into place. She set her down so Georgie lay on her back. Trevor could hear James's breath had also hitched.

In that position, she was exactly like every vestal virgin on every pagan altar in every ancient rite. Her chest rose and fell as if she were in the midst of a great battle. Tears streamed down her face, disappearing into her short blonde hair.

Ansi smoothed her hands all over Georgie's body with ample amounts of a scented oil. She palmed her legs, massaged her hips, caressed her breasts, and tenderly leaned down near her face to kiss her lightly on the lips. George's cry rose from somewhere deep and desperate inside her. Her hips jerked up, her body so blatantly certain about what it wanted, and her mind still far behind, crying and confused.

Then Oni dipped a sponge into the basin and began the ceremonial bath. The scent of lavender and myrrh and other fragrances Trevor didn't recognize began to waft through the room. Slowly and methodically, the two women dipped the sponges in the warm, scented water and cleansed every inch of Georgie's body. From her fingertips, along the strong, lean muscles of her arms, then lifting her arms to let the water and the smooth texture of the sponge trail across the sensitive skin under her arms.

The slab of marble where she lay was long and wide, smooth from many centuries of use. Even with her hands extended above her head, the table still had ample room for Georgie's long frame. The two Egyptian women continued to wash her, singing a low and beautiful melody, sultry and sensual.

By this point, Georgie's sobbing had reached a higher pitch. Her hips were rocking in a desperate imitation of lovemaking, and Trevor leaned forward to get up from his seat and go to her. He couldn't bear it any longer.

Before he could stand, James and Khalid each placed one strong hand on either of his shoulders.

"Not yet," James whispered. "Wait for her to call out for you."

Khalid let go of Trevor's shoulder, but James pulled Trevor's face to his and kissed him with deep, passionate thrusts of his tongue. Trevor moaned into the kiss and heard an echoing moan through the grillwork that separated him from Georgie. They were connected even now—she must feel it.

She must know that he was there watching her—on some deep, primitive level, she must know.

James finally released his face after leaning in for one last, quick kiss. James stared into his eyes, silently checking to make sure he was well. He nodded. James smiled and released him. When Trevor turned his attention back to Georgie, she was writhing and twisting in desperate pleasure.

When they had finished bathing Georgie, Ansi set down her sponge and picked up one of the vials. She removed the glass stopper and smelled the contents, then smiled and tipped a bit of the oil onto her fingertip. The fragrance obviously evoked some happy memory, as Ansi's eyes drifted closed when she brought her fingertip to her own sex. Khalid exhaled as well, obviously recalling the same shared experience.

Ansi held the vial near Georgie's nose to get her attention. Georgie's eyes flew open and her back arched. Her head began to swing from side to side. Whatever Ansi was whispering to her had cast some sort of invisible spell upon Georgie. The way her wrists and ankles remained against the wet marble, it looked as though invisible shackles were pinning them to the surface. In truth, Georgie was perfectly free to get up and walk away any moment she chose.

Georgie's cry pierced the evening air. The sun had set, and Trevor could see the early evening stars beginning to fill the sky above this magical place, this place where Georgie would finally release all of the knots and snares with which she had hindered herself her entire life.

James held on to Trevor's hand, both to anchor himself to the moment and to prevent Trevor from crashing through the thin, delicately carved wooden screen that separated them from the woman they loved. Georgie's suffering was exquisite. James had never realized he could find so much pleasure in someone else's pain—to actually feel joy while this beautiful creature writhed and struggled only a few feet away.

"What is the oil?" James asked in a low whisper.

"It's a very powerful camphor —" Khalid's quiet explanation about its highly arousing effect was interrupted by another shriek from Georgie. Ansi had traced the oil around Georgie's nipples and lips and had then passed the maroon glass vial to Oni, who waited for Ansi's signal to apply it to Georgie's pussy.

"No!" Georgie cried.

Ansi smiled and spoke in soothing Arabic.

"She's asking Georgie to confess," Khalid translated softly, "to declare her love for you."

James watched as Georgie fought it, as she fought those invisible restraints at her wrists and her ankles, as she fought a lifetime of repressing her own complex desires, of trying to parse them instead of weave them together.

Ansi continued speaking to her in that soothing, persistent way.

"No!" Georgie cried out again.

"Now," Khalid whispered, "Ansi is telling her she will never be free until she is free of her stubbornness."

Babbling in rapid Arabic, Georgie was obviously pleading with Ansi, trying to negotiate some way out of her fate. Ansi merely shook her head and smiled at Georgie, then looked down toward Oni and motioned for her to proceed.

Georgie's wail sounded like some ancient cry, a desperate plea to the vacant, soulless universe. James watched her back arch and her neck tense, her fists ball above her head, her arms and legs stretching tight. She held on like that as Oni continued applying the devilish oil, and James watched, proud, as Georgie rode wave after wave of pain and pleasure, her face beginning to take on an almost trancelike quality.

James now recognized the word that Ansi was repeating over and over. *Confess confess confess.*

When Oni was satisfied with the amount of oil she had applied to Georgie's sex, she handed the glass vial back to Ansi without taking her attention away from Georgie's swollen pussy. The beautiful young woman smiled as she leaned in and let her tongue pass gently over Georgie's clit.

The dam broke.

"Trevor! James! *Bahebbuku*!"

"She says she loves you," Khalid whispered.

Georgie's body was rigid with pleasure—her hands flexing open, her breasts heavy and full, her thighs quivering—unable to hold back her crushing release. Oni worked her mouth against Georgie's pussy with an endless sweep of those tender kisses and licks, driving her higher and higher toward ecstasy until she exploded with it.

Ansi leaned down and kissed Georgie on the lips. James would never forget that kiss: Georgie starving, desperate for it, for that connection to humanity she had denied herself for so long. Eventually, Ansi pulled away slowly from the kiss, caressing Georgie's forehead and smoothing her hair away from her face. Georgie's eyes were glassy and beautiful, glowing in the starlight as James watched the tension in her body subside.

Oni finished licking Georgie's pussy, and then she too moved to the top end of the table. She stood across from Ansi, also smoothing George's neck and shoulders to help her calm.

Khalid spoke softly, jarring James from his complete absorption with Georgie and her explosive release. "I believe I'm going to take my wives to my private chamber now," Khalid said. "I will leave you both to enjoy the baths at your leisure with your wife." Khalid imitated a trilling bird song, and his wives looked at one another and smiled.

Georgie was far from having recovered her faculties and barely noticed when the two women helped her move—groggy and dreamlike—over to one of the satin beds alongside the far wall. They pulled a silk sheet over her, and each of them kissed her on the lips.

James watched the women turn to leave, and then he and Trevor got up to follow Khalid. His wives had already passed through another door when Khalid opened a secret door in the carved grillwork screen. He gestured for James and Trevor to enter the baths and smiled, but he did not join them. "Enjoy."

Khalid pulled the door shut behind them, and Trevor and James began removing their clothes immediately. Once they were undressed—both of them hard and eager to be with Georgie and one another—they crossed the stone floor and approached the daybed where she lay.

Georgie's face was blissful. Without turning to see them, she said, "James and Trevor?" The words came out on a sigh of relief as she rolled to face them. "Is it really you?" Her beautiful amber eyes fluttered slightly, but her words were surprisingly clear. "I wanted you so desperately. Could you hear me? You were all I wanted." Her voice was dreamy and far away, but no less honest for it.

"We heard you, love," James said, reaching out to touch the edge of her lips. She grabbed his hand and began kissing the tip of each finger, then his palm and his wrist.

"And you came for me . . . " Her voice was filled with blessed gratitude. No more questioning or skepticism of the joy which had fallen in her path, thought James.

"We will always come for you, Georgie." Trevor's voice was thick with emotion. "Please say you will stay with us, really stay."

She moved onto her side to make room for both men on the wide bed. Trevor climbed over her and stretched out against her back, with the pillows against the wall behind him. James faced her, naked and aroused. All three of them were pressed against each other, melding into one another.

"We don't want to imprison you, Georgie. We want to love you." James leaned in and kissed her lips. Trevor's fingers were there, touching both James and Georgie. "Can you see that now? Can you feel it?"

Her eyes gleamed, and a few tears had left streaks down her cheek. "I can feel it now," she whispered on a choked breath. "I can feel everything. I can feel how much I love you. Can you feel it?" She twisted to face Trevor, to include him in her declaration. "I love you. I believe we have always loved each other."

Trevor kissed her temple. "Yes, my love, I believe we always have. And you will return to England with us?"

"I will go wherever you are," she whispered, as if in awe of her own words. "It all feels so obvious now, doesn't it?" She looked back at James with wide, curious eyes. "So obvious how much I love you?"

"Yes, love. It seems very obvious now," James agreed, kissing the turn of her cheek and the edge of her jaw.

"But I hope we will return to this place as well." She stretched and reached behind her to rest her hand at the back of Trevor's neck. "Don't you, darling?" She turned her head slightly so Trevor could see she was addressing him. "Don't you want to return to this magical place that freed me, freed my soul?" She kissed Trevor, then turned and kissed James again, while her hips pushed back against Trevor with burgeoning need.

"Yes, my love," Trevor whispered close to her ear, where James could also hear. "We will always come back to visit the wonderful place that finally set you free. We will go anywhere we please. Together."

Epilogue

September 1811
Mayfield House, Derbyshire

Georgiana, Lady Mayson stood in the dim corridor and tried to catch her breath. She'd been in any number of scrapes over the course of the past year—contending with an unexpected marriage that landed her not one, but two husbands; falling in love against her will, against her reason, and even against her character.

She smiled and took another deep breath, forcing herself to calm after running from the main house. If she had survived the wicked sorcery of Khalid's two wives, she could certainly handle a bit of intimacy between the two beasts in the room behind her.

She pushed open the stable door and saw Cyrus and Bathsheba rearing back and preparing to attack each other in the wide central section of the building.

"That is quite enough!" Georgie called out. Her voice settled them down somewhat, but they both stamped their feet and laid their ears back as flat as they could to show the extent of their displeasure. "I see you," Georgie added more calmly.

Three grooms were hovering near the far wall, obviously terrified of the large, unpredictable Arabian horses. Bathsheba's eyes went wide and white, and Georgie watched in amazement as the mare's stomach rolled and turned, as if an earthquake were preparing to take place inside her huge belly.

"We cannot wait any longer for Lord Mayson's return," Georgie explained. "You there." She pointed at the new youngster who'd just started working at Mayfield. "Go find Mr. Rushford—I believe he's down at the Sackett cottage—and tell him the foal is about to come and I'll need his help."

"Yes, m'lady." The boy sidled past Bathsheba and Cyrus, then broke into a fast run when he was clear of them.

"What's to be done about Cyrus, Lady Mayson?" the head groom asked. "None of us can even touch him without a ruckus."

She turned to look at the big brute. He lifted his long black head and stared down at her, as if to say he would not be doing her bidding anytime soon. He only answered to one master now, and that was Trevor. "I know, I know," she said to him in a soothing tone, slipping him a bit of apple she'd pilfered from the pie Mrs. Daley was making in the kitchen. "He's coming back soon. We all miss him."

Bathsheba's eyes widened again, and she turned to enter her stall. The men had put in fresh hay and water, and the poor mare looked like she was ready to deliver the foal within minutes. Cyrus tried to get close to her again, and she kicked up one of her rear hooves and nearly got him in the jaw, whipping her head around and showing the stallion her teeth. Even the lord of all horses he surveyed appeared to be properly humbled by the poor mare's obvious discomfort and ire. Bathsheba collapsed into her stall with a grateful exhale through her flared nostrils, her oversize body resting in the hay bed with her legs outstretched.

"*Where is she?*" Trevor's unexpected voice whipped straight up Georgie's spine; she shut her eyes briefly and let herself feel the thrill of it. He sounded stern, and his temper was being let loose on one of the poor stable boys.

"She's just there, m'lord." The boy pointed in her direction.

"Damn it, Georgie! I told you not to go into the stalls until I got here. It's too dangerous." Trevor tossed his hat to one of the grooms and pulled off his coat and tossed that as well. She felt his approach like fire licking at her palms. He'd been in London for six long days, and she and James had been missing him like mad. They'd made do with one another, of course, but none of them felt whole unless all three of them were together.

Trevor rolled up his sleeves as he strode across the remaining few yards that separated them. Without losing his pace, he kissed Georgie hard on the lips, then turned to look at Bathsheba. Having finished with his sleeves, shoving them up above his elbows, he fisted his hands on his hips and took stock of the situation. "She's close."

Georgie nodded, touching her lips lightly. God, how she loved this man—beyond reason, beyond anything. What a fool she'd been to put off their joy those first few months.

"Are you all right?" He had turned from Bathsheba to give Georgie a similar once-over. His eyes—those green-gold shards of his that saw everything about her, had always seen right through her—were taking her measure. A slow smile spread across his beautiful face. "You missed me," he stated with a hint of masculine pride.

Yes, he saw that too.

Her fingertip was still tracing the edge of her lip, and she nodded slowly.

"Come here." He pulled her into his arms, and when his lips touched hers, tender and full of promise, she felt her insides begin to settle back into place. "Where's James?" he whispered against her lips, so the grooms couldn't hear.

"On his way . . ." she murmured between more kisses, pressing the length of her body against his, loving the familiar strength and warmth that made her feel anchored and free all at once.

"Is everything all right?" James called down the length of the stable.

Trevor turned to see him, and Georgie felt it, that magical connection that all three of them shared. As James walked toward them, Trevor's arm gripped tighter around Georgie's waist, and she reached out for James with her free hand.

"We will take care of the mare and foal from here on out, gentleman," Trevor said, dismissing the grooms. "Thank you for standing by until we arrived."

The grooms shuffled off to their various quarters. James looked over his shoulder to make sure all of them were out of sight, then turned and dug his fingers into Trevor's hair at the base of his skull and pulled his lips into a kiss.

Georgie let her cheek rest against Trevor's heart and melted into the blissful feeling of James snaking his arm around her waist as well. When the three of them were together like this, in one another's arms, Georgie knew peace at last.

AUTHOR'S ote

There are notes upon notes upon notes to do with this little book! Early on, I envisioned Georgie as a sexually charged homage to the heroine in Judith McNaught's *Whitney, My Love*. Whitney is what's commonly known—in romance community lingo—as an Unlikable Heroine. For better or worse, I tend to adore Unlikable Heroines. They can be thorny or selfish or petulant or blind to their own best interests, but they're also strivers, characters who are eager to be out in the world—they want to *live*! It turns out they are also very hard to write. Georgie was *difficult* in almost every conceivable way—her sexual preferences, her emotional hurdles, how others saw her, how she saw herself. Then, once I got all that internal stuff sorted (sort of), I had to sort out how she was going to fit—however uncomfortably for her—into a plausible historical context. Research commenced!

First off, it was necessary to find (at least one . . . please at least one) example of a woman who was able to wield Georgie's financial independence in the face of existing coverture laws. Jackpot—thank you for existing, Harriot Mellon (1777–1837). Georgie's ability to negotiate for her own financial freedom prior to her marriage (aka Regency Reimagined Prenup) was inspired by the scintillating actress who married Thomas Coutts, of Coutts Bank, in 1815. Upon his death in 1822, he left her 750,000 GB pounds, equivalent to 70 million US dollars today. In 1827, Mellon then married the Duke of St. Albans (who happened to be twenty-three years younger than she was—*cough*—go Harriot!), and she was able to put her Coutts inheritance into a trust over which she retained complete authority.

I also wanted to weave in a few nods to another favorite Old Skool romance, Bertrice Small's *Skye O'Malley*—hence the midnight-at-the-oasis sheikh element. Again, history provided some precedents with women like Lady Mary Wortley Montagu and Lady Hester Stanhope, who spent much of their lives traveling in and writing about the Middle East.

As always, I spent many happy hours with my great, dear friend, the *Oxford English Dictionary*, getting swept away by countless #oldwords searches. Yes, *come* was used as a verb as far back as 1650 to indicate orgasm; *rogering* has been around since 1788; *tup* since 1549; *waffle* meant "waver" starting in 1803; and *slewed* denoted drunk as of 1801.

All of that said, none of this is real! I know, shocking. This is first and foremost a wild tale that's intended to divert and amuse and titillate and entertain. So, while I loved researching and weaving in some wonderful historical elements, I mostly hope you simply enjoyed the characters and their story. Thank you for reading!

Explore more of the *Regency Reimagined* universe at
riptidepublishing.com/titles/universe/regency-reimagined

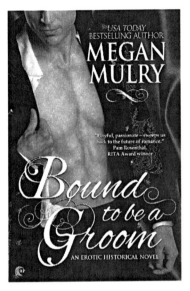

Dear Reader,

Thank you for reading Megan Mulry's *Bound with Passion*!

We know your time is precious and you have many, many entertainment options, so it means a lot that you've chosen to spend your time reading. We really hope you enjoyed it.

We'd be honored if you'd consider posting a review—good or bad—on sites like **Amazon, Barnes & Noble, Kobo, Goodreads, Twitter, Facebook, Tumblr,** and your blog or website. We'd also be honored if you told your friends and family about this book. Word of mouth is a book's lifeblood!

For more information on upcoming releases, author interviews, blog tours, contests, giveaways, and more, please sign up for our weekly, spam-free newsletter and visit us around the web:

> **Newsletter:** tinyurl.com/RiptideSignup
> **Twitter:** twitter.com/RiptideBooks
> **Facebook:** facebook.com/RiptidePublishing
> **Goodreads:** tinyurl.com/RiptideOnGoodreads
> **Tumblr:** riptidepublishing.tumblr.com

Thank you so much for Reading the Rainbow!

RiptidePublishing.com

Acknowledgments

Thank you so much to everyone at Riptide—Sarah, Del, Rachel, Alex, Amelia, Kelly, and L.C.—I couldn't have done this without you!

ALSO BY
Megan Mulry

Regency Reimagined
Bound to Be a Bride
Bound to Be a Groom
Bound with Love
Bound with Honor

Historical
The Wallflowers

Contemporary
A Royal Pain
If the Shoe Fits
In Love Again
R is for Rebel
Roulette

ABOUT THE  Author

Megan Mulry writes sexy, stylish, romantic fiction. Her first book, *A Royal Pain*, was an NPR Best Book of 2012 and *USA Today* bestseller. Before discovering her passion for romance novels, she worked in magazine publishing and finance. After many years in New York, Boston, London, and Chicago, she now lives with her family in Florida.

Website: meganmulry.com
Goodreads: bit.ly/1boncLy
Facebook: facebook.com/meganmulry
Pinterest: www.pinterest.com/meganmulrybooks
Twitter: twitter.com/MeganMulry
Email: megan@meganmulry.com

Enjoy more stories like *Bound with Passion* at RiptidePublishing.com!

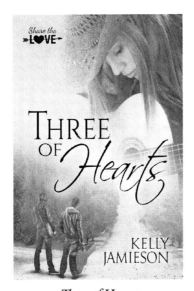

Three of Hearts
ISBN: 978-1-62649-255-4

Squamous with a Chance of Rain
ISBN: 978-1-62649-227-1

Earn Bonus Bucks!

Earn 1 Bonus Buck for each dollar you spend. Find out how at RiptidePublishing.com/news/bonus-bucks.

Win Free Ebooks for a Year!

Pre-order coming soon titles directly through our site and you'll receive one entry into a drawing for a chance to win free books for a year! Get the details at RiptidePublishing.com/contests.

566305044

CPSIA information can be obtained at www.ICGtesting.com
Printed in the USA
LVOW07s2124060915

453083LV00004B/115/P

9 781626 493155